If Chad could manage to approach this case with professionalism and some measure of detachment, so could I.

Until the forensics report came in, I would avoid speculating about who the murder victim—and the murderer—might be. I would investigate this crime just as I'd investigate any other crime. I would work with Chad and we would build our case carefully and meticulously. Basing it on facts, likely circumstances and evidence.

And if the investigation pointed to someone I loved? Threatened to expose facts long buried?

My stomach did a half twist, destroying my sense of calm.

Just do your job, I told myself. The way you were taught. One step at a time. Follow the evidence wherever it leads.

Then deal with the consequences.

Dear Reader,

Have you been lost and alone in a forest at night?

During a search-and-rescue training exercise, I put myself in that situation, experiencing the disorientation and terror that real victims often feel. My imagination ran wild as small forest noises became threatening sounds and uneven darkness tricked me into seeing shadowy forms. At one point, I was sure that ticks were raining down on me from the trees overhead and I fought the impulse to run away screaming. You can imagine my relief when a young German shepherd crashed through the underbrush with his human handler fast at his heels.

That night and my love of dogs were the inspiration for *Too Close to Home*'s heroine, rookie cop and search-and-rescue volunteer Brooke Tyler. Brooke's fictitious adventures play out against a real and often treacherous backdrop—the atmospheric Shawnee National Forest area of southern Illinois. From the murky water of a cypress swamp to towering river bluffs to forested hills cut with jagged ravines, Brooke must confront and overcome challenges.

An intriguing geography of the heart is as important to me as the story's physical geography. Brooke's world is complicated by her family's commitment to helping abused women escape to safety. No sooner than she's found the man she'll love forever, she's sacrificed that relationship to protect her family's dangerous legacy. The question is, can she live with her heartbreaking decision and overcome perils that strike *Too Close to Home?*

Maureen Tan

MAUREEN TAN
TOO CLOSE TO HOME

Published by Silhouette Books

America's Publisher of Contemporary Romance

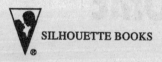

SILHOUETTE BOOKS

ISBN-13: 978-0-373-51422-9
ISBN-10:   0-373-51422-0

TOO CLOSE TO HOME

www.SilhouetteBombshell.com

Printed in U.S.A.

Books by Maureen Tan

Silhouette Bombshell

A Perfect Cover #9
Too Close to Home #108

MAUREEN TAN

is a Marine Corps brat, the eldest of eight children and naturally bossy. She and her husband of thirty years have three adult children and two grandchildren. They currently share their century-old house with a dog, three cats, three fish and a rat. Much to his dismay, their elderly Appaloosa lives in the barn. Most of Maureen's professional career has involved explaining science, engineering and medical research to the public. To keep her life from becoming boring, she has also worked in disaster areas as a FEMA public affairs officer and spent two years as a writer for an electronic games studio. Maureen's first books, *AKA Jane* and *Run Jane Run,* detail the exploits of a female British agent.

For the kind and hospitable folks of Elizabethtown, Illinois. For my family and friends of all generations. For my mother, who taught me reading and courage and love. And especially for Peter, who still looks good in jeans.

Prologue

I was sixteen. Old enough that I no longer believed in story-book monsters. Young enough that, despite plenty of evidence to the contrary, I didn't quite believe in human monsters.

Dr. Porter changed that.

"I'm getting tired of waiting," he called from the vicinity of the living room. "Come take your punishment like a good little wife."

His coaxing, reasonable voice was accompanied by the rhythmic slapping of a leather strap against an open hand. The sound echoed off the glossy, hard surfaces of the expensive suburban home and carried clearly into the kitchen at the back of the house.

"Obviously, you've forgotten who your master is," he continued. "You must be reminded."

From where I stood, I couldn't see Dr. Porter. Or the strap. But I'd seen the welts and bruises left by the strap. Left by

Dr. Porter on his wife's flesh. So maybe that was why it was all too easy to imagine what *he* looked like. No matter that I knew better, that Aunt Lucy and Gran had more than once reminded me that appearance was a poor predictor of behavior, I couldn't help but picture bulging muscles and twisted, lunatic features.

Nothing about his voice convinced me otherwise. And because my upbringing was Baptist and biblical, I imagined it was the same voice the serpent had used in the Garden of Eden. Low, vaguely seductive and absolutely evil.

"It will only be worse if I have to come get you, Missy."

My name was Brooke. Not Missy. Missy Porter was gone. And monster or not, devil or not, I stood my ground and waited for her husband. Because that was what I'd promised Missy I would do.

Just moments earlier, when the lock had turned in the front door, she'd been standing beside me in the kitchen. I'd watched as the blood drained from her face and she began trembling.

Missy was terrified. With good reason. Earlier that day, her husband had come home unexpectedly and found her packing. Missy's punishment began before he'd left the house and he'd promised to continue it when he returned. In the meantime, he'd taken their twin sons away with him, confident that she would never run away without her children.

When we'd first arrived, she hadn't answered the door. Fearing that Dr. Porter's escalating abuse had turned homicidal, Gran and I crept around the house trying to get a glimpse inside. We found an open window, shouted Missy's name again, and heard a woman sobbing.

Right then, I'd seen in Gran's face that she wished Aunt Lucy was at her side. But Aunt Lucy was home with a broken leg and—no matter that I was nothing more than a gawky adolescent girl with boring brown eyes and chopped-off brown curls—I was her replacement on this rescue. Mostly because, unlike Gran, I could see well enough to drive after dark. I was also undeniably more nimble than Gran. Reluctantly, she agreed that I should crawl inside. Without saying a word, she gave me the big leather handbag that concealed my grandfather's gun.

I'd found Missy in the kitchen, sitting naked on the stool where her husband had ordered her to stay, urine puddling on the floor beneath her. Horrified and unsure of what to do or say, I ran to the kitchen door and let Gran in. Valuable time passed as she convinced Missy to leave the stool, to escape as planned. Then Gran stood guard on the front porch and I waited inside as Missy got dressed.

We were almost to the foyer when the doorbell rang three times. A warning that Dr. Porter was approaching. Gran's usual tactic—posing as a neighbor in search of a lost cat— bought us enough time to backtrack to the kitchen. And in that time, Missy lost her nerve.

As her husband bellowed for her from the front of the house, she stood, indecisive, unable to chose between the promise of escape and the certainty of abuse, between the risk of directing her own life and the terror of letting her husband control it. With her children in the balance, the decision was agony. And it was hers alone. In the end—with the sound of her husband's heavy steps echoing down the hallway toward us—she chose survival.

"Run to the blue van parked down the street," I whispered just before she bolted out the kitchen door. "I'll slow him down, give you time to get away."

I pulled my grandfather's gun from the handbag.

I waited for the monster to come get me.

* * *

Dr. Porter's cool tone warmed with growing anger.

I flinched at the obscenities he thought he was directing at his helpless wife, used both hands to support the weight of the bulky Smith & Wesson Victory revolver and waited for him. His breath, I was certain, would smell like rotting meat. His face would have flaring nostrils and pointed teeth. His eyes would be reddened by bloodlust and fury. It was the stuff of horror flicks and nightmares and novels by Koontz and King. But it was happening to me.

He screamed as he rushed through the doorway.

"You little bitch! I'll drag your fuc—"

The sight of me and my gun brought him slamming to a halt.

"Missy's not home," I said into the sudden silence.

Between us was the polished granite counter, six empty plastic water bottles and the stool where he'd left his wife sitting for several agonizing hours. He'd compelled her to drink every bottle, then ordered her to remain on the stool until he returned. After years of being battered into submission, she'd done exactly as he'd said.

The revolver trembled in my hands as I pointed it past the water bottles to a spot where a blue silk tie was framed by the V of his gray vest. His light brown eyes stretched wide as his lips formed a moist O surrounded by the short, wiry hairs of his beard.

I returned his stare, as surprised by his appearance as he was by mine. He was ordinary. Absolutely, horrifyingly ordinary. Medium height, slightly pudgy and dressed in a three-piece suit. Mouse-colored hair had receded enough to make his forehead look tall, and his neatly trimmed mustache and beard were shot through with gray. His right shoulder was slightly humped, but not so much that he would stand out in a crowd of other middle-aged, average-looking men.

No matter how he looked, I told myself, he was still a monster. A threat to Missy. And to me.

"Drop the belt," I said.

He surprised me again by immediately opening his hand and releasing the thick leather strap. Its buckle clattered noisily against the tiled floor, but he didn't take his eyes from me and the gun I held. The bright spot of the task light above the counter glinted off a string of spittle at the corner of his mouth.

It was then, suddenly, that I realized the monster was terrified. Of me. And that I—Brooke Tyler—was utterly in control.

My hands steadied as my fear was replaced by an awareness of my own power. And the power of the weapon I held. With just the slightest pressure of my right index finger, I could kill this monster who looked human but took pleasure in torture and pain and humiliation. I could keep him from hurting Missy—or any other woman—ever again.

It wouldn't be murder, wouldn't be a sin. It would be justice.

Something in my expression told him what I intended.

He raised his hands in front of his face, arms crossed at the wrist and palms faced outward as if they could shield his face from the impact of a .38 caliber bullet. And he whimpered.

Maybe that very human reaction saved his life. Or maybe it was the sound of a horn blaring outside. Three times, then twice again. The signal that Missy was safely inside the van. A reminder of the promise I'd made on the family Bible on my last birthday. With Gran, Aunt Lucy and my seventeen-year-old sister, Katie, as witnesses, I'd placed my hand on the worn leather cover and sworn to protect the Underground. To keep its work secret. To continue our family's legacy, begun during the Civil War, of aiding the helpless and abused.

Killing Dr. Porter could betray us all.

Missy would surely be blamed for the murder, but a police investigation might expose the Underground, forcing our network of safe houses to shut down. Jeopardizing the women we were supposed to be helping.

In the space of a heartbeat, reason supplanted rage. Or, at least, controlled it. But part of me still lusted for a small measure of revenge. That, as much as the desire to escape town unimpeded by Dr. Porter, inspired me.

I ordered him to strip.

Without the tailoring of his suit coat to hide it, the curve in his back and the hunch in his shoulder were even more obvious. But I felt not a moment of sympathy for this hateful, ordinary man.

There were two large crystal water pitchers in the buffet. I made him fill them before he took Missy's place on the kitchen stool, then kept my grandfather's gun pointed squarely at him as I demanded that he drink both pitchers dry. And I watched, unmoved, as he gagged in his haste to please me.

"I'll be right back," I said and had no problem matching the menace I'd heard in his voice. I simply imagined the way he'd spoken to Missy hours earlier. "If you move from that stool or if you mess yourself—" I stepped behind him, pressed the tip of the gun against the bare flesh where his spine twisted just below his shoulder blades "—you will be punished. I swear."

Then I backed out of the kitchen.

The engine was running and Katie had just crawled over into the passenger's seat when I yanked the van's driver-side door open. I climbed inside, dropped the purse that concealed my grandfather's gun on the floor between me and Katie, and glanced over my shoulder.

Gran was seated behind me. An empty row separated her from Missy, who huddled into the corner of the bench seat at the very back of the boxy van. There was more metal frame than window there—a comforting location for someone who wanted to hide.

I flashed a smile at my grandmother and my sister. Success, I thought. My very first solo extraction for the Underground and everything had gone right. Before long, our van would blend into the heavy interstate traffic moving away from the St. Louis metro area. Away from Dr. Porter.

I couldn't help feeling a bit self-satisfied. Within hours, Missy would be tucked into one of the guest rooms at the Cherokee Rose Hotel, our family home. Our family's business. Within days, she would continue her journey along the Underground network, moving from one privately owned hotel or bed-and-breakfast to another until she reached her final destination. There, she'd be given a new identity, a job and a safe place to live. And we'd arrange for her children to be snatched from their father and returned to her.

Before I could pull away from the curb, Katie tugged at my arm.

"Where are the little boys?" she said urgently.

"They weren't at home," I said simply.

"So she just abandoned them?"

Katie made no effort to keep her voice down or to disguise her outrage. And there was no doubt that what she said carried clearly because Missy began sobbing.

I looked over my shoulder in time to see her struggle up from her seat, move forward past the empty row of seats, reach for the handle that opened the van's side door. Then Gran's hand darted out and I saw the sinewy muscle beneath her leathery skin flex with effort as her long, bony fingers caught Missy's wrist and held it captive.

A fit, lean sixty-three years old, Gran was undoubtedly strong enough to force Missy back into her seat. But that would turn a rescue into a kidnapping and we, like Dr. Porter, would be denying Missy control of her own life. If her life was to change, Missy had to make her own decision.

The van was already running, so I shifted it into Drive. But I kept my foot on the brake, my hands on the steering wheel, and my attention split between the rear of the van and the front door of the Porter home. I couldn't help wondering how long fear would control Dr. Porter's fury, how long he would remain where I'd left him.

A frozen eternity passed as Gran simply looked at Missy, her expression one of utter sadness. She shook her head slowly and I knew that the intensity of her pale blue eyes would be magnified by the thick lenses she always wore. She lifted her hand away from Missy's hand as she spoke. Missy leaned forward just enough to grasp the door handle but she didn't pull it.

"You did what you had to do, Missy. You escaped," Gran said. "You're no good to your children if you're dead. Or horribly injured. We have to get you to safety. First. Then we'll get your babies back."

Tears were streaming down Missy's cheeks, but she nodded. Maybe it was the strength of Gran's voice and the utter conviction of her words that returned Missy to her seat. Or maybe it was the sight of her husband—red-faced, barefoot and dressed only in his trousers—emerging from the house. He saw the van and raced across the lawn toward us.

I pulled away from the curb and the tires squealed as I floored the gas pedal. Inside the van, my passengers huddled down in their seats. Outside, Dr. Porter stood screaming obscenities in a cloud of exhaust smoke. There was nothing he could do to bring his wife back except, perhaps, call the police. But then he might have to explain why she'd fled. And I doubted he'd want to do that.

I rounded a corner, putting Dr. Porter out of sight. Another stretch of residential street, another quick turn, and I joined the heavier traffic on a main thoroughfare and headed for the interstate.

A glance in the rearview mirror briefly revealed Missy's blotchy, tearstained face. Then she covered her face with her hands. I changed lanes, then checked the mirror again, seeking Gran's eyes. But I was distracted by a quick movement beside me as my sister turned back around in her seat to stare at Missy. Her golden hair framed a face twisted ugly with anger. Her hazel eyes were narrowed, and her full bow lips were pressed into a tight line. Then she opened her mouth.

"Hey, you! Missy Porter!" she said, her usually soft, breathy voice sounding tight.

Certain that she would say something we all would regret, I reached quickly for the dashboard, cranked the volume setting on the radio up to maximum and turned on the power. Noise blasted through the van's interior and drowned out Katie's shrill yelp as I pinched her hard.

"Behave," I mouthed as she jerked her head in my direction.

Katie surprised me by doing as I said. She faced forward again, sat rigidly with her hazel eyes fixed on the view out the front window. The muscles along her jaw flexed as she gritted her teeth.

I reached out again and dialed the radio down several notches.

"Sorry," I said loudly in no one's direction.

Then I fiddled with the controls until I found a country-western station where Toby Keith was singing something bawdy. The song was just loud enough to cover a front-seat conversation.

"What's wrong with you?" I said to my sister once both of my hands were back on the steering wheel. "You don't have any reason to be mean to her. You weren't inside that house, didn't see what she had to endure. She didn't have a choice."

"Oh, yes, she did," Katie hissed. "She could have stayed with her children. Protected them. That's what a good mother is supposed to do. Isn't it?" And then more urgently, she repeated: "Isn't it?"

That's when I realized that she wasn't really talking about Missy Porter.

"This is different," I said. "Missy's not like her."

Eleven years earlier, our mother had left us alone with a stranger. Just for a little while. While she got a fix with the money he'd given her. She didn't bother asking him what the money was for, didn't wonder about his generosity.

When he began touching me, Katie had attacked him with teeth and fists.

"Get Momma!" she screamed as I broke free.

I ran as fast as I could. I searched for our mother in all the places I knew. The alley. The street corner. The bar at the end of the block.

I couldn't find her anywhere.

So I did what she said we should never do. I found a cop and showed him where we lived.

I took him into our building, dragged at his hand so he would hurry, hurry, hurry. I told him to ignore the roaches and, instead, to concentrate on not falling through the traps that Momma and her friends had cut into the stairs and in the upstairs hallway. To keep the police from sneaking in and throwing everyone in jail.

Momma had said that the police put children in jail, too. But I didn't care. Because even then I knew there were far worse things.

I'd brought help as fast as I could, but the stranger had already gone.

He hadn't left right away.

Briefly, I looked away from the traffic, reached across the front seat of the van and covered Katie's hand with mine. Our eyes met, and the smile that passed between us was sad and full of memory. And though I was sixteen and old enough to know better, I wished that I could go back in time. Wished for a chance to run faster, to find a cop sooner, to be brave enough to stay and fight by Katie's side. I wished for a chance to save my sister just as she'd saved me.

Gran always said to be careful what you wished for.

Chapter 1

Eight years later

Lust.

That's what any thought of Chad Robinson's muscular six-foot-two frame, copper hair and green eyes inspired. The sound of his deep voice with its down-home drawl inevitably notched lust up another level, pushing almost-nostalgic warmth in the direction of aching desire. Not a particularly good way to feel about a man I was determined not to fall back in love or in bed with.

So when I answered the phone on a hot, humid evening in mid-June and heard Chad's voice on the line, I kept my thoughts focused on the business at hand, not the memory *of* his hands. It was a good strategy for ex-lovers who were determined to remain friends.

In the time it had taken me to cross the kitchen and lift the cordless phone from its cradle, Chad had apparently been distracted from his call. When I put the phone to my ear, he was already speaking to someone in the background.

"Yeah. Good idea. The water gets pretty deep in those ditches. As soon as Brooke and her search dog are headed this way, I'll take the southbound stretch and do the same...."

"Hey there," I said by way of greeting, personal issues abruptly irrelevant as the snatch of conversation hinted at the reason for his call. "What's going on?"

Chad's attention returned to the phone.

"We've got a missing toddler, Brooke. Family lives northwest of town. The forest is right in their backyard. I checked the map. The house is in Maryville jurisdiction."

As a deputy sheriff for Hardin County, Chad usually patrolled the southern Illinois towns of Humm Wye, Peters Creek, Iron Furnace and everything in between. When no cop was on duty in Maryville, his patrol looped a bit farther south to include the town where the two of us had grown up. Undoubtedly, that had happened tonight. Because, at the moment, Maryville's entire police force was off duty and standing barefoot in the middle of her kitchen, considering dinner possibilities.

Chad gave me directions that started at the intersection of two meandering county roads. From there, he described his location in tenths of a mile and natural landmarks.

"How fast can you and Possum get here?" he said.

Away from the bluffs of the Ohio River, where the original town had been built, Maryville's ragged boundaries were created by fingers of human habitation jamming deep into the vast Shawnee National Forest. I lived at the tip of one of those fingers. The missing child's home was on another, in an area of expensive, very isolated homes. Even with four-wheel drive and a native's intimate knowledge of the area's back roads…

"I need half an hour," I said, then asked him for details.

With the receiver held between my ear and shoulder, I listened to him talk as I walked halfway down the hall to my bedroom. There, I snatched a pair of jeans and a long-sleeved denim shirt from the closet. Though the T-shirt and cutoffs I'd changed into when I'd gone off duty were more appropriate to June's hot and humid weather, they were poor protection against branches and thorns. I wasn't even tempted to change back into my uniform. Maryville's budget paid for one replacement uniform annually. Not quite a year as a rookie cop in the town's newly created one-person department, and I was already out-of-pocket for two uniforms.

But uniform or not, and although Chad was the responding officer, the location of the house meant that I was not just a searcher, I was also the police officer in charge. So I began gathering the information I needed for both those roles as I exchanged shorts for jeans and slipped the long-sleeved shirt over my T-shirt. I clipped my shiny Maryville PD badge onto the shirt's breast pocket.

"When the call came in, I had dispatch contact the forest service and pull some rangers from the Elizabethtown district office," Chad said. "They're searching the immediate area."

"You've already searched the house?"

"Yep. First thing," Chad said matter-of-factly. "Every room, every closet, behind the furniture and under all the beds. I checked the garden shed and the garage, too."

I nodded, pleased by the information. All too often, cops and inexperienced searchers focused their attention on searching areas beyond the house right away, only later discovering a lost child fast asleep in a closet or in the backseat of the family car. Or, more tragically, overcome by heat in an attic crawl space.

"The parents are sure Tina's wandered off," Chad continued. "That's her name. Tina Fisher. Did I tell you she's four years old? The parents have been searching for her since sunset. Sure wish they'd of called us right away."

But they hadn't, which was typical.

Chad provided me with a few more sketchy details as I recrossed the kitchen, snatched two bottles of lime-flavored Gatorade and a handful of granola bars—tonight's dinner—from refrigerator and pantry. Then I moved my shoulder to hold the phone more securely against my cheek as I sat down on a wooden bench by the back door and laced on a pair of oiled-leather hiking boots.

From his nearby cushion, my old German shepherd, Highball, wagged his tail and woofed twice, ever hopeful that when I put on boots it meant playtime for him. But Highball was too old for this kind of search. Too old, really, for any kind of search.

"Brooke? You still there?"

"Yeah," I said slowly. "Give me a minute…."

I spent that minute trying to figure out if I was seeking feedback from a cop far more experienced than I, one who'd been on the force for three years and in the military police before that. Or if I was simply looking for the kind of reassurance that only an old friend or an ex-lover can provide. In the end, I gave up on sorting it out and simply blurted out what was on my mind.

"What's your feeling on this one, Chad? Do you think she's really lost?"

It was his turn to hesitate. And I suspected that he, too, was recalling a cool day in early spring more than a year earlier.

Back when I was still a civilian, when the county police force knew me as that gal who helped out when folks got lost. Or maybe as the gal that Officer Robinson intended to marry, if only she'd get around to saying yes. Back then, I already suspected that the only possible answer I could give Chad was no. But I still hoped that when folks said that love conquered all, those conquests might include guilt and deception. The reality was, love couldn't stand up to either.

Anyway, on that particular spring day, Highball and I had been called in to look for another missing child. Possum was still more puppy than adult, and the older dog had always been a marvel at in-town searches, capable of ignoring the distractions of traffic and onlookers and the confusion of scents.

We found the body near a sagging post-and-wire fence that did a poor job of separating a run-down trailer court from a field that was shaggy with the remains of last year's corn crop. The two-year-old boy was wrapped in his favorite blanket and buried beneath a pile of damp, winter-rotted leaves nearly the same color as the blood that crusted his hair.

I helped Chad stretch yards of yellow plastic tape from one tree to the next. CRIME SCENE. DO NOT ENTER. Then I walked slowly back to the street where the little boy lived and stood on the curb, just watching, as the ambulance arrived.

Usually, when I found a missing person—living or dead—there was a moment of primitive glee, a flash of adrenaline-spurred triumph. But this time, as the paramedics loaded the tiny body into the ambulance, I could think only of the terrible loss. Then the rear doors were slammed shut and the ambulance pulled away without screaming sirens. Without haste.

The media was at the scene to cover the story of the missing toddler. Reporters and camera crews from papers and TV stations as far away as Evansville and Paducah trolled the crowd, hungry for one more detail, a unique angle, an award-winning photo, a bit of footage dramatic enough to make the national news. Desperate to avoid their prying eyes, I tugged Highball's leash and quickly walked away. When the tattered gray trunk of a century-old sycamore was between me and the media, I stopped, dropped to my knees and buried my face in the thick fur of my dog's ruff.

I thought I was safe, so I wept. But within moments, voices—urgent and demanding—surrounded me, and I feared that my private tears for a dead child would make someone's news story complete. Then, unexpectedly, Chad was there. He hunkered down beside Highball and me and wrapped his arms around both of us. His snarled commands had kept the reporters at bay.

Now, another young child was missing.

I stood by the back door, looking out its window, waiting for Chad's reply.

"I don't know, Brooke. I really don't. The parents seem real upset, but…"

His words trailed off as he left unspoken the reality we both understood. Upset parents didn't mean that one of them hadn't murdered their child.

I sighed, fingered my badge for a moment. My job no longer ended with the rescue or recovery of a victim. If Tina was dead, my responsibility was to find out how and who and maybe why. Any tears would have to wait.

"Finding Tina is a priority," I said. "But if you haven't already told them, would you please remind the rangers that we could be dealing with a crime? If they find the child dead, tell them not to move her body. I know they'll have to check for vitals. But after that, they need to back off and leave the scene as undisturbed as possible. And Chad, maybe assign one of the rangers to sit with the Fishers. Call it moral support, but don't let them do any cleaning up that might impede a murder investigation, okay?"

In all likelihood, Chad didn't need me to tell him any of that, either. And I understood that, whether they knew what to do or not, a lot of seasoned male cops would have resented taking direction from a female and a small town's rookie police officer. But Chad and I had never had a problem where our professional lives were concerned. When I'd first pinned on a badge, we'd worked out the ground rules. Almost a year later and, despite the recent upheaval in our personal relationship, those rules and our friendship still worked.

In this situation, the rule was simple. My jurisdiction. My responsibility. Chad apparently also remembered the rule and responded accordingly.

"Will do," he said. "Another county cop is on the way to back me up, so I'll have her keep an eye on the parents. Anything else?"

"I don't think so," I said, my tone inviting feedback.

Apparently, Chad had no advice to give.

"Then see you soon," he said and disconnected.

Out in the kennel area and seemingly oblivious to the heat, Highball's replacement was bouncing around on the other side of a six-foot-tall chain-link fence and barking up a storm. The young dog's excitement was most likely prompted by one of his namesakes searching for grubs in the woodpile.

"He walks like an old fat possum," Gran had observed as my new German shepherd puppy waddled his way across the room to greet her. And though he'd grown up to be a graceful and athletic dog, the undignified nickname stuck. Possum.

I turned away from the window to pick up a powerful compact flashlight from the far corner of the kitchen counter.

Everything else I needed, including my webbing belt and its assortment of small packs, was already in the white SUV that doubled as Maryville's only squad car and my personal vehicle. That was a fairly standard arrangement for small-town police departments.

Customizing the SUV to accommodate a dog wasn't. But the city council members had observed that my volunteer work to locate the lost, complete with search-and-rescue dogs, was just as important to the citizens of Maryville as the job they'd now be paying me for. So the modifications to the SUV had been made, and I'd been grateful.

"Come on. Kennel time," I murmured to Highball.

His kennel area was outside, adjacent to Possum's, and going there always meant a meal. Or a treat. And a tennis ball to chew on. Highball raised his graying head, rose slowly to his feet and wagged his tail as he joined me at the back door.

I pulled a ball cap over my cropped brown curls, then reached into the stoneware bowl on the kitchen counter and snatched up the keys to my squad car.

I was ready to go.

The Fishers lived on top of a rise in a modern, two-story log home, deliberately rustic and heavy on the windows. Out front, a low fence of flat river rock enclosed the yard and lined the approach to the house.

When I pulled into the drive, I saw Chad on the front porch, uncomfortably perched on the front edge of an Adirondack chair and leaning over a low wooden table. He was in uniform, which was short-sleeved and dark blue, but had set his billed cap aside, exposing crew-cut coppery-red hair. Thousands of insects swarmed around him, attracted by the yellow glow of the light mounted above the door. His attention was so com-

pletely absorbed by whatever was on the table that he seemed
oblivious to them.

I turned off my headlights, cut the engine and sat for just
a moment.

In my rearview mirror, I could see flashlights bobbing—
rangers searching through the cattails and tall rushes growing
in the swampy ditch that paralleled the road at the front of the
property. The only other illumination in the area shone from
the windows of the Fisher family's home, where all of the
interior lights seemed to be on.

I climbed down from my SUV and walked around to the
back to lift the door of the topper and drop the tailgate. From
inside his crate, Possum whined excitedly, eager for the search.

"In a minute," I said, and he settled back down.

I pulled the items I needed from the bed of the truck and
sprayed myself with insect repellent. My utility pack was on
a webbing belt. I slung it around my waist, tied my two bottles
of sports drink into the pack's side pockets, and slipped my
flashlight through one of the belt loops. A canteen of water
for Possum was added to my load, along with a small, folded
square of waterproof fabric that cleverly opened into a water
dish. I took a pair of two-way radios from the locked box near
the tire well. One, I'd leave with Chad. The other, I clipped
to my belt.

Then I released Possum from his crate.

He jumped down from the bed, mouthed my hand briefly
in an affectionate but sloppy greeting, then stood with his tail
wagging and his body wiggling. For him, searching for a
missing person was the ultimate game of hide-and-seek, its
successful conclusion rewarded by the praise he craved.

I bent down to clip a reflective neon collar with a dangling
bell around his neck, then slipped a reflective orange vest over

his head and secured the belly straps. The lettering and large cross on each side of the vest proclaimed Possum's status, RESCUE DOG. Then I stood and, with Possum at my heels, joined Chad.

He was concentrating on using a ruler and a narrow-tipped red marker to extend a line on a topographical map. Tomorrow, I knew, the grids that he was drawing would be used for a more comprehensive search. If I failed to locate the child, a full-scale ground search would be organized and mounted at first light.

"Sure hope we won't be needing this," I heard him murmur as I stepped in beside him. Briefly, I rested my hand on his shoulder in greeting, then leaned in closer to get a better look at the map.

He finished the line, turned his head, smiled up at me. And I tried not to think about how much I still loved him.

"Hey there, Brooke," he said. "Thanks for coming."

Tina Fisher was wearing pink.

Pink cotton slacks. A T-shirt printed with pink bunnies. Pink barrettes in her straight blond hair. Her shoes were pink, too—rubber-soled Stride Rite leather sneakers—and they were gone. Maxi was also missing, and Tina's mother explained that the bedraggled, one-eyed teddy bear was Tina's constant companion.

The Fishers stood close to each other as they spoke. Her hand periodically moved to pat the hand that he'd rested on her shoulder. When I asked when they'd last seen Tina, Mrs. Fisher's composure crumbled. She turned and smothered her sobs against her husband's chest.

"It's all my fault," I heard her say. "I should have watched her more closely...."

Mr. Fisher wrapped his arms around her, then looked over her shoulder at me.

"Can you give us a minute?" he asked.

I nodded.

"No problem," I said.

And I meant it. As a searcher, I was pressed for time. But as a cop, I welcomed the opportunity to take a long, hard look at the pair. To add my perceptions to what Chad had already seen. To begin building my case should *lost* turn out to be *murdered.* It would be my first murder investigation, and I wanted to do everything by the book. As I'd been taught.

"Your instincts about people are better than mine," Chad had said before he opened the front door and waved me inside ahead of him. "They claim the little girl wandered away while they were fixing dinner. The more time I spend with them, the more I'm inclined to think they're telling the truth. But see what you think."

Just inside the door, I'd spent a moment glancing around the first floor. The interior and its country-chic furnishings confirmed what the exterior had suggested. The house was modern and expensive. Living, dining and food-prep areas blended seamlessly in an open floor plan, and I'd wondered how a small child could have wandered away unnoticed by either parent. Then I'd reminded myself that children were fairly adept at doing just that kind of thing.

Mr. and Mrs. Fisher had risen from a clean-lined, cocoa-colored sofa as Chad and I had entered the living area. Chad had made quick introductions, then he'd gone back outside. A young woman in a uniform that matched Chad's had been listening from a nearby easy chair. She'd acknowledged me with a quick nod, then excused herself to make coffee, leaving me alone with Tina's parents.

I'd acted like a volunteer, not a cop, kept my voice sympathetic and my tone unaccusing. But still, my gently asked questions had reduced Tina's mother to tears.

As his wife buried herself in his arms, Mr. Fisher half turned so that his broad shoulders sheltered most of her upper body from my view. Then he pressed his lips to the top of her head. Which still left me plenty to look at.

They were both lean and blond and had narrow noses, even white teeth and golden tans. Each wore short-sleeved designer-label knit shirts—his white and hers pale pink— over khaki shorts and athletic shoes designed for a fitness-club workout, not trekking through rough terrain. But their appearance made it clear that they had, indeed, been in the woods. Their clothing was grubby and perspiration-stained and their shoes were streaked with grass stains. Socks, which he wore and she didn't, were hung with burrs and her ankles were raw with mosquito bites.

Tina's mother and father were also both bloodied by the wild roses and raspberries that invaded sunny boundaries between cultivated yards and the forest. Away from tended trails, their whiplike branches were difficult to avoid, especially if one wasn't paying attention to them. The couple's bare arms and legs were crisscrossed with long, thin scratches, and a tear on the back of Mr. Fisher's shirt still had a few large thorns embedded in the ragged fabric.

I tipped my head, considered the possibilities. Hope and instinct supported Chad's assessment—ignoring their own welfare, Mr. and Mrs. Fisher had searched frantically through the nearby woods for their missing child. Missing because she'd wandered off, or because some human predator had exploited an unlocked back door or an untended child in the yard.

Bitter experience suggested an alternate scenario. Tina

was murdered in the house and one or both of her parents had been so intent on hiding her body that physical discomfort was irrelevant.

"Please, honey," the husband was saying, "don't do this to yourself. I didn't know she'd figured out how to unlock the back door. Did you?"

"No," came his wife's muffled reply. "But she's smart."

"Yes, she is. So she probably went outside and saw a butterfly or a bunny and followed it into the woods. Nobody's fault. So now, what we need to do is help Officer Tyler find her. Okay?"

"Okay," she sobbed.

A moment later, still remaining within the circle of her husband's arms, Tina's mother turned her tearstained face back in my direction.

"I'm sorry," she said, still sniffling but once again coherent. "What else do you need to know?"

I shook my head.

"Nothing else. But I do need a piece of Tina's clothing. Something she's worn recently. That hasn't been washed. Like socks. Or pajamas. Or underwear."

"I'll get it," she said eagerly.

As she scurried into a nearby room, I opened the small, unused paper sack I'd carried with me into the house. When Mrs. Fisher returned, she had a pair of socks clutched in her hand. They were pink, ruffled at the cuffs and obviously worn.

"Thanks," I said, dropping the socks into the sack.

With the Fishers in tow, I walked to the front porch where I'd left Possum waiting. With my body propping the door open, I held the open bag at his level. He nosed the fabric, memorizing the scent of this particular human being.

"Possum, find Tina," I commanded.

As I tucked the sack into one of the exterior pockets of the search pack, Possum trotted past me to nuzzle each of the Fishers, his tail moving in a rhythm that I recognized as concentration. They stared, unmoving, probably unbelieving, as Possum walked past them and into the house.

"Possum's comparing your scent to Tina's, sorting Tina's smell from yours," I explained. "Now he's following Tina's scent."

"Why doesn't he keep his nose on the floor?" Tina's father asked.

"Sometimes he does, but mostly he picks up scents carried by air currents. When you're searching for someone who's lost, it's more efficient not to have to follow the—"

I caught myself and didn't say *victim*. But the truth was that Tina was in terrible danger.

"—Tina's exact route."

Even without the possibility that her parents were involved in her disappearance, there were plenty of deadly natural hazards in the deep forests, wooded ridgetops, steep rocky slopes and narrow creek bottoms of the ancient Shawnee hills. And there was also the possibility that she'd never entered the woods, that she'd ended up somewhere along the road and a human predator had happened by at just the wrong moment.

I dragged my mind away from that bleak train of thought, concentrated instead on Possum's progress through the house. He circled the living room, then headed upstairs, with me and the Fishers at his heels.

"But Tina's outside," the mother said, her voice traveling in the direction of despair.

"Don't worry," I said, knowing that Possum was seeking the place where Tina's scent was most heavily concentrated. "He knows his job."

With four rooms to choose from at the top of the landing,

Possum made a beeline into a bedroom where the wallpaper was decorated with intertwined mauve flowers. He went directly to the twin bed, nuzzled the pillow and a wad of soft blankets, then wagged his tail.

Easy enough to guess that the room belonged to a little girl, but I made sure.

"Tina's?"

The mother nodded and the father didn't look as panicked as he had just moments earlier.

Possum emerged from the bedroom.

"Good boy," I said. "Find Tina."

Possum went back downstairs, pushed his way beneath the dining table and nosed several stuffed toys that were gathered around a plastic tea set, then made his way quickly and very directly to the nearby patio door. He scratched at the glass and whined.

"That's the door we found open," the father said, sounding as if he'd just witnessed magic.

I told the parents to wait in the house as I opened the door wide for Possum. With little more signal than a half wag of his tail, he crossed the deck, negotiated a set of shallow steps and then angled across the lawn toward a split-rail fence separating the backyard from the forest. Easy enough for Possum—or a small child—to slide between the rails. I climbed over, staying just behind my dog as we crossed the brushy perimeter separating the yard from the deeper shadows of the woods.

Before we plunged into the undergrowth, I switched off my flashlight, giving my eyes a few moments to adjust to the darkness that confronted us. Then I breathed a quick prayer asking for guidance for my feet and Possum's nose. And protection for the child.

Chapter 2

Mosquitoes.

I couldn't see them, but their high-pitched whine was constantly in my ears. They swarmed around me, a malevolent, hunger-driven cloud on the humid night air. Time was on their side. Trickles of salty perspiration would soon dilute the repellent I wore. Then they would feed.

I was used to itching.

Ticks.

The forest was infested with them. Sometimes, they were a sprinkling of sand-sized black dots clinging to my ankles. Often, they were larger. I carefully checked for them after every foray into tall grass or forest, pried their blood-bloated bodies from my skin with tweezers, and watched for symptoms of Lyme disease.

Ticks, too, were routine.

Spiders.

Their webs were spun across every path, every clearing, every space between branch and bush and tree. A full moon would have revealed a forest decked with glistening strands—summer's answer to the sparkle of winter ice. But the moon was a distant sliver, weak and red in a hazy sky, and I found the webs by running into them. The long, sticky wisps clung to my face, draped themselves around my neck, tickled my wrists and the backs of my hands.

I'd feared spiders since childhood, remembered huddling beside Katie as a spindly-legged spider lowered itself slowly from a cracked and stained ceiling. Back then, I'd pounded on that locked closet door, screaming for my mother to please, please let us out. Maybe she hadn't heard me or maybe she simply hadn't cared. But now, with each clinging strand I brushed away, I imagined the web's caretaker crawling on me, just as the spider in the closet had. I wanted to run from the forest, strip off my clothes, scrub myself with hot water and lye soap.

Of course, I didn't.

I ignored the silly voice that gibbered fearfully at the back of my mind and concentrated on following Possum, guided mostly by the reflective strip on his collar. Periodically, I paused long enough to take a compass reading or tie a neon-yellow plastic ribbon around a branch or tree trunk at eye level. The markers would enable me to find my way out. Or help Chad and his people find their way in. Sometimes I spent a minute calling out to Tina and listening carefully, praying for a reply.

She didn't answer.

When I wasn't shouting Tina's name, the only sounds besides my breathing and the crunch of my footsteps were Possum's panting, the tinkle of the bell on his collar and his steady movement through the brush. Overhead, the canopy of trees thickened, almost blocking the sky. Night wrapped itself around us like an isolating cocoon, heightening awareness and honing instincts. Ahead, the inky blackness was broken only by the erratic flash of fireflies that exploded, rather than flickered, with brightness. Behind us, humans waiting beneath electric lights became distant and unreal, irrelevant to the search.

Possum picked up the pace, moving steadily forward, detouring only for tree trunks and the thickest, most tangled patches of roses and raspberries. I struggled to keep up with him, knowing that calling him back or slowing him down risked breaking his concentration.

I ignored the thorns I couldn't avoid, dodged low-hanging branches, skirted tree trunks and stepped over deeper shadows that marked narrow streams, twisted roots and fallen trees. Sometimes I used my flashlight, running it over the ground to judge the terrain ahead. Always, I paid for that indulgence with several minutes of night blindness, and I didn't turn the light on often.

As I made my way through the forest, fragmented thoughts of Tina—fragmented bits of hope—floated to mind. Maybe we'll find her easily. She'll be tired and cranky and mosquito-bitten, but okay. She'll be okay. Possum and I will take her back to her parents. To the parents who love her. Who would never harm her. She'll be okay. We'll find her, and we'll go home. I'll take a hot shower and have a cold beer. Possum can have a dog biscuit. Maybe two. If we find Tina. Alive.

Ten minutes later, Possum's pace slowed.

He wavered, whined and stopped. He had lost the scent. A more experienced search dog, like Highball, would have known what to do next and done it. But Possum was still young and not always confident.

I hurried to his side and gave him a brief, encouraging pat, then checked him for signs of heat stress. Youth had its advantages—he was doing fine. Then I pulled Tina's socks from my pocket. When I held the bag open for Possum, he sniffed the fabric again, lifted his head, put his nose in the air, and wandered in an erratic little circle. He whined again, definitely frustrated.

I oriented my body slightly to the left and pointed.

"Go on," I said. "Find Tina."

Possum followed my direction. I counted ten, slowly. When nothing about the dog's movement hinted that he'd rediscovered Tina's trail, I called him back. Then I turned to the right and sent him off that way.

Still nothing.

I moved forward several yards and we repeated the process. Left, then right. On each sweep, I sent Possum farther away from me. After that, he needed no direction and followed the ever-expanding pattern on his own. The night was still and humid—bad search conditions for any air-scenting dog. And although he was fit, Possum's heavy coat made him susceptible to the heat. If he didn't pick up the trail soon…

Patience, I told myself. Patience.

Minutes later, Possum rediscovered a wisp of Tina's scent. His ears pricked, his tail wagged and his pace suddenly became faster and more deliberate. He continued through the woods with me at his heels.

Between the darkness and the terrain, it was difficult to know how far we had gone. I knew where I was, generally. Knew that I could turn around and find my way back to the Fishers' house. But, at the moment, the physical landmarks that were so clearly marked on Chad's map had little to do with the reality of the forest.

Possum's collar disappeared. And didn't reappear.

I could still hear his bell, so I assumed he was simply blocked from my view. I hurried forward, not considering what I wasn't hearing—the sounds of his movement through the brush.

A spider's web, strung between two trees at shoulder level, probably saved my life. I walked into it. And somehow noticed that, rather than trailing back over my neck and chin, the strands tickled my cheeks and nose, driven by the slightest stirring of upward-moving air. I stopped in my tracks, heart pounding from a sudden rush of adrenaline, my body sensing danger before my conscious mind registered it.

I switched on my flashlight and, with hands trembling from reaction, aimed it two strides forward. And down. A long way down. Maybe forty or fifty feet. I'd nearly stepped off a soil-covered outcrop of crumbling limestone, nearly tumbled to the stream bed below. Now that I was standing still, I could hear moving water.

The seeping groundwater that fed the stream had carved deep scars into the ravine's limestone walls. Horizontal fissures marked places where softer rock had been washed away between layers of less porous stone. Soil had collected on the exposed ledges, creating islands of ferns and a network of slippery, narrow paths. In some places, water-weakened towers of limestone had sheered away from the walls, taking mature trees down with them. Everywhere, shattered trunks and branches were wedged across the ravine, creating a crisscross pattern of rotting and overgrown bridges.

I told myself that Tina had not fallen into the ravine. I told myself that Chad was right—that my instincts *were* good—and that no human monster had abused and then discarded her over the edge.

Possum's bell jingled in the distance, and my flashlight beam made his collar glow. He had entered the ravine south of where I stood and was moving back in my direction, moving steadily along a ledge that would eventually put him six feet below me.

Just a few steps away from me was a tree that leaned precariously over the ravine. An old cottonwood whose trunk was probably seven feet around. There was a ragged hole in the trunk, partially obscured by vines, that narrowed to a point at the height of an adult's waist. The wider opening at the base was just large enough that it might look inviting to a child seeking shelter. I got down on all fours and bent my elbows to peer inside the dark scar, hoping to find Tina curled up asleep. Safe. And discovered that eroding soil, crumbling limestone and twisted roots had created a natural chute inside the rotting trunk. A chute that would send a body downward...

I wrenched my light away from the interior, aimed it over the nearby precipice. A tapering curtain of long, thick tendrils hung directly beneath the old tree, the longest of them trailing down to the narrow ledge below.

Impossible to see what those roots might be hiding.

"Tina!" I called urgently.

The slightest echo of my own voice answered me.

She might be lying there unconscious. Or sleeping. She might not be there at all.

The slope beside the tree was steep but not absolutely vertical.

I checked the ledge carefully for signs of her as I considered my strategy. I could walk along the ravine's edge until I found a place where I could climb down more easily. That would take time and I risked losing sight of Possum, but I'd probably not fall and break my bones. Or I could climb down right here, using the strongest of the tree roots to slow my descent.

I put one hand on the cottonwood for balance and leaned way out into the darkness. Four feet below the first ledge was another jutting outcropping that was at least double the width of the one immediately beneath me. If I could make it down to the first ledge, it was an easy jump to the next one. If I slipped and tumbled past the first ledge, the second one would be my safety net, though reaching it that abruptly was not part of my plan.

And from there? I asked myself. Too easy to imagine me sitting, stranded and broken-limbed, suddenly needing rescue myself. Embarrassing and certainly not helpful to Tina. Especially if she wasn't even down there.

Air currents in and around ravines are complex, I reminded myself. It was impossible to know if the scent Possum was following was actually directly below me. Or upwind. Or maybe, though unlikely, drifting from the opposite side of the ravine. Common sense overcame urgency, and I decided to spend a few extra minutes searching for a safer way down. I played the light around my feet, taking one last, close look at the terrain before turning off my flashlight.

That's when I saw the shoe print.

It was tiny, rounded at the toe and angled into the soft earth between two thick roots. The words *Stride Rite* were lightly embossed into the soil.

That changed everything. Now I knew, without doubt, that Tina had been here. Standing. Walking. Impossible to know if she'd been accompanied or alone, but at the moment she'd stepped next to the tree, Tina had been alive.

And in the next moment? I asked myself. I grasped for hope, for some thought that didn't involve Tina climbing inside the tree and then tumbling down into the darkness. Or being pushed…

But Possum was intent on working his way down into the ravine.

Trust your dog. That was a fundamental rule of canine search-and-rescue work.

I radioed Chad, told him what I'd found and where I was going, and asked him to head my way. Now.

I spent another minute calling out for Tina and listening. Cicadas shrilled. Mosquitoes buzzed. Frogs trilled. But besides the sound of my own breathing, I heard nothing human. So I climbed down into the ravine. With my belly pressed against the crumbling edge, I controlled my descent by wrapping one hand around one of the thicker exposed roots, then digging the fingers of my free hand and the toes of my boots into the limestone wall. My passage triggered a miniature avalanche of pebbles and soil that poured down on my feet when I landed on the narrow ledge.

It was a sloppy descent—unsafe, poorly planned and scary. But it got me where I needed to be. I shook the loose soil away from my boots, brushed the worst of it from my face and the front of my shirt, and retrieved my flashlight. Then, turning my back on the twisted mass of tree roots, I looked toward Possum.

Instead of rushing to greet me as I expected, he stopped just out of reach. He cowered, tucked his tail between his legs, turned his head and one shoulder away from me and whined.

He wasn't reacting to me.

Only one thing triggered that posture in a search dog. Possum hadn't been trained as a cadaver dog, but if death had laid its distinctive scent nearby, he would pick up that less familiar but still human smell and understand at some level what it meant.

I understood exactly what it meant.

My first thought was: Oh, dear Lord! The child is dead.

Then I caught myself. This was no time for the handler to

fall apart. I pushed aside my feelings, ignored the painful tightening in my gut. I pressed my eyes shut as I took a deep breath and let it out slowly. When I opened my eyes again, my emotions were back under control. I could do what needed to be done.

Certainly, recovering Tina's body was urgent. But now, comforting my dog was more important than that. It was up to me to make sure that he was rewarded for finding a victim, living or dead. So I went down on one knee and called Possum closer. I took his big head in my hands, put my cheek against his soft, warm muzzle and ruffled his shaggy fur.

"You're a good boy," I murmured. "A very good dog. You found her."

Then I lifted my head and dug in my pouch for Possum's favorite treat—bits of crisp, thick-sliced bacon. Almost absentmindedly, I fed him tiny pieces as I considered how air currents might move in and along a ravine. Upward, certainly. But eddies of air would form on each ledge, creating pools of scent that might not have originated there. When Possum reacted, there'd been nothing visible between him and me but bare soil and a few maidenhead ferns growing from tiny cracks in the limestone wall. So unless he had sensed particles of flesh or bone or drops of blood that were invisible to me—something that was possible but unlikely in this circumstance—the body was probably below us.

Before moving again, I took careful note of exactly where Possum and I stood and what we were disturbing. If this was a crime scene, our very presence was destroying forensic evidence, our every movement overlaying traces left by a killer with traces of our own. My priority was to find Tina, to recover her body. But after that, I wanted justice. More, I wanted the child's death avenged. Which meant that I needed a crime scene that was as intact as I could leave it.

Possum finished up the last of the bacon.

I wiped my greasy fingers on my jeans, ran the back of my shirtsleeve across my eyes, then stood and played the flashlight's beam along the ledge just below us. Visually, I divided it into grids, carefully checking each square. I saw nothing unusual. But below that barren outcropping, detail disappeared. Whole sections of the ravine were hidden by foliage and fallen trees. If Tina's body was down there somewhere, there was only one way to find out.

But first, there was an area of the ledge we were on that had to be searched more thoroughly. Just in case. I poured Possum a dish of water, noticed that his tail was moving again, and knew that he would be okay. Then I turned, concentrating the flashlight's beam on the cascade of roots obscuring the limestone wall.

Behind me, Possum moved.

In some detached part of my mind, I felt his nose press briefly against the back of my thigh, heard him jump down to the ledge below. But most of my attention was on a bedraggled toy bear caught among the first layer of roots. Mint-green with a white belly and an embroidered pink smile. Tina's teddy bear, Maxi. One of Maxi's fuzzy arms was nearly torn away and his single yellow eye reflected the light.

I knelt, squatted back on my heels and angled my body forward so that I could look into the dark cave beneath the tree without disturbing anything. My flashlight's beam was broken and diffused, so I peered in closely, trying to penetrate the veil of roots and soil.

I saw a body.

Headless.

A tangle of trailing roots wove together a spine, rib cage and pelvis, holding them almost upright. On the ground beside the pelvis were the double bones of a forearm with a skeletal hand and a few finger bones still attached. Nearby, half buried by soil and debris, my flashlight's beam revealed a cheekbone, a dark eye socket and the rounded dome of a fleshless skull. A creeping vine grew like a shock of curly hair through a jagged hole in the forehead.

Tears of relief blurred the grisly scene in front of me.

Not Tina. Thank God, not Tina.

An adult, long dead.

Then my stomach twisted at a sudden and uninvited notion. These bones were Missy Porter, come back to haunt me.

Angrily, I pushed aside the preposterous thought.

Don't be stupid, I told myself. Though she was long dead, too, Missy's body hadn't been concealed within the cocoon of an ancient cottonwood. She would never be embraced by warm, dry earth. Her remains were entombed in steel, hidden where water tupelo and bald cypress sank roots deep into still, oily water. A place where black vultures, frogs and water moccasins were the only witnesses to human secrets.

I knew that because I'd put her there.

Possum barked and barked again.

A child cried out, and the sound was one of surprise rather than pain.

"Go 'way!"

The voice was slurred with sleep.

Yanking my thoughts away from remembered horror and my flashlight's beam away from newly discovered horror, I directed the light over the edge of the ledge. Below me, all I could see of Possum was his enthusiastically wagging tail. The rest of his body was hidden by the overhang I was on.

"Stop dat!"

A child's voice.

"Tina?" I called, and then louder, "Tina!"

"I want my mommy!" she said.

I climbed down to the next ledge with more haste than care. And found her.

She was sitting tucked back into a shallow cave that was little more than a depression in the limestone wall, yelling at Possum, pummeling my dog with tiny fists and sneaker-clad feet. Possum had stretched out beside the child, trapping her against the ravine wall. The more Tina struggled and flailed, the more Possum was determined to care for her, mostly by licking her face.

I called Possum to me, ruffled his fur, patted his head, told him he was a fabulous, wonderful, marvelous dog. His body wiggled with such enthusiasm that I briefly feared he might send us both toppling over the edge.

After a few moments, I pointed at a spot a few feet from the child.

"Now sit," I said, "and stay."

Tina added to the command sequence.

"Berry bad dog," she wailed. "Berry, berry bad."

I knelt beside her and pulled the teddy bear from my belt.

"Oh, no. Possum's a good dog. Aren't you, Possum? See, he found Maxi for you."

Tina quieted immediately as she grabbed the teddy bear. She hugged the poor, torn thing to her chest and covered its grubby head with kisses.

Chapter 3

There was nothing to do but wait.

Too hazardous by far to carry Tina out, risking the narrow ledge that Possum had followed down into the ravine. Foolish and probably impossible to climb back the way I'd climbed down. Chad, I knew, was already on his way. And I admitted to myself that that was a comforting thought.

I looked at the luminous numbers on my watch, saw that Possum and I had been in the woods for just under two hours. Chad and his people, using my markers to find their way, would probably only take half that long to reach us. Though the nighttime temperature was probably still in the mid-eighties, the face of the ravine and the limestone outcropping were damp and cold. So I settled Tina onto my lap and wrapped my shirt around her. Possum curled in beside me and I was grateful for the additional warmth.

As I checked Tina for injuries, we chatted about teddy

bears and big trees and missing bedtime and adventures in the woods. By the time I'd determined that Tina's tumble down to the ledge had miraculously cost her nothing but a few scrapes and bruises, I'd learned most of what I needed to know. Maxi, it seemed, had gotten hungry, so he and Tina had gone into the woods looking for a honey tree. Just like in Winnie the Pooh. It had gotten dark. They'd walked and walked. And then they'd fallen down. Now Tina and Maxi were really, really hungry.

There was no honey for her that night, but the granola bar and lime-flavored sports drink I shared with Tina seemed to do the trick. We offered Maxi and Possum crumbs, which Possum ate with tail-wagging enthusiasm. Tina announced that her teddy bear judged the snack yummy. Then, with Maxi wrapped in her arms, she fell asleep.

I was tired, physically and mentally tired. But I stayed awake anyway, irrationally alert to the presence of predatory spiders on the ledge where we sat. More rationally intent on protecting Tina and listening for the sounds of approaching rescuers. When I heard them, I would aim my flashlight's beam into the sky to mark our exact location.

In the meantime, I waited.

Time passed slowly in the dark. I held Tina, embracing her warm, soft weight and listening to her breathing. And though it seemed inappropriate to think anything but bright and beautiful thoughts with a successfully rescued child in my arms, my mind quickly drifted to the dark, dirty business of the skeletal remains on the ledge just above me.

"Did you walk into the woods with your murderer?" I murmured under my breath.

Possible, I thought, but it didn't seem reasonable for a murderer to lure or force a potential victim very far from a road or a trail. Why travel all the way to the ridge when the forest offered adequate, plentiful and more convenient places?

I considered another scenario.

"Were you killed somewhere else, then carried here?"

I shook my head, immediately dismissing the idea. A body is awkward and heavy to carry. My mind veered away from the reason I knew that, and I focused on the idea that no one carries that kind of weight any farther than they have to.

Killing someone in this place made no sense, I told myself. Unless the murderer had chosen the particular spot, the particular tree, for reasons that only a disturbed mind could fathom. But after nearly a year in law enforcement, I had great faith in the human impulse to do things the easy way.

Then it hit me. The ridge simply wasn't as inconvenient as it seemed. Unless you were searching for a lost child, there was no reason to approach it from the Fishers' backyard, to crash through the underbrush or walk along deer paths that were easy only for a child as small as Tina to follow. It was an indication of how exhausted I was that I hadn't immediately considered that the murderer could approach the ridge from other directions.

I shifted slightly, settled Tina more comfortably into my lap, then pressed my eyes shut, picturing the map that Chad had laid out on the Fisher's front porch. I thought about it, working to recall each of the roads and formal trails that crisscrossed the area. Then I visualized the route Possum and I had followed and estimated the distance we'd traveled.

Camp Cadiz, I realized, was actually much closer to us than to the Fishers' house. Park a vehicle at Camp Cadiz, walk into the forest along the well-marked River-to-River Trail and cross the footbridge that spanned the ravine. After that, I figured the spot where Tina and I waited was no more than a quarter of a mile along the ravine from the bridge.

At gunpoint, a living victim could be forced to walk to this very place. And, if one was strong and determined enough, a body could be carried from the parking lot at Camp Cadiz to the place where I'd found the bones.

The campground—the most primitive of all the campgrounds in the Shawnee National Forest—was remote and only occasionally used by backpackers making the days-long river-to-river trek between the Ohio and the Mississippi. It was the kind of place where a murder could easily go unwitnessed.

I'd visited Camp Cadiz. Once. Eight years earlier. And I hadn't been hiking. I'd been driving Gran, Katie and the woman we had just rescued to the safety of the Cherokee Rose. The detour to Camp Cadiz had been brief and unexpected, but the events of that night had seared the campground's layout into my memory.

I cuddled Tina closer—comfort for her, comfort for me—as I remembered.

Gran had to pee.

Like many such urges, it presented itself at a most inconvenient moment. We were about thirty minutes away from Maryville. And that, as Gran was fond of saying, put us exactly at the hind end of nowhere. Certainly, we were an uncomfortably long way from the nearest public restroom.

The road, lit only by the headlights of the boxy, blue passenger van I drove, cut through a densely wooded and virtually unpopulated section of the Shawnee National Forest. As we slowed to round curves, our lights skimmed undergrowth that, from the van, looked impenetrable. Given Gran's poor night vision and the city suit she was wearing, it probably was.

Gran was as outdoorsy as I was. Lean and athletic, she was an amateur naturalist who had spent most of her life exploring the forest, hiking alone for hours. But no matter that she'd willingly spend hours in a bog or scramble up a rocky slope in search of a medicinal plant or climb high into the branches of a tree to glimpse some endangered species, Gran wasn't the kind of person who would relieve herself in public. And— no matter how unlikely it was that anyone would see her— she considered the side of the road as definitely public.

I mulled over the problem, but before I could come up with an alternative, Gran offered one.

"The turnoff for Camp Cadiz should be close," she said.

We'd gone less than a quarter of a mile when I spotted the small, reflective green sign pointing the way to Camp Cadiz with white letters. A quick turn down a gravel road and we were there.

Seven decades earlier, when F.D.R. had been president and long before southern Illinois bothered itself with concerns about tourism, Camp Cadiz had been a Civilian Conservation Corps camp. The shadowy remains of half a dozen old barracks still dotted the campground. River-stone foundations and clumps of trees and brush provided privacy between a dozen primitive campsites. Along the camp's perimeter, thick foliage joined with the night to create a wall of darkness beneath a starry sky.

The outhouse was at the far edge of the campground.

Missy was curled up sleeping on the bench seat at the very rear of the van. She straightened when I turned into the rutted lot and shifted into Park. I looked over my shoulder in time to see her confused and panicked look as her eyes darted around the interior.

Gran, who sat just behind me, turned her head and spoke before I could.

"It's all right, honey," she said, her tone as soothing as the slow, soft syllables that marked her speech and belied her energetic personality. "You're safe. We're just stopping so that I can use the facilities."

"We'll be at the Cherokee Rose in under an hour," I added. "Where there's a nice, clean bathroom. With a toilet that flushes. But if you can't wait…"

Missy shook her head and managed a weak, exhausted smile. Then she turned to rest her forehead against the side window and stared out at the darkness.

Katie was beside me in the front seat, still snoring softly. Even half-asleep, my sister was beautiful—petite and curvy with pale yellow hair, hazel eyes flecked with gold and a peaches-and-cream complexion. An angel, people were always saying. And I agreed, not only because she was pretty but because she'd been my guardian angel during the earliest years of our childhood. Maybe that's why I'd stood up for her that morning when she'd stripped off her apron, come running from the kitchen and unexpectedly climbed into the van.

"I'm going, too," she'd announced breathlessly.

Gran shook her head.

"You and I have talked about this before, Katie. You have to accept that there are things that you simply can't manage."

I hated it when Gran used that tone with Katie. Katie's asthma, according to Aunt Lucy, was the only reason her involvement with the Underground was limited to playing hostess and cooking—something she already did for the paying guests at the Cherokee Rose. But there was more to it than that.

"She's not like Brooke," I'd once overheard Gran tell Aunt Lucy. "Katie's not strong emotionally. You've seen it yourself. Tears one moment, anger the next. Face it, Lucy. She's never gotten over her mother abandoning her. Or the abuse."

As I looked at my sister, I saw uncharacteristic determination in the way she lifted her dimpled chin. Just a couple months short of her eighteenth birthday, Katie was my senior by a year and a half. But over the past couple of years, she'd grown so timid and unsure of herself that I'd begun to think of her as much younger than me.

Now I wondered if the root of that problem was not our mother, but Gran. Although she pushed me to be independent, to take on challenges and pursue my ambitions, she still made most of Katie's decisions for her. And encouraged Katie to stay close to home. Where it was safe. Usually, Katie seemed content to do whatever Gran wanted.

But not today.

"Go back inside, Katie," Gran was saying, and her tone made it sound as if she were speaking to a child. "Like a good girl."

Though twin red blotches were already standing out against her pale cheeks and she'd started wheezing, Katie didn't move from the backseat. Nothing about her expression changed as she dug in a pocket, took out the inhaler she always carried and gave herself a puff of medicine before tucking it away again.

In that one quick action she reminded me that she *was* fragile, at least physically. I opened my mouth, ready to suggest to Katie that she'd be more useful if she stayed at home, when she did something she'd never done before. She leaned forward and stretched out her hand to clasp my shoulder.

"Please, Brooke. Don't leave me behind. I can help, if you'll let me. I want to make Gran and Aunt Lucy proud of me, just like they are of you. I'm a good driver. When you and Gran go to the house, I'll sit with the engine running. In case we have to leave fast."

Maybe it was Katie's courage that inspired me. Or maybe it was the yearning I heard in my sister's voice. But it prompted me to do something I'd never done before. I told Gran that Katie was brave and helpful and that she was going with us. I was surprised when Gran hadn't protested.

Now, I nudged Katie's shoulder.

"Hey, sleepyhead."

Katie yawned, stretched her arms upward until they touched the van's ceiling, then yawned again as she turned her head slowly, blinking the sleep from her eyes as she looked around.

"Pit stop at Camp Cadiz," I said. "You interested?"

"Ugh," she muttered. "An outhouse. No way."

She snuggled back down into the seat and put her arm across her face.

I turned off the engine and the radio, but left the headlights on, aimed in the direction of the outhouse.

I'd planned to sit and wait for Gran. But I shifted in my seat just in time to see her step out and nearly fall headlong into a pothole that she hadn't noticed in the dark. And it occurred to me that the stretch of weedy meadow between her and the outhouse would present similar hazards, without benefit of the van's door to grab onto.

I scooted out from behind the wheel and met Gran as she was carefully stepping over one of the logs that kept cars from driving into the campground. I took her arm and held it tight. We walked across Camp Cadiz together, our bodies throwing long shadows in the headlight beams.

Tina kicked and cried out in her sleep.

"Mommy! Daddy!"

I tightened my hold on her.

"Soon, little one. You'll see them soon."

I dug through memory, came up with the lullaby that Aunt Lucy had sung to Katie and me when she'd first brought us home to the massive, redbrick hotel. Our great-grandfather had built the Cherokee Rose back when Maryville had been a center of river commerce and no one had thought the swampy northern Illinois town of Chicago would ever amount to much. Gran had grown up there, as had Aunt Lucy and our mother, Lydia. It would be our home, too.

I began singing softly to Tina.

Soon, her body relaxed and her breathing grew deeper and more regular. Asleep again, I thought, allowing my voice to trail off.

I began thinking again about the skeleton that lay on the ledge above us. If nature hadn't undermined the makeshift grave and eventually deposited the remains onto the ledge below and if I hadn't been desperately searching for Tina, I would never have found the body. And someone's guilty secret would have remained hidden forever.

I wondered suddenly, horribly, if my own secret might someday be exposed in just that way. By accident. It was too easy to imagine Missy's bloated corpse somehow escaping its tomb of steel, floating to the surface within sight of human eyes.

I shook my head, tried to clear away the flood of grim memories by focusing on Tina. I pressed my face down against her sleep-dampened curls and listened to the deep rhythm of her breathing as I inhaled her odd, slightly sweet baby scent. An innocent kind of smell. Perspiration and talcum powder, I thought. Or maybe baby shampoo. The kind that doesn't sting eyes.

I'd rescued her, I reminded myself. Rescued an innocent. The way I'd rescued so many others in the years since Missy's death. I'd preserved the Underground and, over the past eight years, helped many dozens of helpless women escape to new, better lives. And I'd given up the only man I'd ever loved because I couldn't tolerate lying to him and I dared not tell him the truth. Wasn't that enough to make up for breaking the law, for abusing in death someone who'd been so badly abused by life?

I couldn't convince myself that it was.

The rescue, with enough people and the right equipment, was quick and safe. Tina, Possum and I left the ravine at a place several yards distant from the exposed root system of the massive tree. I handed Tina over to a paramedic and then, with Possum by my side, followed the tree line to the yellow-taped perimeter that Chad was creating several yards back from the ravine. The tape was a standard item in my pack. Chad always seemed to have it with him, too. And I wondered briefly what that said about our expectations.

Chad paused in his work and reached down to ruffle the fur on Possum's head.

"Good job, Possum," he said. "I'm going to get you a big rawhide chew. And maybe a tube of new tennis balls."

Possum responded as he would to anyone whose voice was so full of praise. He wiggled most of the back half of his shaggy black-and-tan body.

Then Chad straightened and turned toward me. His body blocked the glare from a high-powered lantern that was set up nearby, but there was still enough light to see the dark patches of perspiration staining his uniform shirt and the long, bloody gouge that some branch had carved beneath his right eye. It nearly intersected the puckered, white line that paralleled his strong jaw—a scar that Chad's daddy had put there more than a decade earlier.

"Thank you," he said. "You're fabulous."

I felt my cheeks redden and my pulse quicken in response

to the admiration I heard in his voice, and I knew without doubt that I wouldn't have reacted that way to just anyone. Only Chad.

Quickly, I focused my attention on Possum, who was butting Chad's hand with his broad head in an attempt to get more petting. I ordered him to lie down and stay—probably more firmly than I should have—and waited until his body was sprawled comfortably on the ground. Then I helped Chad finish tying off the tape. I took my end all the way back to the dangerous edge, finally wrapping it around a sapling that was about fifteen feet from the cottonwood tree where I'd found the bones. After rejoining Chad beneath the lantern and taking a moment to survey our work, I turned and looked him squarely in the eyes.

"Okay, now let me take a look at your face."

He shook his head. "No big deal," he began. "We need to—"

"No," I said, cutting him off midsentence and probably midthought. "Before we do another thing, you let me take care of that cheek."

From long experience, I knew just how stubborn he could be. So I didn't wait for his reply. Or his permission. I grabbed his chin, tipped his injured cheek in my direction and peered at the wound.

"It's only a scratch," he said.

"Bull. Shit. Hold. Still."

I gave his chin a quick pinch to make my point.

One way or another, I'd been dealing with Chad's stubbornness and patching him up for years. The first time was just after he'd come to live with a family that took in foster kids. Their house was down the hill from the Cherokee Rose. Even though Chad had been a boy—and, at twelve, I'd written off the opposite sex as pretty much useless—I'd been predisposed to like him. His family situation had distracted most of Maryville from their ongoing gossip about ours. Our mother was merely a runaway and a thief, who'd abandoned her children in a crack house in Los Angeles. Chad's father had murdered his wife, attempted to slash his son's throat and then had claimed that God had told him to do it.

The wound on Chad's cheek was ragged and deep. I pulled an antiseptic pad from my emergency pack and began gently washing blood and bits of debris away from it.

"It doesn't look as if you'll need stitches," I said when the cheek was clean.

"Oh, good," he said, self-mockery evident in his voice. "I was real worried that another scar would ruin my ruggedly handsome good looks."

"It'd take a heck of a lot more than that," I muttered, contradicting him as I always did, knowing that when he looked in the mirror all he saw was a face with a scar. And maybe felt again, just for a heartbeat, the hatred that had put it there.

But, as *he* always did, he shrugged.

Stupid man, I thought. Why can't he see that despite the scarring along his jaw, or maybe because of it, he was utterly desirable?

Too desirable.

At almost nineteen, when he'd joined the military and gone away to fight in the Middle East, he hadn't been at all desirable. At least, not as far as I'd been concerned. I'd watched him grow from a scrawny, carrot-topped boy to a rangy acne-prone adolescent male. I missed him only because he was my best buddy and the boy next door, never anticipating that a few years away would transform him into a six-foot-tall hunk with green eyes and copper hair. I hadn't expected that old friendship would eventually evolve into new intimacy. Or that in a matter of months, our enthusiastic lust would abruptly transform itself into troublesome love. But that's exactly what had happened.

Get over it, I told myself.

I looked away from his expressive eyes and back at his bloody cheek.

He did a good job of pretending that he didn't feel anything when I smoothed a layer of antibiotic cream over the wound. Then, as gently as I could, I used several butterfly closures to pull together the edges along the deepest part of the wound.

He flinched.

"Sorry," I murmured.

"Doesn't hurt," he lied.

"Have I ever accused you of being accident prone?"

"Often," he said, flashing me a smile.

Halfheartedly, I scolded him for moving as I grinned back. It was an old joke and a good memory. We'd met when he'd crashed in front of the Cherokee Rose while attempting a skateboard stunt involving empty wooden peach crates and a plywood ramp.

Chad's expression grew serious, though he was careful not to frown.

"You and I have a jurisdictional issue to resolve," he said. "Fact is, you'd need a surveyor to figure out whether we're standing on county land or if this is still Maryville Township."

I made a sound that was more acknowledgment than an answer as I concentrated on anchoring a square of gauze across his cheek with a final strip of tape. Then I used another antiseptic pad to wipe away the blood that had smeared across his face. Finally, I stepped back to survey my work.

"That should hold you for a while," I said.

Chad slanted his green eyes in the direction of his cheek

as his fingers sought the gauze pad and briefly explored that side of his face.

"Thanks," he murmured "Now about jurisdiction…"

When I attended the statewide police training institute, I'd heard a lot of talk about interdepartmental politics and jurisdictional disputes. Boiled down to its testosterone-spiked essence, the unwritten rule was You Don't Piss on My Turf; I Won't Piss on Yours. But in southern Illinois—where a mile-long stretch of roadway might cross federal, state, county and local jurisdictions—cooperation between law-enforcement agencies was not only customary but essential. So there was no reason, besides the personal, that Chad and I shouldn't work together.

"A shared investigation would keep you from screwing up," I said.

"Might keep the rookie out of trouble, too," he retorted.

A couple hours later, I headed for home.

Chapter 4

I lived on a three-acre tract that had been hewn from the forest. From those felled trees came the logs that built the original cabin. Over the years, plumbing had been brought indoors and electricity had been added. Now the cabin was snug and modern, with a spacious living area, an eat-in kitchen and a bedroom that was an easy fit for one. Or two.

Before I went inside, I settled Possum into his kennel, made sure his water bucket was full and left him happily chewing on a rawhide bone. As was my habit, I brought Highball inside with me—his age and arthritic limbs had earned him a spot in the kitchen. I fed him a snack, patted him on the head and turned off the kitchen light. For a moment, I stood in the doorway between the kitchen and the hallway, listening to the soft chuffing and whining sounds Highball always made as he prepared for sleep.

The big dog had been my confidant, comforter and protec-

tor since I was fourteen. So many things in my life had
changed since then, but Highball's unconditional love was a
constant. For a moment, I considered walking back across the
darkened kitchen and settling down on the cool floor beside
his bed. As I had so often in the past, I would stroke his velvet
ears and pretend he understood when I told him all about the
evening's events. But a trickle down the inside of my shirt—
a tickle that I tried to believe was perspiration, not a spider—
convinced me that my time could be better spent.

I made a beeline to the bathroom.

I stripped off my clothes, put them in a plastic bag destined
for tomorrow's laundry and washed off sweat and grime under
a stream of lukewarm water. Then I washed again. I ran the
water so hot that it almost scalded, stood beneath a shower of
needle-sharp droplets and scrubbed my skin with a loofa
sponge until I was pink. No amount of soap and water could
purge emotion or chase away unclean images of violent death.
But still, I scrubbed. Finally, when the hot water ran out and
my flesh turned to goose bumps, I stepped from the shower.

As I toweled myself dry, I checked carefully for ticks and
found one. It had embedded its tiny head in the soft flesh
behind my right knee, and its body was already swollen with
my blood. Ignoring a twinge of nausea, I grasped it with
tweezers, exerted steady pressure to pull it free, then crushed
it. I disinfected the site with alcohol, then conducted another
careful, paranoia-driven body search and found nothing.

After dressing in underwear and a soft, oversize white
T-shirt that smelled comfortingly of bleach, I walked down
the long hall to the front of the house and sat down at my desk.
Now that I was clean, my attention turned back to the crime
scene. I pulled a yellow pad from the bottom drawer and a
blue pen from the middle drawer, then jotted down details

while they were still fresh in my mind. When I'd finished filling a page with notes, I pushed away any thought of the evening's events. But I couldn't help remembering the moments before I'd left Chad at the scene.

"It's going to be hours before the state forensics team arrives," Chad said. "And, once they're here, there won't be much for us to do besides stand around and watch. You and Possum gotta be worn out. So why don't you take the kid to her parents and let me do the waiting?" Then his lips twisted into a half smile. "On your way back to their house, you could make sure the trail's flagged in a real obvious way. The state guys are city boys, all of 'em. It wouldn't do to have to call you and Possum out for another search."

The idea, even in jest, was appalling. And confirmed just how exhausted I was.

"Call me—" I began.

"In the morning. Sooner if something turns up tonight. Okay?"

Then, in a gesture that blended cop and friend seamlessly, Chad put his arm around my shoulders and gave them a quick squeeze.

"Be sure to get yourself something to drink, maybe something to eat," he said before pushing me gently in the direction of Tina and the waiting paramedic. "Hell, eat and drink something for us both."

Mostly because I'd promised I would, I went back to the dark kitchen for a snack. The light from the open refrigerator slanted across the room and touched Highball's bed. Though in years past, the sound of my bare footsteps would have awakened him, he snored on undisturbed.

The contents of my refrigerator hadn't changed since I'd surveyed them hours earlier. Except now—and despite missing dinner—food held absolutely no appeal. I shook my head as I let the refrigerator door swing shut and left the kitchen empty-handed.

If Chad were relying on me to eat for him tonight, he was out of luck. Besides, missing a meal wouldn't hurt him. His uniform was getting a bit snug through the waist again, and I briefly wondered if anyone else would tease him about his love handles. Or count push-ups for him.

Despite the smile I managed, the thought of Chad with someone else—anyone else—hurt. But most unguarded thoughts about Chad hurt. Especially lately. Though he still kept a change of clothing in my hall closet and used my sofa and my shower when exhaustion made the treacherous drive into town seem impossibly far, it had been several months since we'd shared a bed.

My decision. The right decision.

"Please, Brooke," he'd said on the last night that we'd spent together. "Let's get married."

The request was a familiar one.

His first proposal had involved champagne, soft music and candlelight. He'd knelt down on one knee and offered me a ring. This time, he simply whispered across the pillow as we lay in my bed, quiet and relaxed after lovemaking.

I said no.

Amazing how so small a word, so softly spoken, could hurt so much. Hurt to say. Hurt to hear. Hurt more each time it was repeated.

That night, I decided that I'd said no to Chad for the last time. Perhaps I should have figured it out sooner, spared us both the pain. But, for a time, I'd convinced myself that a happy ending was possible. Now I knew that I would never say yes. Could never say yes. Because of what I'd seen. Because of what I'd done. Because of the secrets I was bound to keep.

I shook my head at my reflection in the medicine-cabinet mirror, told myself that I'd done the right thing and now it was time to move on. As if determination was all that was needed to drive away longing and tears. Then I popped several vitamin C tablets, washed them down with a large glass of water and headed for bed. After pulling the bedroom door closed behind me, I crawled beneath the blankets and closed my eyes.

Gun fire shattered the night.

Three shots. Coming from the direction of our old blue van.

Gran and I were on our way back from the outhouse and I was a little ahead of her, walking on the path back across the campground. When I heard the shots, I froze and, for a heartbeat, stood illuminated by the van's headlights, unwittingly presenting the perfect target. For a moment I was sure that Dr. Porter had somehow followed us, found us and was attacking my Gran and me. That was my thought as I grabbed Gran's arm, pulling her down beside me as I flattened myself on the ground.

More shots shattered the night, but this time I glimpsed the hot muzzle flashes within the van.

My grandfather's gun.

I'd left it in the purse on the floor of the van. Next to Katie's feet. But there was nothing for her to shoot at—

That was when I scrambled to my feet and raced toward the parking area, half-raising my arm to shield my eyes from the bright headlights and raced across Camp Cadiz. As I ran, I prayed that I was wrong.

Gran's frantic cry came from somewhere behind me.

"Katie!"

Impossible to tell from her voice if her fear was the same as mine.

I didn't wait for her to catch up.

I swerved to avoid the water spigot at the campground's center, pushed myself to run faster though I was already running as fast as I could. Just as I had when I was so much younger, when I hadn't been able run fast enough to save my sister. But this time I knew that the situation was hopeless and that I would be too late.

It was too easy to remember how angry Katie had been. Angry at our mother, who'd abandoned us for her own selfish reasons. Left us alone and unprotected in the hands of a child molester. But our mother was long gone, and tonight there was only Missy who had also abandoned her children. I'd left her unprotected in the van. I should have known better.

A final few steps took me abruptly out of the headlights' glare. Darkness closed in around me as I leaped over the log that separated grass from gravel and stumbled to the front passenger-side door. I yanked it open.

Katie was kneeling up in her seat, facing the rear of the van. Her elbows were braced on either side of the headrest, and she held Grandfather's gun clutched in both hands. Her wheezing was counterpointed by the hollow click, click, click that echoed through the van each time the heavy hammer fell on an empty chamber.

I followed the direction of her gaze.

The dome light was more than enough to illuminate Missy's body. Bullet-riddled and covered in blood, she was still held securely in place by her seat belt. There was a gaping hole where a blue eye had once been.

"My God, Katie!"

I couldn't tell if my own words were a prayer or a curse, a thought or a scream. But my sister heard me.

She turned her head and stared at me.

I stared back.

"Brooke," she whispered, and her tone told me nothing.

Then, suddenly, Katie went limp.

She collapsed down into the front seat, half turning as she pulled her knees up toward her chest and huddled on the seat. She was gasping, fighting to drag more oxygen into her lungs and not succeeding, no longer pulling the trigger but cradling the gun against her chest. Just as she used to hold on to her rag doll whenever she was scared.

I leaned into the car as I decided what to do.

Missy was dead. I couldn't help her.

My sister might die. I owed her more than my life.

The decision was surprisingly easy.

I ignored Missy, frantically searched the front seat for the small purse Katie always carried with her. But I saw only the larger purse, now wide open. So I pulled open the glove compartment and dug through its contents, finally locating one of the backup inhalers we carried in every vehicle. From long habit, I gave it a quick shake, then shoved it between my sister's bluing lips and pressed down on the plastic plunger.

I heard Katie's quick intake of breath, knew she was trying to pull the medication into her lungs. She didn't resist when I took the gun from her and replaced it with the inhaler. Then I supported her shoulders and helped her lift her trembling hands to her mouth once again. Another quick blast of medication, another gasping breath, and I began to believe that Katie might live.

By then Gran was there, standing in the doorway behind me. I turned my face toward her, expecting her to elbow me aside, to take charge as she usually did. But she just stood there, her wrinkled face illuminated by the wash of light from the interior of the car, light bouncing off her glasses, her head slightly tipped. She was slack-jawed and openmouthed.

"She didn't take care of her children," Katie said in a whispery voice. As if that explained it all. "Bad mommies must be punished."

Gran stared at me and Katie, then at Missy, then at me and Katie again.

"No," Gran said. "No, no, no…"

She said the word over and over again. Quietly. Tonelessly. Volume and cadence unchanged as she just shook her head. Back and forth. Back and forth. Slowly. While I held my sister, who was now a cold-blooded murderer, in my arms. And wondered what I was supposed to do next.

Katie's eyes filled with tears, the skin around her nose reddened, and she began sobbing, forcing out words between ragged, gulping breaths. She held her arms out toward our grandmother.

"Don't be angry, Gran," she wailed. "Katie's still your good girl, isn't she?"

Katie's plea snapped Gran from her stupor. She took a breath, squared her shoulders, gave her head a quick shake. Suddenly she seemed more focused. Less aged.

"Yes. You're still my good girl," Gran said, her voice weary and terribly sad. Then her eyes sought mine. "Get on out of there, Brooke. Let me take care of your sister."

By now, tears were plugging Katie's nose and throat, and she was choking, wheezing, panicking again.

As soon as I slid from the van, Gran crawled in. She grabbed Katie's chin, lifted it, forced Katie to look at her.

"Stop that at once. You're making your asthma worse."

Katie, like the good girl she was, hiccupped, sniffled and did as she was told. Gran reached past her to turn off the dome light, then the headlights and plunged us into darkness.

It was still dark when I disposed of Missy's body in a place many miles away from Camp Cadiz. The only light I had was the emergency flashlight that had been in the glove compartment. I released the brake, then watched as the van disappeared beneath the water. Soon, I told myself, crayfish would strip the flesh from Missy's body and silt would cover her bones. The secret would be hidden forever.

Most of the flashlight's remaining life was used up as I tried to assure myself that, come daylight, no hint of my crime would be revealed. Only a dim glow lit my path away from the steep bank of the swampy river basin. So I walked as quickly and far as I could before the light gave out.

Then I was alone. There was no moon and no stars. And dawn was hours away.

I settled beneath a tree whose trunk was as large as a garden shed, whose height I could only guess at in the darkness. I leaned against the tree, the flashlight clutched in my hand, now useless for light and probably equally useless as protection. Gran had taken Grandfather's gun with her. When I'd dropped her and Katie at the Cherokee Rose, she said she'd hide it somewhere safe. For a moment, I regretted not having the gun now. But I wasn't all that sure I'd be able to use it. Not after seeing what its bullets had done to Missy.

The night wrapped around me. Not private or comforting, as I'd always found it before, but crawling with unseen terrors. Exhaustion and fear honed my hearing and dulled my ability to think rationally. Every moment that passed was potentially the moment just before Missy escaped her grave and came after me with mud-caked fingers, her bloody mouth stretched in a silent scream of revenge.

At daybreak, the forest was once again transformed into a safe and familiar place, and Gran could see well enough to drive. I hiked back to the intersection where she had promised to pick me up with Aunt Lucy's car.

I climbed into the car, settled wearily into the passenger seat, and no doubt looked as exhausted as I felt. But the emotions I saw on my grandmother's face—emotions that tightened her lips and narrowed her pale blue eyes—had little to do with my disheveled condition. Mostly, I suspected, her expression reflected frustration and anxiety. Her night blindness had forced her to rely on me to hide a murder that, if revealed, would expose the Underground and destroy the secret network that Gran had protected all her life.

But I knew, even then, that the Black Slough would not easily give up its dead.

"Don't worry," I said before she could ask. "It's all taken care of. No one will ever find her. The Underground is safe."

My eyes opened to the familiar darkness of my bedroom. For a moment, I lay very still, staring at the luminous numbers on my clock. Afraid, but not sure why. The memory of Missy's murder was so familiar that it no longer produced fear. Only sadness and regret.

Three-twenty in the morning.

For another few heartbeats, I continued to wonder what had awakened me. Then the out-of-place noises registered above the hum of the window air conditioner. The scrunch of tires on the gravel driveway. The sound of an approaching car.

I rolled over, suddenly alert. The view out the bedroom window was of the side yard and woods, so I didn't bother peering outside. Instead, I slipped my hand beneath the bed, immediately locating the locked box that held my SIG-Sauer P239. As I listened to the engine turn off and a car door slam, I twisted the key that remained in the lock unless I had company in the house and slipped my hand around the security of the compact pistol's rubber grip.

I listened as Possum briefly woofed a greeting. A moment later, the back door opened, then closed softly. Highball didn't raise an alert, which meant that either the noise hadn't roused him from his deep sleep or he, too, recognized my visitor.

"It's just me," a familiar male voice said. The announcement was loud enough that, if someone in the house was awake, it would be heard and quiet enough that it was unlikely to awaken a sleeper.

By the time I heard Chad's footsteps across the kitchen floor, my gun was under lock and key and my heart rate was back to nearly normal. Though I was tempted, I didn't leave my bed.

The hallway light was switched on and, as Chad walked past my room, his shadow broke up the sliver of illumination that peeked beneath the bedroom door. A moment later, I heard the bathroom door close and the shower running.

Ignoring the thrust of pure lust that accompanied the image of Chad naked in my shower, I rolled over, thumped my pillow and tried to go back to sleep.

A few minutes later, the shower stopped running.

My renegade mind offered images of Chad stepping from the shower and me there with him. How long had it been since I'd used my tongue to catch the droplets that caressed his muscular, golden body? How long since his lips had followed some rivulet's errant path down my breasts and along my curves?

Too long. Far too long.

I turned my head as I heard footsteps in the hallway, this time the sound of bare feet on a hardwood floor. Once again, Chad's shadow blocked the light flowing from the hallway. He stood there for a time, on the other side of my bedroom door.

My breath caught in my throat as I waited in the bed we'd often shared. Wanting him. Determined not to want him. If there had a been a future for us—if the two of us had married—I already had Gran's permission to reveal the secret of the Underground's existence to him. *That* secret, I knew he would willingly protect. But he was too good a cop—too good a man—to condone murder. And a cover-up. I'd always known I could never reveal the secret of Missy's fate. It had taken longer to realize that I couldn't build a happy life on such a horrific deception.

"Brooke?"

It was Chad's voice on the other side of the bedroom door. He spoke only that single word and it was not much more than a hoarse whisper. But in it I was certain I heard the echo of my own longing.

Don't be stupid, I told myself. He probably just wants to talk.

I was in no mood for talk.

I couldn't trust myself just to talk.

So I buried my face in the pillow, gritted my teeth as I willed away an ache I couldn't ignore but would not give in to. For many months, lust had happily coexisted with my lies. But then came love. And love deserved better than lies. Chad deserved better than me.

Eventually, he walked away.

Eventually, I slept.

Chapter 5

The smell of frying bacon awakened me.

I opened my eyes, glanced first at the window—still dark outside—and then at the clock. It was 5:00 a.m. I shut off the alarm, which wasn't due to ring for another thirty minutes, stretched, then slid from my bed. When I opened the bedroom door, the aroma of hickory smoke was joined by mellow undertones of coffee and a hint of sweet vanilla. Pancakes or French toast, I guessed, as much from experience as from an intimate knowledge of the groceries I had on hand. Though I couldn't smell them, I knew that there would be scrambled eggs, too. Chad enjoyed a big breakfast and was an enthusiastic cook. Something I'd never complained about.

Lack of barking from the kennel and the kitchen meant that he'd already fed the dogs, too. No doubt he'd doubled Possum's morning ration because Possum would have greeted Chad—and the sight of the food dish—with a brown-eyed, starved-puppy look and tail-wagging enthusiasm. Highball was far from being a puppy of any kind and definitely more dignified. But he would undoubtedly have received a double ration, too, because Chad took pride in being a fair man and, besides, loved the old dog almost as much as I did. As I got dressed, I thought about the canine ability to manipulate mere humans. Especially soft-hearted guys like Chad.

As a distraction from my too-sentimental thoughts, I concentrated on washing my face, brushing my teeth and getting dressed. Before leaving the bathroom, I checked my reflection in the full-length mirror mounted behind the door.

Unfortunately, my uniform didn't look nearly as good on me as Chad's did on him. His muscular body filled out his uniform, made him look buff and young-cop tough. Add dark glasses and a frown and he could be positively intimidating. The best I could hope for was not to look like a pudgy teenager. The color wasn't bad—the light tan shirt and darker tan slacks were so neutral that they'd look fine on anyone. But despite the small size, the uniform was cut with a man's body in mind—a flat-chested look that was only enhanced by my bulletproof vest. My arms seemed particularly scrawny hanging out from beneath the short sleeves.

Cute, Chad had judged the outfit the first time he'd seen it. Especially the way my curls tumbled out from beneath the uniform's matching ball cap. And then, because I'd been modeling for him in our bedroom and he'd always said I was irresistible when I pouted, he'd demonstrated how quickly the entire uniform and everything beneath it could be removed. After that, he'd spent a little more time—

I shook my head, briefly scowled at my reflection and then went to stand unnoticed in the kitchen doorway.

Chad was standing at the stove, singing a Tim McGraw

tune off-key. Something about being a real bad boy, but a real good man. He was wearing my red-and-white-gingham chef's apron over a clean uniform and was keeping time by moving his hips. He should have looked silly. In fact, he looked so sexy it made my body ache.

Briefly, I questioned the wisdom of our open-door policy. But Chad very rarely took advantage of it. Each time, he'd been dangerously exhausted. Or briefly overwhelmed by some horror he'd encountered on the job. Offering each other a safe place to sleep and a sympathetic ear were acts of friendship. A favor that Chad willingly returned.

I'd lost so much already. I didn't want to lose the precious little bit of our relationship that still remained. That had been ours from childhood.

So maybe it's time you got your hormones under control, I scolded myself. Obviously, *he's* managed it.

I crossed the kitchen and tucked in next to him.

"G'morning," I murmured.

On the stove, the percolator was chugging away, producing coffee that was stronger and hotter than any mere automatic drip coffeemaker could produce. But before lifting the pot from the burner, I touched Chad's face, made him hold still long enough for me to get a good look at his injured cheek.

"Good. You changed the bandage."

"Yes, ma'am," he retorted, flipping me a quick salute. "Got it wet in the shower, and I didn't want to get into trouble."

I reached for the percolator and concentrated on pouring scalding-hot coffee into my mug. Trying not to burn my tongue, I slurped the first sip and kept sipping steadily as I made my way to the round oak table that was tucked into a corner opposite the stove.

"Good coffee," I said, sighing dramatically. "Thank you."

Chad laughed, but kept his eyes on the bowlful of eggs he was beating.

"You might be a cop if—" he paused for a beat, then went on "—you wish caffeine was available as an IV drip."

The game was a familiar one, begun during the months when bed and breakfast were a shared activity. Chad had posted a list he'd found on the Internet to the refrigerator. You Might Be a Cop If… Within a week, the original list became so familiar that we'd begun offering variations. And that, like so many things we shared, evolved into good-natured competition. Unofficial rules dictated that a game period lasted for twenty-four hours and that quips—from the list or our own—had to be situation-appropriate.

"I heard you come in," I said as I settled down into one of the bentwood chairs. "You must have been exhausted."

Chad shredded some cheddar cheese into the eggs.

"*Exhausted* is an understatement," he said. "When the call from the Fishers came in, I was just minutes away from going off duty for the day." He grinned suddenly. "You might be a cop if your idea of a good time is a murder at shift change."

I stuck my tongue out at him, then laughed. Now he was two up on me.

"Yesterday, even before the little girl went missing, the day'd already gone to hell. First thing in the morning, I dealt with a shitload of vandalism complaints."

As he spoke, Chad threw a handful of finely chopped chives into the bowl. They grew wild in the sunny field that lay between the back of the house and the forest, and Chad was fond enough of their mild, oniony flavor to pick them fresh.

"Some kids in a pickup truck apparently took out most of the mailboxes along Route 3 near Iron Furnace. Probably with a baseball bat. I also got to spend some quality time at the county courthouse, testifying against a shade-tree mechanic who likes fixin' folks' cars with stolen parts. His way of keeping the prices down for his customers, he said."

Chad paused as he dumped the eggs into a pan, then began pushing them around with a wooden spatula as he continued speaking.

"After that, I made some traffic stops, arrested a guy for shoplifting cigarettes at Huck's and helped out a couple of women who'd locked their keys in their car. So, business as usual. Until the Fishers called. And after that…" His shrug covered territory that didn't need recapping. "Anyhow, when I finally left the scene and headed toward Maryville, I still figured I could make it back to my apartment, no problem. But I started drifting, closing my eyes just for a second or two, jerking awake, braking for deer that weren't there…. You know the drill."

I knew it only too well.

"You might be a cop if," I said, "your favorite hallucinogen is exhaustion."

"Good one. I'd say the caffeine is kicking in."

"Speaking of, do you need a warm-up?"

"Yeah, that'd be great."

In the midst of cooking, he'd parked his mug in an odd but momentarily convenient spot and forgotten about it. It was a habit that I'd always found entertaining. Now I suppressed my smile as he glanced away from the frying pan, his eyes darting around the room in a futile attempt to locate a mug that I'd spotted the moment I'd come into the kitchen.

I didn't want to risk his burning the eggs, so I waited only another moment before laughing.

"Top of the fridge," I said. "I'll get it for you."

I crossed the room, rescued his mug and poured us both a

refill, then sat back down at the table and reminded him where we'd left our conversation.

"So you realized that, as tired as you were, the next accident scene you were going to visit was likely to be your own."

"That's about it," Chad said as flipped off the gas flame beneath the skillet. "Your place was just down the road. I was going to call, but I realized what time it was and figured you'd be sound asleep. So I let myself in."

He was in the process of splitting the eggs between two plates and paused, pan held midair, to turn his head and search my expression.

"I hope you don't mind—"

I lifted my hand to stop the flow of his words. Now—away from my bed, stoked by caffeine, with the pale beginnings of dawn peeking through the yellow café curtains over the sink—I didn't mind at all. In the morning light, a platonic relationship between ex-lovers seemed entirely possible.

"If I ever have a problem with it, I'll let you know. Deal?"

"Deal."

We'd had breakfast together often enough that the only question Chad needed to ask before filling our plates was how many pieces of French toast I wanted. Everything smelled wonderful and, though I hadn't awakened with much of an appetite, my mouth was watering by the time he brought the food to the table. After a quick detour back to the counter for syrup and more coffee, he settled into the chair opposite me. For a time, we ate in companionable silence.

"So, did the state's crime-scene techs tell you anything interesting about our victim?" I said finally. Then I grinned, suddenly realizing that I could tie the game. "You might be a cop if discussing skeletal remains over breakfast seems perfectly normal to you."

Chad muttered, "Tie," then shook his head. "They never showed up. One of them radioed and—after sounding surprised that we'd been competent enough to secure the scene—announced that they'd been rerouted to a murder-homicide in Effingham. They finished processing *that* scene, but decided to check in to a motel and get some sleep. They promised they'd be out our way sometime this morning."

I sighed.

"I suppose old dry bones aren't a priority compared to a couple of nice, juicy bodies."

Chad agreed.

"The surprise, really, is that they are responding so quickly. A few more murders up north, and it could have been days."

"Maybe it's a blessing," I said. "I don't know about you, but I wasn't looking forward to another long trek from the Fishers' place. You want to take an early-morning hike with me? It shouldn't take us long to find our way from Camp Cadiz to the scene. It's relatively cool now, but the heat index is supposed to climb into the triple digits again. By noon, I'm sure we'll all appreciate a more direct route."

"I'll take care of it, Brooke," he said. "Alone. Okay?"

Odd, I thought. Not that Chad wasn't capable of making his way safely to the scene now that it was daylight. But he'd always been an enthusiastic advocate of hiking with a partner, especially if you planned on straying from marked trails. Too easy to get hurt. Or simply disoriented. It was the kind of precaution that Chad and I often wished aloud that all backpackers would take. If they did, Possum and I would spend considerably less time hunting through the forest.

My expression must have reflected my thoughts.

Chad offered an explanation. A poor one.

"No point in both of us wasting our time," he said a little

too quickly. "You've got work to do. So do I. But I have backup, and you're the only cop that Maryville has. It just makes sense. I can mark the trail myself, then run my usual patrol. Dispatch can contact us both when the state guys arrive. We can meet them at the scene."

Though I was still puzzled, I was willing to accommodate him.

"Okay. As long as—"

He cut in, reading my expression again and half laughing. "Don't worry. I'll be careful."

For a time, we went back to our food and relative silence. I was down to a strip of bacon and a bit of French toast when I noticed that Chad had abandoned the last of his eggs and was staring into his coffee cup, apparently fascinated by whatever was in the bottom. And he was busily and unconsciously rasping his fingers along his jaw. Another habit, one that made the long scar that paralleled his jawbone stand out vividly white against irritated, reddened skin.

He rubbed his face like that whenever he was upset. Which wasn't often. Chad was no stereotypical redhead given to outbursts of emotion or temper. In fact, he usually held his feelings close and guarded them carefully. But early on, I'd learned to pick up on the clues.

Back when we were still kids, he'd walk up the hill to the Cherokee Rose and sit on the porch steps beside me, rubbing his cheek and making small talk. Or not talking at all. Eventually he'd tell me what was on his mind, worrying aloud about missing an easy pass during a football game or getting a bad grade in math or breaking up with whichever girl he'd fallen in love with that month.

I used the side of my fork to cut off a corner of my remaining piece of toast and slipped it across the plate to pick up a little more syrup. Then I put it in my mouth, chewed carefully and waited for him to spit out whatever it was he had to say.

After a while, Chad's fingers slowed. But they didn't relax as I expected them to. Instead, his right hand shifted until his palm cupped the angle of his jaw and his fingertips dug into the ridge just beneath his right eye. That gesture, I hadn't seen for years. But it was something he used to do all the time, back when people around town were still talking about how he'd come to get that scar, back when most of him had been trying to forget how it had happened.

What's dragging you back to the worst moments of your childhood? I wondered. But, even as I asked myself the question, I began to suspect that yesterday's discovery had resurrected a piece of Chad's past, too. And I thought that I had, in fact, been right about the reason for Chad's late-night knock at my bedroom door. Not lust, but an urgent need to talk.

I had finished the last bit of food on my plate before he stopped punishing his face. He gave his head a quick shake, then lifted his mug right-handed and tossed back the last of his coffee as if it were a shot of whiskey. Finally, he met my eyes, and his, I noticed, were intensely green. Then he began talking right in the middle of his thought, as if I knew him well enough that I would understand without being told what had brought him to that point. Within a sentence or two, I usually did. This time was no exception.

"The location works, Brooke. A big tree. Though I suppose the forest is full of them. But the ravine...remember? He told the cops that he threw the gun into a ravine. Though as drunk as he was and as dark as it was, how he managed not to fall over the edge is anyone's guess. Anyway, I know it's a long shot, but I can't help but think that maybe—"

Then, suddenly, Chad must have heard something in his

own voice that he disapproved of. Or that scared him. And I suspected…no, I *knew* it was hope.

Chad snapped his mouth shut, tightened his lips, then noisily pushed his chair back from the table. He stood, turning away as he took a step—

I put my hand over his wrist, stopping him.

"Forget what I just said, okay?" he said flatly, his back still to me. "I'm just being stupid. Acting like a damned fool rookie. There's no way anyone's going to know anything before we process the remains."

"There's nothing stupid about what you're saying. Or feeling," I said quietly. "Talk to me, Chad. So we can deal with it."

Together. Just as we always did. Friend to friend. Cop to cop. That was what I thought and didn't say.

He looked back toward me, hesitated for another moment, then found his voice. A deep, unwavering voice that didn't even hint at the scars that a murderous father had left on a son's soul.

"I think maybe you and Possum finally found my mother. Just like you said you would."

We left the house together, each snatching a uniform cap from the hooks beside the door. I pulled on my tan ball cap and Chad put on the less comfortable billed hat that matched his blue uniform. We walked across the little porch with its sturdy built-in bench and down several steps to the gravel path that crossed a patch of lawn. Midyard, the path split. Several yards to the right, it ended near the dogs' kennel area. Go left for about twice that distance, and the path merged with the end of a wide, U-shaped gravel drive where two official police vehicles were parked. One bulky and white. One sleek and blue.

Possum barked and bounced against the chain-link of his kennel the moment it became apparent that we weren't headed in his direction. Highball barked, too, but with less urgency, less hope. He understood the early-morning owner-goes-to-work routine.

"Quiet, you silly dogs," I said.

But I said it halfheartedly, more from habit than conviction. Not unexpectedly, I was ignored. The nearest neighbor was almost a mile down the road, so no one was going to be disturbed by dogs barking. And I knew that Highball and Possum would stop as soon as we got into our vehicles. Denied the possibility of playtime or more food or a car ride, they would occupy themselves by gnawing at a tough rawhide bone or chewing the softer rubber of a tennis ball until it popped.

Chad and I had reached the driveway and the dogs were still barking when Chad turned toward me, put his hands on my shoulders and leaned in to kiss me goodbye.

He caught himself almost immediately.

"Sorry," he blurted, "bad habit—"

Then he realized that didn't sound really good, either.

Embarrassment was rapidly staining his cheeks when he salvaged the awkward moment by giving my shoulders a quick little shake, then releasing them.

"Do as I say, not as I do," he said. "Don't you go spending your time speculating about our victim or forming any opinions that aren't supported by fact. And until forensics is done at the site, we don't have any facts. Got it, rookie?"

"Got it," I said, grateful that he was too rattled to realize how very close I'd come to returning his kiss as heedlessly as he'd offered it. A bad habit, indeed.

I climbed into my SUV. As I pulled away, Chad was already sliding into his car. He followed me to the end of the wide gravel drive and pulled up beside me. Just before I turned right, in the direction of the highway that would take me into Maryville, I lifted my hand in a casual wave. He returned it, swung left, heading farther into the forest toward Camp Cadiz.

For a moment, I watched his dust in the rearview mirror. I thought about his desire to mark the trail to the crime scene on his own, and realized that I knew why he wanted to go without me. Last night, after I'd left the forest with Tina, a handful of rangers and other cops had remained with Chad. They'd undoubtedly stayed within eyeshot of him the entire time. Later today, he knew the crime-scene techs would arrive, remove the remains and take them to the state forensics lab for processing. So this morning would be his only opportunity to be out there by himself.

I braked at the stop sign that marked the intersection with the highway, and waited for the traffic to clear as I thought about Chad and the hope that I'd seen in his green eyes. Hope, and a hint of reflected light along his lower lashes that suggested something more tangible, but expertly controlled.

Chad had a right to be alone, I thought as I stepped on the accelerator and made my turn onto the highway. A right to some small measure of privacy. Because even the possibility that the remains belonged to his murdered mother was enough to make a grown man cry.

Chapter 6

Ed Statler was an insomniac.

The sign posted in the front door of Statler's Fill-Up announced that business hours were from 6:00 a.m. until 10:00 p.m. and that absolutely no personal checks would be accepted. In fact, the store was generally open for business from predawn until past midnight, and if Ed knew you—and you'd never stiffed him—he'd take your check. Or, in a pinch, extend you credit. Between customers, Ed would sit at the counter looking out his big plate-glass window, watching the traffic on the highway.

It wasn't quite 6:00 a.m., but the lights were on inside the convenience store and the sign in the heavy glass door was turned so that it read Open. I was confident that inside the store, the coffee would already be brewed and the doughnuts that Ed made every morning to sell to his customers would be hot out of the fryer.

Outside, there weren't any vehicles in the lot except Ed's. Which wasn't unusual at almost any hour of the day, except for Wednesdays. A chain of convenience stores had opened up and down 146, their uniformity and predictability luring all but the locals away from eccentric little places like Statler's. But I suspected that, for the past several years, running the place was more hobby—or perhaps habit—for Ed. Talk in town was that his wife's stock-market investments had guaranteed the couple a comfortable retirement. In any event, Ed seemed content with the business he had, even if that meant going for hours without seeing a customer.

The gas pumps at Statler's offered diesel, premium and a ten-percent ethanol blend that—according to a corn cob–shaped sticker near the credit-card slot—supported the local farm economy. I pulled under the aluminum canopy that sheltered the pumps, turned off my engine, slid a city of Maryville credit card into the usual slot and watched the numbers on the pump flip as I poured gasoline into the less-than-fuel-efficient SUV. As usual, I felt a twinge of gratitude that I wasn't out of pocket for the fuel. After that, I headed for the store to make a purchase with my own money.

I intended to begin my investigation of the remains up near Camp Cadiz with a bit of gossip. And Ed Statler was just the man to provide it. Ed always bragged that most days, if asked, he could tell you where half the town was based on who'd stopped in or driven by. Add to that the fact that Ed was an easy man to talk to and, like many such men, was also a good listener. And the fact that for the last thirty years, Ed had sold homemade ham and beans and corn bread at lunchtime every Wednesday.

Ham and beans had always been a particular favorite in small-town southern Illinois, and Ed's missus did a particu-larly good job with that old favorite. So anytime after about ten o'clock on Wednesday morning, a sizable segment of the local population drove up the highway to Statler's. Those who couldn't spare the time or preferred not to eat elbow-to-elbow with other customers at one of the long, oilcloth draped folding tables at the back of the store carried away warm, heavy foam containers.

Beyond the opportunity to eat good food, Statler's on Wednesdays was a regular social event. Even folks who just stopped long enough to pick up food greeted neighbors and gossiped with friends. And Ed listened. But unlike a good part of Maryville's population, Ed only passed that information on to a select group. Fortunately, Chad and I—even before we'd become cops—were among Ed's chosen.

It was too early for the rush. Too early, in fact, for Ed's missus to drive over to deliver the big iron pots and battered baking pans that would fill the convenience store with a smoky smell of ham overlaid with a sweet, toasty whiff of corn. And although Mrs. Statler was probably in the midst of frenzied food preparation at their home near the center of town, Ed was sitting at the counter with Maryville's weekly newspaper spread out in front of him.

Ed lifted his head and a broad smile split his dark face when he saw me come in. For as long as I could remember, he'd favored Hawaiian-print shirts—he said they made him feel cheerful. Today's shirt was a retro masterpiece of cherry-colored gardenias with bright yellow stamens against a background of lime-green.

The shirts were cheerful. Like Ed. And I had no problem admitting to myself that, most days, Ed's upbeat attitude was more important to me than keeping abreast of local gossip. It was, in fact, the real reason I made a habit of stopping by to chat with Ed almost every morning. But not today.

"Nice shirt," I said.

His smile expanded into a grin that revealed a single gold front tooth bisecting a row of bright white.

"Bought it on e-Bay. Man, I *love* technology."

I twisted off the lid of my thermal cup and began filling it with coffee. Like no one else in town and probably few in all of southern Illinois, Ed understood that coffee should be something more than brown-tinged water. He ground the beans for every pot, even brewed his decaf dark, and had probably addicted more than a few Maryville residents. I'd discovered coffee—real coffee—sitting in the Statlers' kitchen when I was in fifth grade. He'd fixed me and his daughter, who was about my age, a big cup cut with sweetened, condensed milk. She'd grown up and moved to Chicago. I'd stayed in Maryville and discovered I preferred my coffee bitter.

I lifted my chin in the direction of Maryville's weekly paper.

"Anything interesting?" I asked.

I figured that Chad and I had discovered the remains near Camp Cadiz late enough in the evening that we hadn't made the local paper. And a crime scene that was a decade old wasn't likely to get much more than a paragraph or two in any of the regional daily newspapers.

"Nope," Ed said.

But then he thumped the tip of a knobby, black finger on the black-and-white photo of the state's current governor. A man so hopelessly a big-city northerner that he refused to leave Chicago to live in the governor's mansion in Springfield, a town that was significantly larger and farther north than Maryville. As far as I knew, no one in Maryville had ever admitted voting for him.

"Unless you consider the latest thing those Chicago Democrats are proposing to make life difficult for us folks down here," Ed added.

I leaned against the counter, sipped my coffee and idly considered the tray of doughnuts just a few inches from my elbow. You know you're a cop if you consider doughnuts a food group, I thought with a smile and awarded myself a point. I had a particular weakness for the ones coated in chocolate, but I was too full from breakfast to be tempted.

"Aren't you feeling well?" Ed asked, real concern apparent in his voice.

"I had a big breakfast at home."

One of Ed's grizzled eyebrows crawled up his forehead as his dark brown eyes slid in my direction, making his face a human question mark.

If he asks me how Chad is, I'll scream, I thought. Ed, like most of Maryville, knew that Chad and I had lived together. It was the kind of arrangement that raised eyebrows in conservative Maryville and, I supposed, kept us very much in the prayers of our local Baptist congregation. But they'd been praying for marriage, not separation, and I doubted anyone had celebrated when Chad had moved into an apartment over one of the businesses on Main Street.

Now the locals could only guess about our relationship, which inspired more gossip than merely living together had. Except for Ed, who didn't need to speculate because he could use the number of doughnuts I ate to gauge the state of my personal life. And there was no doubt that I ate fewer doughnuts when Chad—and his hearty breakfast habit—were in residence.

Even Ed, as astute as he was, could sometimes put two and two together and come up with five. But I'd apparently misjudged the man. He didn't ask me about Chad or tell me how pleased he was that we'd gotten back together. Instead, his eyebrow slipped back down into its usual location and his expressive face grew serious.

"A ranger stopped by here for coffee real late last night. On her way home from an emergency call out. She said you and Possum went searching for a little, lost girl and got her back to her parents safe and sound."

I nodded, thinking of the number of people on the scene last night. Multiply that by colleagues, families and buddies, and a significant part of Maryville had probably been buzzing with the news of the search—and the newly discovered remains—before I'd gone to sleep last night. Just as well, I thought cynically, that the crime scene was as isolated as it was. Otherwise, it'd quickly become a local tourist attraction.

"Possum's a good dog," I said.

"Yeah, he sure is," Ed said. "There was also some talk about a climb down into ravine—a climb that the gal I was talking with said no one else she could think of would have attempted solo and in the dark. Suppose it just wouldn't do, though, to call the handler heroic."

"No," I said, though I smiled at the compliment, "it wouldn't."

"Coming from a Tyler, I'm not surprised. You folks have always been real quiet about all the good you do. And the risks you all take doing it."

Except for the risks, which I supposed might have been thrown in to describe my day job or search work, Ed might have been talking about all of the volunteering Aunt Lucy and Gran did in our town. Or he might have been talking about something else altogether. Something like the Underground.

Despite the precautions our family took to keep the organization secret, I suspected that there were people in town—especially old-timers like Ed—who had caught on. Who knew

that not all the guests at the Cherokee Rose were paying customers and noticed the disproportionate number of scared
and battered women who stayed with us for just a night or two.
And who had figured out that the occasional bruises that Gran
or Aunt Lucy or I couldn't hide weren't, as we always
claimed, the result of clumsiness or bad luck.

Before I could muster a denial or come up with a response
that contradicted or deliberately misinterpreted him, Ed
shifted to a new subject.

"Heard you also found some old bones buried up near
Camp Cadiz. You figure it's Chad's momma?"

Though it was unusual for Chad to jump to that conclusion,
that was usually the first question asked when any body was
discovered within a hundred-mile radius of Maryville. Chad's
father hadn't remembered exactly where he'd left his wife's
body. In the forest somewhere, he'd said. But he did remember
that he'd made her kneel and beg God aloud for forgiveness
that he'd assured her wouldn't be forthcoming. Then he'd put
a bullet in her head.

"Don't know yet," I said. "Is that what folks think?"

He shrugged.

"You of all people should know…folks hereabouts like to
talk. Not much else to do, I suppose. Doesn't really matter if
they've got anything to say."

I couldn't argue with that. If gossip were illegal, most of
Maryville would be jailed as chronic offenders.

"What do you say?" I asked.

"I say, it'd be good if that boy could bury his momma
proper after all these years. And Lord knows, those bones
might just be her."

Then he picked up the tongs that shared the tray with the
doughnuts, lifted a white paper sack from the stack next to

the tray, and tucked a chocolate-iced doughnut into it. Handed it to me.

"For later," he said. "So, do you think this weather'll be breaking soon?"

End of discussion, I thought with a stifled sigh. I knew from experience that Ed couldn't be bullied into saying one more word than he wanted to and, unlike so many others in town, wouldn't talk about what he didn't know about. So I didn't bother pushing him. Maybe tomorrow or the day after, when I had a little more information and Maryville gossip had cranked up another notch or two, Ed would have more to say. But until then...

We talked about the weather for a bit, then moved on to speculate about the price that local farmers would be getting for a bushel of corn this season, then got down to our usual argument. He thought that my doughnut and coffee should be on the house. I told him, as I often did, that I wouldn't come by anymore if I couldn't pay.

"I'd sure miss your coffee," I added. Then I patted my waist, which was made considerably thicker by my bullet-proof vest. "But I could probably do without the doughnuts."

I won as I sometimes did, handed Ed a couple of dollars and got back change. As I left the store with coffee mug and doughnut bag in hand, it occurred to me that not only had I managed to pay for my purchases, but I'd actually just had a conversation with Ed where he didn't have the last word.

I congratulated myself too soon.

The door hadn't quite swung shut behind me when I heard his voice.

"You be sure to say 'hey' to Chad for me. He's a real nice boy. 'Bout time you two got back together."

I raised my hand in a wave, but didn't look back. As I climbed back into my SUV, I was still shaking my head and laughing. Mostly at myself. How could I have believed, even for a moment, that my personal life wasn't everyone else's business?

A quarter mile down 146, I pulled into a used-car lot at the northeast edge of town, tucking my SUV in between a rusted El Camino that I doubted had ever seen better days and a once-blue Chevy truck with oversize tires and a jacked-up frame that I doubted was street legal. The curb in front of me was fairly low, and the location put my radar gun in the right place to catch early-morning commuters speeding toward the ferry.

I spent the next hour making money for the city treasury and keeping the roads safer for the good citizens of Maryville. It was the kind of task I usually enjoyed because it gave me time to think. Today was no exception. And, like so many of my thoughts lately, I couldn't help thinking about Chad. But today, I thought not of us and the immediate past, but of the circumstances of his mother's murder.

The trial had been such a popular topic around town that sometimes I felt as if I'd actually witnessed it rather than simply eavesdropped on adult conversations. Like everyone else in Maryville, I knew that Chad's father was a mean-tempered drunk. And the night he murdered his wife and tried to do the same to his son, he'd been drinking heavily. That was something he'd admitted in court, prompted by a defense lawyer who wanted to blame the alcohol, rather than the man, for what had happened. When the bars along Dunn Street closed at 2:00 a.m., he drove his battered pickup back home.

It was storming that night. Figuring that the thunder had muffled the sounds of his arrival, he'd taken the opportunity to peer in through the tattered curtains of his home and spy on his wife. As always, he expected to catch her with another man. Instead, he saw her talking on the phone that she was forbidden to use except to reach him in an emergency. She hung up when she heard him come in, thus confirming his paranoid suspicions.

Chad's father had always questioned the parentage of his only child. That's what the lawyer told the jury. It didn't matter that his wife swore she'd never been with another man. Or that even the most casual observer could see a strong resemblance between father and son. What mattered was that, in his alcohol-poisoned mind, Chad's father thought he finally had proof of his wife's infidelity. So he dragged the sleeping boy from his bed, then forced the child and his wife at knife-point through the rain and into the truck.

With his family held captive in the cab of the old pickup, Chad's father sped northward along Big Creek Road. As he drove, he raged at his wife, screaming about adultery and betrayal and brandishing a razor-sharp skinning knife in her direction. He told her he was going to kill her and the boy and leave their bodies out in the forest for animals to gnaw on. Their souls, he assured her, would burn in hell. As befitted a whore and her bastard child.

That's when Chad, who was almost thirteen, lunged past his mother and grabbed his father's wrist. But the boy wasn't as strong as his rage-maddened father, and the man shook him loose. He used the back of his hand to knock the boy aside, then raised the knife—

Maybe it was God's will that the boy lived, Chad's father told the court. Just as it had been God's will that Abraham not slay his son, Isaac. More likely, the prosecutor rebutted, it was the determination of the boy's mother that had saved his life. There were deep scratches on her husband's arm where she had grabbed it in an attempt to deflect the deadly blade away from her son.

In the midst of his parents' struggle for possession of the knife, the truck hit water where Big Creek had overflowed onto the road. Chad's father grabbed the steering wheel with both hands, fighting to regain control of the skidding vehicle. That was when Chad's mother opened the passenger-side door and pushed her son out of the truck.

He landed in the water, somehow scrambling to his feet in time to watch as his father brought the truck under control. Then the driver-side door opened. Chad watched as his father jumped from the truck and waded through the knee-deep water toward him. For a moment, Chad was sure it would be all right, was sure that his father had regained his senses and come to rescue him. But as his father reached his side, a flash of lightning revealed that the knife was still clenched in his hand. He struck at his son again, a heartbeat before the boy flung himself into the deeper, fast-running water of the creek. That time, the blade sliced flesh.

A red Toyota sped by, the radar gun registering sixty. The posted limit was forty-five, so I hit the siren and the accelerator, and pulled the car over.

The driver was a pretty gal from up north who accepted the ticket philosophically. The gray-muzzled black Lab riding on a big cushion in the backseat of the car seemed predisposed to liking cops. After I'd issued the ticket, the driver and I spent a few minutes chatting about dogs in general, Labs and German shepherds in particular. But there was no doubt in my mind that she wished I was male, preferably young and cute. Chad, I suspected, would have let her off with a warning.

I smiled as I thought of a quip I wouldn't repeat to Chad.

You know you're a male cop if...you consider traffic stops a social event.

I crossed the street and spent a little time monitoring the speed of northbound motorists who today didn't seem to be in the same hurry as those heading south. My thoughts turned toward the remains near Camp Cadiz. Within a day or two, we'd have definite information about sex and age and a more accurate determination of height. There were no dental records—Chad's mother had never gone to a dentist. But if everything else fit, a test might just match Chad's DNA— already on file—with the unknown victim's.

For Chad's sake, I hoped the victim was his mother, that he could finally lay her to rest. But, realistically, the remains probably belonged to someone else. Most likely a stranger. For many decades, bodies had been disposed of with some regularity in the forest. The sparse population, difficult terrain and dense woods made it likely they wouldn't be found. Except by accident.

If the DNA didn't match—if our victim wasn't Chad's mom—maybe we could send the skull off for facial reconstruction and eventually have some idea about the victim's appearance. But chances were we would never discover the identity of the victim. And a murderer would continue to walk free.

Just like Katie.

Chapter 7

A call from dispatch saved a tanned, lean-faced young man from Ridgway from a ticket. I'd just pulled the white-on-cream three-quarter ton Ford pickup over and was discussing the need for a safety sticker on a vehicle registered as a farm truck when the radio crackled to life.

"Your lucky day," I murmured as I waved him on his way, then turned my full attention to a report of bad news from a familiar address.

"They're at it again," the female voice on the radio added to the end of one of her characteristically businesslike messages.

Feeling every bit as exasperated as she sounded, I acknowledged the call as I pulled out into traffic with lights and sirens clearing the way. As unlikely as it was that the call was, in fact, an emergency, I did my job and treated it as if it were. Minutes later, I left Route 146 and headed for an old neighborhood of neatly kept bungalows and—for the most part—law-abiding senior citizens.

I slowed down when I turned onto Honeysuckle Drive and parked my car between the two houses on the cul-de-sac at the end of the street. The emergency call had been made by the owner of 1231 Honeysuckle, but I had no doubt that I'd end up talking to the neighbor at 1233.

As I opened the wrought-iron gate and walked up the flagstone path to the first house, it occurred to me that the front porches of 1231 and 1233 accurately reflected the homes' owners. The porch I was stepping onto was glossy white and furnished with wicker furniture, cushy floral pillows and hanging baskets of cascading petunias. Next door, the other porch was pony-spotted with multicolor layers of peeling paint, had rusted milk cans and cracked ceramic crocks overflowing with bright flowers decorating its sagging steps, and supported an old sofa. Also floral. No car in front of Marta Moye's impeccably kept house—she no longer drove. A vintage yellow Cadillac was the only thing that was impeccably kept on the property next door.

Marta, who had recently celebrated her sixty-eighth birthday, was sitting on the wicker sofa, obviously waiting for me. Today, she was the one who had called 911, so hers was the story I needed to hear first.

Despite the flowing woven cotton jumper she wore, her usually pale, round face was flushed bright red beneath a halo of pink-toned gray hair. As much with agitation as with heat, I thought. She sputtered as she stood, still clutching her tiny Yorkie, Peanut, against her ample breasts.

"That…that…*man*…urinated on my hedge!" she shrilled the moment I set my foot on her porch.

That man was Larry Hayes, the proprietor of the Antique

Attic and Marta's senior by at least a decade. I glanced at my watch knowing that, these days, Larry opened the Attic closer to noon than ten. That was, when he bothered opening it at all. I shook my head slowly, thinking that his retirement hours were leaving him plenty of time for his feud with Marta.

Rumor had it that there was a good reason that the break in the fence between their backyards had remained unrepaired for decades. Scandalous, the usual local gossips maintained. Such carrying on—especially at their age! And they wondered if the affair had been going on before Marta's husband had died and Larry's young wife had deserted him.

But a month earlier, on my first official visit to the two frame houses, I'd noticed that the passageway had been crudely repaired—on both sides of the fence. A neat square of latticework on Marta's side. Mismatched scraps of lumber on Larry's. And the same ladies who had been happily outraged now happily discussed the inevitable consequences of "that kind of behavior."

The feud between the two seemed to be escalating. In the past week, their calls to 911 had almost become a daily event. Most of them in the morning, when the two seemed to take particular pleasure in annoying each other. Usually, I tried to be patient. I liked Larry. I liked Marta. But today, with the memory of a root-ensnared skeleton fresh in my mind, their complaints were particularly irrelevant.

Twenty minutes later, after taking enough notes to keep Marta happy, I climbed the steps onto Larry's front porch. He looked utterly relaxed as he sat on his battered floral sofa, sipping extra-sweet iced tea. He was dressed in slim jeans, aged and bleached to a soft blue, and a short-sleeved shirt in a shade of pearl-pink. The V of the shirt revealed a turkey neck and a curl of white chest hair. Given the proximity of their yards and Marta's volume as she'd spoken with me—and assuming that Larry had turned his hearing aid on—there was no doubt in my mind that Larry had heard every word of her complaint.

Difficult to know if it was friendship or anticipation that brightened Larry's face when he saw me, but it prompted him to offer me tea from a nearby pitcher. When Katie and I were younger, Larry's tea had ranked as one of our favorite beverages, though I'd probably had gallons to her quarts. I drank it to wash down the peanut-butter-and-cheese sandwiches that Larry and I ate while we sat in his battered, flat-bottomed boat and fished for anything that'd bite.

Katie had hated fishing. Hated, she'd said, to see defenseless things die. Not just the fish we caught, but even the worms that baited our hooks. At the time, I'd thought that odd. I still did, but for a different reason.

Today, as usual, the aluminum pitcher was stacked with ice and sparkled with beads of condensation. I was hot, sweaty and sorely tempted. But I'd turned down Marta's lemonade just minutes earlier, so I couldn't accept a cup of tea from Larry. There'd be no end of trouble if I appeared to be taking sides.

"Thanks, but no," I said.

I perched on the porch railing just across from the tanned, skinny old man. I spoke in a normal voice and judged from his posture and expression that he was having no problem hearing this morning. A change from the visit I'd had to make a few days earlier, when I was sure he'd deliberately turned his hearing aid off. And he'd made a point of keeping his bad ear turned toward me.

"So, tell me, what's going on?"

It took a few minutes for him to gather enough enthusiasm

to tell his side of the story, but he eventually endorsed Marta's account. With a single addendum.

"I peed on *my* property, on *my* side of the hedge."

Which explained it all, I supposed.

The day before, Larry had called 911 and, when I'd arrived, had complained about Marta encouraging her dog to relieve itself in the vicinity of the very same hedge. I had pointed out—quite moderately, I'd thought at the time—that there was no law against Peanut doing his duty on *his* side of the hedge as long as Marta didn't allow the waste to pile up. Which she didn't.

I allowed my exasperation to color my voice.

"Goddamn it, Larry."

He raised an eyebrow at me, not because I'd called him by his first name—he'd given me permission to do that when I was ten—but because I'd taken the Lord's name in vain. Larry was proud of being a God-fearing man. Marta, he'd assured me on several previous occasions, was the Almighty's way of testing him. Just like the sores He'd inflicted on poor old Job.

I considered the possibility that Larry and Marta were God's way of testing *me*, briefly rolled my eyes in His direction—toward a hazy blue sky that promised no relief from the already oppressive heat of the day—and prayed for patience. Then I tried again.

"I'll throw you in jail if you pee on the hedge again."

I figured that for a sufficiently unpleasant threat. The town's solitary cell was a windowless room that had formerly served as records storage in the brick city building. At about the time I'd been hired, rows of filing cabinets had been replaced by two cots, a utilitarian sink and toilet and a locking steel door with a barred viewing window. The cell opened into my small office, was a dozen steps removed from the larger offices of

the mayor and the city clerk, and was at the far end of the
building from an auditorium that was used for city meetings
during the week and social gatherings on the weekends.

After a year's worth of occasional overnight occupants
and despite air-conditioning and regular scrubbing, Maryville's lockup now smelled like most every other lockup.
Summer humidity seemed to encourage the oily, persistent
aroma of perspiration, urine, vomit and beer. Not that I served
alcohol to the inmates, but beer was usually what landed them
there. Lately, the smell had been bad enough that the mayor
complained about it to anyone who would listen.

Larry was on the city council, so certainly he had heard the
mayor complaining. He'd probably smelled the odor himself.
So the possibility of ending up as one of the cell's few sober
visitors was, in my opinion, a deterrent. But Larry wasn't
looking deterred. Rather, the expression on his wizened face
rivaled that of a Friday-night drunk-and-disorderly. His beetle
brows pulled together into a wiry V-shaped gray caterpillar
above pale blue eyes, and his lips twisted into a pettish scowl.

"What could you possibly charge me with?"

I thought about it for a heartbeat.

"Public indecency."

I was serious.

He was outraged.

"I made sure she couldn't see my privates."

Based on Marta's account, he wasn't lying.

"He waited until I was out on the steps, watering my
petunias," she'd told me. "Then he shouted to get my attention. I could only see his head and shoulders above the hedge,
but I could tell he was…you know…unzipping. And I could
hear exactly what he was doing. Afterwards, he sighed, then
waved at me!"

I looked down at Larry, who was still scowling, and resisted the urge to throttle him. Instead, I briefly rubbed my thumb across a couple buttons of my uniform shirt in a futile attempt to blot the itchy trickle of sweat between my breasts. The trickle was protected—in fact, encouraged—by a pair of 32Bs encased beneath too many layers for a hot summer day. Bra, T-shirt, vest, uniform. The vest was also layered—sixteen ultra-thin layers of Kevlar rated IIA and guaranteed to stop a .40 caliber Smith & Wesson bullet.

Sadly, the vest offered no protection against the likes of Larry and Marta. But living most of my life in Maryville did. I knew, for instance, that Larry and Marta attended the same Methodist church and that the minister's wife was a reporter for Maryville's gossipy weekly newspaper. The very paper that Ed Statler had been reading.

I took a deep breath, then deliberately slowed my speech and softened my vowels so my drawl was unmistakably southern Illinois. But I kept my tone unyielding. Important that Larry understand: I might be his friend and a hometown girl, but I would do whatever it took to keep the peace.

"This problem between you and Marta, I want you to resolve it, Larry. Resolve it or forget it. Leave each other alone. If I have to come out here again, I will tell Reverend and Mrs. Cox about the little war you two have going on. The Spirit might compel the reverend to bring it up during Sunday services, in the context of loving thy neighbor. But even if he doesn't, his wife will certainly publish the details I'll provide in the Police Blotter."

Minutes later, I made a return trip to Marta's house, delivered a similar message and left her sputtering on her front porch.

Then I crawled gratefully back into the SUV, cranked up the air-conditioning and thought about gossip. And scandal.

And how I now exploited almost daily and virtually guiltlessly the very thing that had victimized Katie and me throughout our childhoods.

No doubt having Katie and me arriving in town too skinny and never having set foot in a school, much less a church, set tongues wagging throughout Maryville. Only Aunt Lucy and Gran knew the actual circumstances that landed us in Maryville. Knew that—most likely scared off by the cops who swarmed our apartment building—our mother had never returned to claim us. No one in Maryville ever knew what had happened to Katie on the day our mother abandoned us. Or what, except for Katie's brave intervention, would have happened to me.

But lack of information had never been a problem where Maryville gossip was concerned. Folks had pretty much always expected the worst from Lucy Tyler's sister, Lydia. You could see it coming, I heard them say. That Lydia Tyler always thought she was better than everyone else. Her, with her Marilyn Monroe looks and too-tight clothing! But with a father not long dead from cancer and a mother who was too busy mourning and putting food on the table to notice much of anything, it was easy enough to understand how a teenager like Lydia might spin out of control.

To hear people talk, it was no surprise to anyone—besides, maybe, Gran and Aunt Lucy—when Lydia ran away with money and jewelry stolen from the Cherokee Rose and its guests. To Hollywood. And every once in a while Katie or I would hear folks snicker about my mother ending up doing *those* kinds of movies. And worse. They wondered aloud if our mother was still alive or if, by now, drugs or alcohol or one of *those* diseases had killed her.

As we got older, the inevitable comparisons between us and our mother began. Mostly because it was apparent to anyone with eyes that Katie was growing up to look just like our mother. Five foot five, blond, beautiful and voluptuous. Fortunately, folks whispered just loudly enough for us to hear, Katie was also quiet and shy and well-behaved. It was her spindly limbed, headstrong sister who had Lydia's personality, who hadn't learned proper respect for almost anyone, who used her fists in the school yard the way no proper young lady ever would. And because I looked nothing like my sister and because gossip always assumes the worst, folks speculated about whether Katie and I shared the same father. A woman like Lydia Tyler wouldn't much care who she slept with if it got her what she wanted, they said. No doubt both girls were bastards.

Who my father might be plagued me, inspired a years-long search for my birth certificate in every nook and cranny of the Cherokee Rose. I stopped looking when I was twelve. That's when I found a bundle of letters tucked beneath a floorboard. They were all addressed to Aunt Lucy at a post-office box address on the other side of the river. From the postmarks, I could tell that my mother had been writing to her sister ever since she'd run away. The series of letters, which ended about a year before Katie and I came to live at the Cherokee Rose, detailed my mother's big career plans and her new clothes, described parties with movie stars and boyfriends who were talent scouts.

Never once did she mention having two little girls.

Not too long after I found those letters, a registered letter was delivered to the Cherokee Rose with a Las Vegas postmark. I never read that letter. Never even saw it. But I didn't have to. Maryville gossip provided me with all the information that I needed.

I was in the library, sitting on the floor between shelves, reading the first pages of *The Blue Sword*. It was an adventure, which was the kind of book I liked. That's when I overheard the librarian talking to the chief of Maryville's volunteer fire department. And I heard my mother's name. The librarian said that a friend at the post office had told her that Lucy Tyler had received a letter from her sister a couple of days earlier. Between that letter and the one that was mailed back—to a *bail bond* company—Lucy had pulled five hundred dollars from her savings account and bought a money order.

I didn't understand, back then, the significance of that transaction. But I did know that my mother hadn't ever bothered writing to *me*. Or to Katie. Certainly, she'd never phoned us. Or sent us gifts on our birthdays or at Christmastime.

My mother didn't care about us.

That's what I decided that day in the library. And that's when I tried to stop caring about her. Tried to stop even thinking about her. Because I knew the truth. Though Aunt Lucy was always telling us that our mother loved us, I'd overheard Gran say more than once that Lydia Tyler cared only about herself.

I believed Gran.

Of course, I never told Katie about the letters or my decision. I didn't want to risk her having an asthma attack and ending up in the emergency room or maybe dying. And I didn't want her crying all the time the way she had when Aunt Lucy had first brought us home to Maryville. So I kept quiet as Katie created soap-opera fantasies about our mother's amnesia or her undercover work in some foreign country or her long imprisonment on false charges. Someday, Katie assured me, our mother would come and find us. Gran would forgive her. Aunt Lucy would hug her. And finally reunited, we would all live happily at the Cherokee Rose.

* * *

When, I wondered idly as I lifted the microphone from its mount on the dashboard, had Katie finally stopped believing that our mother would return? I thought about it for a minute, realized that we'd been in high school before her hope had turned to bitterness. Bitterness that had festered and spread like poison through her mind. And had finally ended in murder.

My bleak turn of thought made it easy to keep my voice serious when I checked back in with dispatch and reported that the 911 on Honeysuckle Drive had been resolved. At least for the time being. In turn, I was told that Chad had just radioed. He and the state crime-scene techs were headed to Camp Cadiz and would meet me in the parking lot.

My trip back through the forest took me along the same route that Chad's father had traveled with his terrified family a decade earlier. Past the narrow, rutted mud road that had once led to a rotted-out single-wide trailer. A few years earlier, a gang from out of the area had set up a meth lab on the property. They'd discovered too late that—unlike many of the rarely traveled roads that crisscrossed the forest and rural southern Illinois—this particular dead-end road was regularly traveled by a big, redheaded county cop.

For a while, I watched the dense green woods flash past on both sides of the gravel road. Then I crossed the narrow bridge over Big Creek. For about a mile, the creek paralleled the road's right shoulder, occasionally visible through the tangle of green foliage. This morning, it sparkled unthreateningly in the early-morning sun. But on the night Chad's mother had died, the rushing current had been strong enough to carry the bleeding boy almost a mile downstream.

It was a miracle that he hadn't drowned, I thought. But he'd managed to grab onto a branch and pull himself from the water. A county cop had found him walking down the road in the dark, headed for town, looking for help to save his mother.

Chad's father had been arrested just after sunrise the morning after he'd killed his wife. He'd been found at home, sleeping soundly in the bed he'd shared with his wife for fourteen years. The Lord, he'd told the cops when they'd questioned him, had commanded him to punish his unfaithful wife and purge her living sin from the face of the earth. He was certain that he'd done just that. Shot her with the critter gun he'd always kept in his truck, then thrown the gun away. Down into a ravine.

"It wasn't the Godly way to do it," he'd explained, "but I lost my knife in the floodwater. Shortly after usin' it on the boy."

He'd seemed distressed by the news that his son had lived.

Chapter 8

There was a stop sign at the next intersection.

In a masterpiece of coincidental timing, Chad pulled onto the gravel road in front of me. But instead of taking my turn and immediately following him, I waited for a second vehicle to pull out onto the road behind him. The unadorned minivan was white and its blue-on-white license plate read Illinois and Official Vehicle.

I stayed far enough back to avoid the dust and gravel thrown by the convoy. After a few more miles of winding road, the taillights of the van flashed as it slowed to turn at the green sign that pointed eastward toward Camp Cadiz. Five miles. I tapped my brakes, made the turn, flipped down the visor to shield my eyes from the sun that hung like liquid fire above the tree line. Not nearly noon and the temperature was already creeping above ninety.

I pulled into the lot at Camp Cadiz and turned off the

engine. Chad slid from his squad car, shrugged his shoulders to settle his bulletproof vest more comfortably around his chest, and adjusted his belt and holster to ride smoothly at his waist. I slipped from my vehicle and did the same. In the meantime, two men had emerged from the van. They introduced themselves and began unloading equipment.

The crime-scene techs were a pair of fiftysomething-year-olds. Male. Both wearing Illinois State Police badges at their waists.

One of the investigators was tall with broad shoulders, a scrawny neck, and thinning blond hair. He was dressed for a walk along city sidewalks in dark slacks, a short-sleeved white shirt and a conservative tie. Two minutes out in the sunny parking lot and he shed his sports jacket, throwing it into the front seat of the van.

The other man, who was more practically attired in jeans and a short-sleeved double-knit shirt, called to mind a bulldog. Short and muscular with bowed legs and a deep chest, he had droopy jowls framing a mouth with small, uneven teeth and a distinct underbite.

Even the shorter route to the crime scene—which, once we reached the bridge over the ravine, Chad had marked by sticking the wire ends of tiny orange flags into the ground—was a hot, uncomfortable hike. All of us were lugging heavy equipment. In the sun, the humidity made breathing almost difficult. In the shade, mosquitoes swarmed hungrily and bit despite the repellent I'd sprayed on all of us. Walking single-file with Chad in the lead and me bringing up the rear, we followed the makeshift trail that meandered its way between trees and avoided thickets of brush, but managed to stay within a dozen yards of the edge of the ravine.

We didn't talk much and we didn't hurry.

I kept an eye on the men in front of me, making sure that neither of the city boys strayed from the makeshift trail or collapsed from the heat. Which gave me plenty of time to recall the promise I'd made to Chad back when we were teenagers. Back when I'd wanted nothing more than to have the best search-and-rescue dog in the county.

Back then, it had been Indian-summer weather—comfortably cool, dry and sunny. Chad, Highball and I had practiced together that morning. It had taken just over an hour for Highball and me to locate Chad, who had hidden himself among the thick branches of a fallen tree. After that, the three of us had hiked along the tree line to the top of a ragged bluff. While Highball napped in the shade, Chad and I had sprawled side by side on a sun-drenched outcropping of sandstone, our bellies warmed by the rock and filled by the sack lunch Aunt Lucy had fixed us, our chins propped on our elbows. From our vantage point, we'd looked out over miles of treetops burnished red and orange and gold.

At some point, Chad began rubbing his cheek. Hard. I still remembered the loneliness I'd glimpsed when he'd finally turned his face toward me.

"My momma's buried out there," he'd said. "Somewhere. She never liked the forest, y'know. She always said it was dark and gloomy. Even this time of year. It was too closed in. That's what she always said. Momma loved sunshine and flowers. She'd want to be buried in a place like that little cemetery up on the hill in Golconda. You know the one. It's planted with lilacs and black-eyed Susans and purple coneflowers. And, hell, you can see practically into the next county from there."

That's when I—naive and overconfident—had promised that someday my dog and I would find her for him.

Now, more than a decade later, maybe we had.

When we arrived, the two techs skirted the scene, taking photos, before ducking beneath the yellow crime-scene tape that Chad and I had put up the night before. Then they stood a little back from the crumbling edge, peering downward.

"Nasty," the taller man observed.

"Very nasty," his jowly partner agreed as he used the back of his latex-gloved hand to brush a trickle of sweat from his forehead.

They both insisted that processing the scene—even on a narrow ledge down inside a ravine—was their job. No offer of help that Chad or I made was going to change their minds. But neither turned his nose up at the safety harnesses Chad had brought with him or the quick lesson on rappelling I offered. Once down on the ledge, the taller man took photographs and the shorter took samples of soil.

Then we gathered up the bones.

With latex-gloved hands and more reverence than I'd expected, the techs removed the bones, one by one, from beneath the curtain of roots and passed each bone up to either Chad or me. We wore gloves, too, and carefully placed the bones in one of the boxes the investigators had brought with them. As routine as processing a crime scene must have been for the two men, they still seemed to feel sympathy for the victim. No matter that our victim was recently found rather than newly dead.

They freed the rib cage by cutting the roots around it, so we placed almost as much tree as bones in some of the boxes. As I handled the bones, I tried to identify them, hoping that I might be able to glean something about the identity of the victim from ribs and vertebrae, from the tiny bones that the investigators sifted from the soil and I recognized as being pieces of hands and feet. But what little I knew about the identification of skeletal remains I'd learned during a short session at a weeks-long training course for rookie cops. On the campus of the University of Illinois, I'd sat in a modern classroom at the Police Training Institute among students—mostly male and all as green as I was—who'd traveled from all over Illinois to learn the basics of law enforcement. Regarding bones, we'd learned mostly that it was our job to preserve the scene for more skilled investigators. That we would never be as skilled as the Illinois State Police's forensic lab rats. They, with their books and charts and mathematical tables, could determine height by measuring a leg bone and age by looking at the seams in a skull.

For a couple of hours, and despite the blistering heat, the two techs worked methodically, communicating in the kind of verbal shorthand that longtime colleagues often developed. Chad and I didn't talk much, either. We stayed busy passing equipment and evidence up and down as requested and simply watching the state investigators as they moved around the narrow outcroppings—the one on which I'd discovered the remains and the ledge below it, where I'd found Tina. We called out a warning whenever either man became so engrossed in his work that he forgot he was on the edge of a precipice. Safety harness or no, an unexpected fall could cause injury and was something to be avoided.

Both ledges looked more hazardous by the light of day. Darkness had only suggested the depth of the ravine, but had left mostly unseen the jutting rocks, ragged dead branches and a rock-strewn stream far below. I realized how very fortunate Tina and I had been.

Finally, Chad and I helped the state investigators back up to safe, solid ground. Then we all stood for a moment, surveying the boxes and bags that they'd collected.

Bones, it seemed, were pretty much all that remained of the victim. Except for a small white button and a section of zipper, nature and animals had stripped away our victim's clothing and scoured away clues.

"No ring?" Chad asked, though it was obvious there wasn't one. His mother had always worn her wedding band and, during questioning, his father had been upset because he'd forgotten to remove it.

"An adulteress should not be allowed to defile such a sacred symbol of marriage," he'd said.

Chad's hand had risen to his face and, when he asked about the ring, he was already working his fingers back and forth along his scarred jaw as he stared down at the contents of the box.

"No," the tall crime-scene technician said.

"Are you sure?"

I expected the investigator to interpret Chad's words as a challenge to his competence, to stiffen his body and snap out a response. But he didn't. Chad was staring down into the box, so he didn't see the flicker of sympathy that I saw on the tall tech's face.

"No ring," he said, and no hint of sympathy colored his voice. "No jewelry of any kind. And we were thorough."

I was fairly certain that Chad hadn't mentioned his suspicions about finding his mother's remains to anyone but me. But cops were a gossipy brotherhood and I knew that this particular tale of duty and devotion had reached near-legendary status statewide. Although few were acquainted with the actual man or even the specific circumstances of the murder, the story of the young cop and his unrelenting search for his mother's body was well-known. I'd heard the story several times and, each time, the facts had been just enough off that I could tell they weren't based on first- or even secondhand information.

Apparently the tale had traveled as far as the Illinois State Police crime lab. Or maybe, I told myself, Chad's chief had simply made a call to the crime lab on behalf of one of his favorite deputies.

"But it's probably not a complete skeleton," the stockier tech added as he began placing lids on top of the boxes of bones.

I noticed nothing about his manner or tone suggesting that *he'd* heard the story.

"I found a few bones on the second ledge," he continued, "but I suspect some of the tiny bones from the hands and feet have been washed away by the rain. Or carried off by rodents. It's surprising, really, that all the major bones are intact."

"We have enough to confirm the obvious," his partner said. "And maybe eventually come up with a description of the victim."

The stockier man nodded, then lifted the skull from the last open box and held it upright in his palm.

"Here's what we can tell you now," he said matter-of-factly, "which is probably nothing that you haven't already figured out. GSW to the head."

He turned the skull to display the hole I'd noticed the night before above the bony ridge of the left eye.

"Entry wound."

Then he rotated it to reveal a much larger hole at the back of the head.

"Exit wound."

For a moment, he lifted his hand a little higher, briefly looked into what had once been a face.

"Alas, poor Yorick! I knew h—"

It was the kind of humor that Chad and I both understood, black humor that kept cops one step removed emotionally from the tragedies they investigated. But this time, at least one of the state investigators knew that the tragedy *was* personal. He interrupted his partner's soliloquy.

"Actually, our vic is a female," he said quickly, his eyes flickering to Chad's expressionless face.

Taking the skull from the hands of his unresisting partner, the taller man hunkered down on one knee beside the box and placed the skull carefully inside. After putting the lid on the box, he rested his right hand on it for the briefest of moments.

A benediction, I thought, though I couldn't have proved it.

"Yeah, definitely a woman," he said as he stood, then concentrated on brushing soil and bits of vegetation from his knees. "Pelvis gave us that much. And based on the general conformation of the face, my bet's Caucasian. Of course, the lab'll have to confirm all that."

"Any idea about her age?" Chad asked.

Both of the state guys shook their heads.

"Adult," the stocky tech said. "Lab guys will look at her teeth and pelvis more carefully, narrow it down for you. But you probably already know that your gal won't get priority treatment. Lab's already got a backlog of recent deaths to deal with. It may be weeks before you'll get a formal report."

Chad nodded. So did I.

"Whatever you can give us informally would be appreciated," I said.

"Yeah. No problem," the tech said.

"Any idea how long she's been here?" Chad asked.

The taller tech lifted his chin in the direction of his partner.

"Nature boy," he said, as if that explained something. And when his partner spoke, I realized it did.

"This is just a good guess, understand? But it might just help you track down a few possibles before you get the official report. Figuring on the size of the roots that grew in and around the ribs and spine, I'd say—" he stopped, thought about it for a moment "—ten years. Give or take a couple of years on either side of that."

Chad nodded, and then his eyes met mine.

Twelve years would be about the right time frame, I thought. But maybe the body had been there for as few as eight. And I was comforted to see more caution than optimism in Chad's expression.

"You didn't find a bullet," I said, hoping that somehow I'd missed them bagging one up.

"No," the stockier tech said. "And given this—"

Briefly, he shook his head as the sweep of his hand took in the forest. Then he stepped to the edge of the ravine, looked downward, and shook his head again as he spoke.

"What we've got here is a decade—more or less—of constant erosion, aggressive plant growth and exposure to the elements. Odds are, any physical evidence is long gone or so deeply buried that there's no hope of finding it. Not even with dozens of people looking for it. And, frankly, this kind of case doesn't warrant the manpower. So anything we find out about this gal is going to have to come from her remains."

As his partner spoke, the taller blond technician had slowly turned in place, his thoughtful gaze taking in the entire area enclosed by the yellow plastic tape.

"Hollow tree," he murmured. And then he said more loudly: "We missed checking the tree trunk. The body was probably stuffed there first, so it'd be a good idea to take a look inside."

Years earlier, a murderer had judged the rotting hole at the base of the massive tree large enough to serve as the entrance to a makeshift tomb. But over those years, woody vines as thick as a man's arm had snaked up and around the dying tree.

Encouraged by the light sifting through the thinning canopy overhead, new growth had crowded the ragged opening. Neither the crime-scene investigators nor Chad looked enthused about flattening themselves on the ground and angling their bulky upper bodies into the cramped hole. And, in fact, I doubted that any of their shoulders were narrow enough to fit.

The taller investigator pointed.

"Is that poison ivy?" he asked. "What is it they say? Something about three leaves?"

"Leaves of three, let it be," Chad answered. "And yes, that is poison ivy."

"I suppose you could avoid it if you were careful," the tech with the jowly face observed.

I hadn't been careful the night before, I thought as I stood listening, waiting for the men to work out the problem and reach the inevitable—and unwelcome—conclusion. Just lucky. I could still make out the impression of my elbows and knees in the humus-y soil next to the tree, and realized that I'd missed crawling through a patch of poison ivy by just a matter of inches. But then, I'd been concerned only that Tina might be inside.

"Hole's too small for a grown man to crawl into it," the taller technician said. "We'll have to enlarge the opening to get a good look inside. A chain saw would do the job. Probably easy enough to get our hands on one. Be messy, though. Faster and easier if one of us was small enough…"

His voice trailed off about the time I noticed that the hole in the trunk was spun with tattered spiders' webs. Only my pride and the three pairs of male eyes turned my way kept me from shuddering.

"I'll do it," I said without enthusiasm.

I waited for a moment, hoping that some valiant man would try to stop me. Would say that, in fact, the chain saw would be a better choice.

Wishful thinking.

Sighing, I slipped my billy club from my belt, then undid the buckle and wrapped the leather strap around my holster. I handed the holster to Chad, stepped over to the tree and, trying not to think about what my uniform—already perspiration stained—was going to look like by the time I finished, I used the billy club to clear the webs and bits of loose, termite-infested wood from the narrow opening.

I exchanged the billy club for a flashlight, turned the brown ball cap that was part of my uniform around so that its bill protected the back of my neck, then lay down on my right shoulder. Avoiding the patch of poison ivy and trying not to think too closely about the eight-legged residents that I might be dislodging, I pushed myself forward into the hollow trunk. I stopped when my head, shoulders and right arm were just inside the opening.

Contrary to what is reported in children's storybooks, there is nothing magical about being inside a tree. A couple feet in front of me was a gaping hole where daylight glimmered upward from the direction of the ravine. Above me, surrounded by the remaining trunk, was a damp honeycomb tunnel of rotting wood that narrowed until it appeared solid. Spindly black ants the size of dimes streamed up and down the interior carrying fat, round pupae the milky color of rotting flesh. That didn't bother me. But the sight of countless daddy longlegs scuttling for cover did.

For a moment, I panicked. I could feel my heart pounding, feel the air trapped in my throat, feel the building scream that would release it. Would release me from the frozen moment that preceded flight. I shoved my fist against my mouth, drove my index finger against my teeth, and bit down. Hard.

The pain cleared my head and, for a heartbeat, refocused my thoughts away from the spiders. Long enough. I let my captive breath rush out around my hand. Then, though my nerves screamed their objection, I shut my eyes. Counted to ten. And ten again. Told myself that childhood had passed. That I had endured the terror back then. That I need not relive it now.

Memory provided a flash of Katie's hand holding mine. Warm and tight and strong. Her voice was strong, too, as she assured me that she'd killed the spider. That she would kill any spiders that dared to come anywhere near me. Because she was my big sister and it was her job to keep me safe.

There was more comfort in that than I was willing to admit, even to myself. But I found the courage to open my eyes.

I took a deep breath, then ignored the spiders and did my job.

I turned slightly, running my flashlight slowly around the interior perimeter of the trunk. To my right, I saw recent droppings that my nose suggested were probably fox. The smell was musty and rank. A clump of red fur that was definitely fox supported my identification of the smell inside the tree. And a scattering of tiny bones and feathers suggested the fox had curled inside the tree to have a snack. I abandoned the flashlight long enough to scoop the bones into a bag. Then I picked up my flashlight again and moved it steadily, ignoring fungus and moss and jagged fingers of corklike wood.

I glimpsed a shape that didn't occur in nature and spotlighted it.

The object lay opposite me and was caught in the lacework of roots that descended into the sinkhole. A smooth and very regular cylinder. About an inch long with a half-an-inch-in-diameter base. And I thought I recognized…

I used my toes to scoot my shoulders farther into the tree trunk.

Chad must have noticed my movement and interpreted it correctly.

"Are you all right, Brooke? Do you see something?"

Even in his muffled voice, I heard concern.

"Dunno," I said, and my voice echoed back oddly at me. "I'm going to take a closer look."

I lay the flashlight down, positioning it so that its beam continued to illuminate the object. Then I stretched out my hand, angled it beneath the cylinder. Using my fingertips, I teased it closer until I was able to enclose it in my hand. Feeling rather than sight told me that a thick plastic tube—dirt clogged, perhaps a quarter-inch long and much narrower than a soda straw—stuck out from one end of the cylinder.

I left the cylinder where it was and backed out of the hole.

"Nothing," I said as I stood and brushed off the front of my uniform. "All I saw was a pile of scat, a bit of fur from a red fox, and a few tiny bones. Probably bird—"

I held up the bag, stopping the objection I saw forming on the shorter investigator's lips.

"—but I bagged them anyway. Beyond that, there were only spiders."

Chad, who knew of my phobia, looked guilt stricken.

I made the effort, grinned at him.

"You owe me," I said. "Big-time."

The techs simply looked grateful that they'd avoided a nasty little task.

Chapter 9

Inside the SUV, the air-conditioning was running full blast.

I sat with a pen in my right hand and my logbook propped against my steering wheel. But I wasn't looking down at the page. Instead, my eyes were on the rearview mirror. I watched the dust cloud kicked up by two departing vehicles—the minivan belonging to the crime-scene technicians and Chad's squad car.

Once the dust settled, I scribbled a few more lines in my logbook. Then I sat for a while longer doing math, thinking thoughts that I didn't much like, and making sure that no official vehicles would return unexpectedly.

After that, I went back into the woods.

At the crime scene—now stripped of the yellow tape that marked the exact place where the remains had been found—I crawled back into the hole in the tree trunk and retrieved the cylinder. The one I hadn't wanted anyone else to see, but that I didn't need to look at more closely.

There was no need for me to rub soil off the cylinder to know what it was. I didn't have to examine the bits of clinging label or to peer at the tiny block letters on the flat end as I searched for some hint about the contents of the vial. I knew already who'd manufactured it, knew that—if it had made its way to the state crime lab—any drug residue would prove to be albuterol. From memory, I murmured aloud the instructions etched into the base.

"This end up. Shake before using."

I shoved the asthma inhaler deep in my pocket and walked back to my vehicle. I climbed into the SUV, turned the key in the ignition and, all the while, kept trying to ignore the suspicion that had been chewing at the edge of my mind ever since I'd found the little cylinder.

It was a coincidence, I told myself. Only a coincidence. Hundreds of thousands of people used asthma inhalers. It didn't matter that neither of Chad's parents had asthma. There was no proof yet that the remains belonged to his mother. The victim— or her murderer—might have had asthma. Or an animal, responding to some peculiar instinct, might have stashed the inhaler in the trunk of the tree. Or maybe the little vial was just a random bit of trash that had somehow found its way onto a crime scene. It was improbable that this particular asthma inhaler had any connection at all to anyone I cared about.

That's exactly what I told myself. And that's exactly why I lifted the microphone mounted on my dashboard, held it with my thumb near the mike as I considered what to say when I passed the bit of missing evidence on to the state police.

Somehow, it got caught inside my shirt, beneath my vest, when I was crawling around beneath that tree, I could say. *I thought it was just a stone or a clump of mud. But when I shook out my vest, I found this.*

It was a good lie. At worst, they'd think the small-town female cop was a bit incompetent.

But I put the mike down instead of making the call. Instead of contacting dispatch and asking the state cops to backtrack to Camp Cadiz, I slipped the inhaler into one of the evidence bags I carried. And I told myself that the cylinder was too weather-beaten and corroded, anyway, to yield any kind of print. No need to send it to the state lab.

After tucking the little bag safely into my glove compartment, I pulled my SUV out of the parking lot and headed for town. And I did the math again.

Ten years, the investigator with the bulldog face had said. Ten years, give or take a couple of years on either side of that. That meant the body had been there between eight and twelve years.

Nine years ago, my sister Katie would have been sixteen.

That year—the year that Katie had gotten her driver's license—was easy for me to remember. In fact, it stood out in my mind. In the spring, just days after Katie's birthday, the Ohio River had flooded many of the low-lying streets in town. That was when I'd found a young German shepherd tangled in a heap of flood-deposited debris, down behind the bars that lined Dunn Street. I'd named him Highball.

I didn't have any problem recalling that summer, either. Mostly because Katie had pretty much stopped talking to me, particularly at night when the lights were turned out in the bedroom we'd shared. For no reason that I could fathom, she'd stopped sharing secrets and complaining about guests or grousing about chores. No longer was I lulled to sleep by the sound of my big sister's voice or comforted by the knowledge of her presence in the nearby bed. In fact, sharing a room with Katie that year had been a punishment. The nightmares that had plagued her when we'd first come to live with

Aunt Lucy and Gran—the screaming awakenings that had wrenched both of us from our sleep—had returned that year.

Hormones and stress, Aunt Lucy had diagnosed. Katie was just having a difficult time growing up. Be patient, she said when I complained. It will pass. And at bedtime she began dosing my sister—and me, for good measure—with steaming mugs of chamomile tea sweetened with wildflower honey. A treat for Katie, who liked the concoction. A torture for me, who didn't. And one more reason for us to bicker. As if teenage sisters needed a reason.

That summer, Katie began taking long, solitary drives in the beaten-up old car she'd bought for two hundred dollars. Back then, I'd figured she had a boyfriend—someone Gran and Aunt Lucy wouldn't have approved of. I still remembered the curious mix of jealousy, envy and anger I'd felt each time I'd watched her drive off and how I'd speculated about who she might have been meeting. Maybe she was seeing that gangly Baker boy who had dropped out of school and was bagging groceries at a store in Paducah. Or the Rosses' youngest son who, that summer, had taken to hanging out with his friends late at night at the little park just up the street from the Cherokee Rose.

I sat with my foot pressed down on the accelerator and the air-conditioning blasting away inside my SUV, wondering with nine years of hindsight if I'd gotten it wrong. Wondering now if the reason Katie had so hotly denied having a boyfriend—the reason no boy had ever surfaced that summer or, in fact, any of the summers after that—was that there had never been a boyfriend. Something else, I now feared, had stolen Katie's attention away from me. Had reawakened memories of our past.

And there was something else that was racheting up the

painful, twisting anxiety I began feeling deep in the pit of my stomach from the moment I'd first wrapped my fingers around the inhaler.

Right after Missy's murder, Gran and Aunt Lucy had moved Katie into an isolated facility in the hills of Montana where she'd stayed for almost two years. After that, she'd traveled to France. To Paris, where she'd learned to cook and bake. She'd worked for a while at a hotel resort in Colorado, and then for a trendy restaurant in Miami. Finally, she'd returned to Maryville and the Cherokee Rose. Because she missed us and she loved us and she was lonely for her family and her home.

Gran, Aunt Lucy and Katie—especially Katie—seemed to have put the past behind them. Katie had been given a second chance, Gran told me. Just like the women we moved along the Underground.

A second chance. That's what covering up Missy's murder had bought my sister. A chance that I owed her. Because she was my sister and my protector. I had willingly paid the personal costs. But now…

I hit a pothole a little faster than I should have. The seat belt tightened across my lap and tugged at my shoulder, jolting my attention back to the winding road in front of me.

For a few minutes, I concentrated on the road and on managing a little more detachment. I dug through my glove compartment, popped a couple of the antacid tablets I stored there, and washed them down with a swig of lukewarm coffee from my Thermos cup. Then I ticked off the facts—only the facts—in my head.

I'd found an inhaler near a female murder victim's remains.

Katie used an inhaler.

The remains were found within an easy drive from Maryville.

Within the time frame that the murder had occurred, Katie had had a car and had often been absent from town without explanation.

The remains were near Camp Cadiz.

Eight years earlier, my sister had committed cold-blooded murder at Camp Cadiz.

It was beyond circumstantial, I told myself. Just random coincidence and paranoid, guilt-driven supposition, all arbitrarily knotted together into an unlikely pattern. There were other explanations. Better explanations.

No matter that, at the moment, I couldn't think of any.

Despite my best efforts, my instincts—or maybe simply my fear—presented a horrific scenario that I couldn't reason away. No matter how reasonable I tried to be.

What if Missy Porter hadn't been my sister's first victim? I asked myself.

What if Katie had killed before?

And if what I feared was true, how many murders was I willing to cover up to protect my sister?

Once out of the forest and miles away from Camp Cadiz, I swung back onto 146 and followed it as it ran south toward town. By the time the highway curved westward to parallel the Ohio River, it was lined with buildings and I'd wiped the back of my hand across my face and convinced myself that it was perspiration that stung my eyes.

The highway curved westward, but I continued south on an abruptly narrowing stretch of roadway that angled sharply downhill and ended, very literally, at the river's edge. At Maryville's ferry crossing, which was the only way across the river for fifty miles in either direction.

The ferry captain saw me and waved as I pulled the SUV

off to the side of the road. There was no real reason for a police presence, but I watched for obvious safety violations and expired tags on the big rigs that lumbered up the heavy steel ramp and onto the deck of the ferry. Cars loaded on, too, most filled with shoppers on their way to the grocery stores and strip malls in Marion and with vacationing tourists mostly driving through Maryville on their way to somewhere else.

The ferry crossing was blisteringly hot. Unfiltered by clouds or shade, the sun beat down on the pavement, the glittering white limestone gravel along the shoulder and the low bluff of bare limestone that framed the roadway. Even on idle, the ferry engine was loud, its deep thrum mixing with the sounds of trucks changing gears and the shouts of the crew as they directed vehicles onto the ferry. And the damp breeze blowing off the river smelled. More accurately, it stank. Diesel fumes, car exhaust and the dank, organic scent of the Ohio River in the summertime permeated the air. It wafted through the streets and even carried to the highest point in Maryville—the bluff where the Cherokee Rose looked down over the town.

I slipped out of my vehicle, rolled my shoulders and stretched my arms, then leaned back against the front fender with my legs crossed at the ankles. I took a deep breath and smiled. The heat, the noise, the odor didn't matter. I loved the river and its distinctive smell. Loved standing on its banks with the sun warm on my shoulders. Loved just doing my job. For a few minutes I stood watching the deep water of the Ohio muscle by and tried not to think, not to feel. Just to be. On the sun-drenched banks of the river, my problems always seemed less complex than they did when I was trekking in the shadowy forest.

Then, when I felt particularly clearheaded, I revisited the promise that I'd made myself as I'd driven into town. Nodded to myself, still satisfied with the strategy I'd decided to follow.

If Chad could manage to approach this case with professionalism and some measure of detachment, so I could I.

Until the forensics report came in, I would avoid speculating about who the murder victim—and the murderer—might be. I would investigate this crime just as I'd investigate any other crime. I would work with Chad and we would build our case carefully and meticulously. Basing it on facts, likely circumstances and evidence.

A big part of that evidence, I knew, would be the report from the state forensics lab. If the remains proved *not* to belong to Chad's mother, I would add the grubby inhaler to the evidence. And let the investigation unfold from there.

And if the investigation pointed to my sister? Threatened to expose the facts of Missy's death? Compromised the Underground network? Sent me or Gran or Aunt Lucy to prison for covering up a murder?

My stomach did a half twist, destroying my sense of calm.

I inhaled again, exhaled slowly as I watched the faster flow of current near the center of the river, then made a conscious effort to unclench my jaw and relax the knot of muscles at the intersection of my neck and shoulders. Just do your job, I told myself. The way you were taught. One step at a time. Follow the evidence wherever it leads.

Then, only then, I would deal with the consequences.

Briefly, I craned my neck to look upward along the nearly sheer face of the limestone bluff jutting up from the river just west of the ferry landing. It was emblazoned with graffiti that was spray painted on by teenagers with little else to do in a small town after dark than risk their lives for the sake of self-expression. Newly applied red paint advertised young love and a pair of initials I recognized.

As I considered whether I should drop in at the kids'

homes, maybe give them a lecture about defacing public property, my eyes unconsciously sought a pair of more familiar initials. B.T. C.R. Their faded paint was in two different colors. My initials, which I'd sprayed on the stone myself, were blue and stood alone, unattached. Chad's were in black, perpetually linked with M.H., a dark-haired girl with bee-stung lips whom he'd loved passionately the summer before he'd enlisted in the military. She'd married someone else and moved away from Maryville, but her initials remained, a visible piece of our town's history.

The ferry blasted its horn and a deck hand scurried to drape a chain across the road as the ferry's vehicle ramp groaned upward, locking in the vehicles parked on its deck. On the road, half a dozen more cars and trucks remained, recipients of a questionable honor—they'd be the first in line for the next crossing. Their turn would come once the ferry reached the opposite bank, dropped its ramp, exchanged eastbound vehicles for ones bound west, and then made its way back across the river.

Maybe it was my presence—the sight of a uniformed cop, mirrored glasses glinting in the sun, leaning against a glossy white SUV that was topped by Mars lights and emblazoned with Maryville's logo. Or perhaps it was simply that today's drivers were all veterans of the process. But in either event, no horns blared, no curses flowed, and no one broke traffic laws trying to back uphill and out of line. The drivers sat patiently, most with their windows shut and their vehicles idling, burning fuel for the sake of air-conditioning.

The noise from the ferry's powerful engines indicated that they were now fully engaged, fighting to navigate across the strong river current. I looked away from the water churning in the wake of its departure and toward the bluffs again. Up near the top, there was a section of rock that staggered outward, like a side view of a sloppy stack of thick, grubby white dinner plates. And at the very top of the stack was a flat stone, just big enough for two. Though there were undoubtedly others of many generations who claimed that spot as their own, I always thought of it as ours. Chad's and mine.

I glanced again at the departing ferry and smiled to myself as I resisted the urge to look down at my watch. But the impulse to time the ferry's circuit from the Illinois side to the Kentucky side and back was a strong one, rooted in the best days of my childhood.

How old had we been, I wondered, when Chad and I had first climbed down onto that outcropping, defying every adult rule about children staying off the bluffs? On days just like this, the two of us would lie on our stomachs, betting pennies on the timing of the ferry, our elbows propped, our bare arms and legs touching. Not all that many years later, we'd snuggled together on that same rock after midnight, two off-duty cops sharing a bottle of Jack hidden in a paper bag and watching the lights of the ferry moving ever-predictably between the two riverbanks. Touching then, too. But in a way that childhood had never imagined.

My mind veered away from that train of thought and I re-focused on the present. Just downriver, a convoy of barges moved slowly down the Ohio, the weight of their cargo making them ride low on the water, the deep hum of their heavy engines echoing off the bluffs.

I pulled my cap from my head and wiped my arm across my forehead. For a moment, I wasted time searching the sky for some sign of a storm cloud. Then I straightened my back, put my cap back on my head and climbed back into my SUV.

For the next half hour, I drove a slow, lazy loop around

Maryville. Just making sure that everything was peaceful in my town. Peaceful and—unlike my personal life—under control. Except for children, few people were even outside. No one lingered on Main Street. And even seniors like Marta Moye and Larry Hayes, who usually sat out on their porches this time of day, had retreated out of the heat and into cooler indoor spaces.

After that, I decided to go to my office and do some paperwork.

My office was a newly remodeled space and all of my furniture matched. Which sounded better than it was. The desk was a gray steel monster that took up about half of the windowless room's square footage. The door that the desk faced was oak with a frosted-glass pane and dark lettering that read Maryville Police Department.

I settled in behind my desk with the door open for maximum ventilation. On the narrow gun-metal gray credenza immediately behind me, the low-volume voices on my scanner crackled on and off. I half listened to them as I polished off a sandwich and began cleaning out the accumulation in my IN box. As usual, I was interrupted. But today it wasn't a series of calls from county dispatch that thwarted my good intentions and made paperwork impossible. It was a persistently ringing phone.

Two out-of-town reporters and half a dozen concerned citizens phoned, all seeking better information than a police scanner and local gossip could provide. I confirmed what they'd already heard—unidentified remains had been discovered in the forest during a successful search for a lost child—and offered nothing more. They hung up disappointed.

Hours later—a stack of paperwork and a dozen more interruptions later—I went home.

* * *

That night, the phone on my nightstand rang as I was crawling into bed and the caller ID flashed the number of the Cherokee Rose. The phone rang again as I held my hand suspended inches above the receiver, knowing that the call might be urgent Underground business, but still hesitating. Because chances were, the caller was my sister.

Earlier, when I'd come home from work, the answering machine had been flashing and the voice on the phone had been Katie's.

"Hi, Brooke. It's me," she'd said at the answering machine's prompt. "Nice work finding the little girl. Call me, okay? I have great news."

My sister's voice had been predictably sweet, upbeat and optimistic. Just like her attitude since she'd returned home to the Cherokee Rose months earlier. Not at all like the depressed, acutely disturbed teenager who had left Maryville eight years ago. Therapy, travel, education, growing up. Some of those things—perhaps all of them—seemed to have transformed Katie. And as for the event that had separated Katie from us? Those who knew of it—Gran, Aunt Lucy, Katie and I—never spoke of Missy's murder. As if not talking about it meant it had never happened.

As I'd hit the button to erase her message, I'd decided that my day had already been emotionally grueling enough. Katie's good news would have to wait until tomorrow. That decision had little to do with the day's events. My reluctance to interact with my older sister was, unfortunately, business as usual.

Despite the changes in her personality, ever since her return to Maryville, the relationship between Katie and me had been strained and distant. My fault, not hers. I loved my big sister as I always had, but a minefield of taboo subjects now lay between us. Our childhood. Missy's murder. The Underground. Chad. I found it difficult to recall a time when the secrets Katie and I shared had united us. Now I feared that there might be a secret that Katie *hadn't* shared with me.

The phone beneath my hand rang for the fifth time and, just as I heard the message tape click on, I answered it. Impulse, perhaps. Or concern inspired by the late hour of the call. Or maybe just to prove to myself that I wasn't going to let coincidence and unfounded suspicion poison my interactions with my sister. So I picked up the phone.

I was surprised and a little relieved to find Aunt Lucy on the line.

"Hey, honey," she said by way of greeting. "Gran and I are going shopping tomorrow. Across the river in Paducah. We'll be meeting a friend of a friend. Would you like to come along?"

I had no doubt that Aunt Lucy was talking about an extraction. And that long habit rather than any pressing need for caution had prompted her to discuss Underground business in veiled terms.

"Okay," I said without hesitation.

Despite the conflict it brought to my life, I'd never questioned my commitment to the Underground and the women it served. Many who traveled along the Underground network were able to walk away from the abusive situation they'd been in. Easy enough, then, for one of our volunteers to help them take the first step toward a new life in a new location. But some women couldn't escape on their own. They—and, sometimes, their children—required extraction from life-threatening situations. Over the past eight years, I'd helped Gran and Aunt Lucy with dozens of such urgent rescues.

"We should probably leave the Cherokee Rose by one,"

Aunt Lucy said as we finished talking about the next day's rescue. "If that works for you."

"Sure does," I said. "Sounds like fun."

Business taken care of, the urgency left Aunt Lucy's voice. Her syllables lengthened as her voice relaxed, and I could almost hear her smile. That smile, I knew, would deepen the laugh lines around her mouth and crinkle the skin surrounding her dark-lashed chocolate-brown eyes.

"I'm sorry for calling so late," she said. "Are you too tired to talk?"

"No. Not at all," I said, and I meant it.

As I settled back against my pillows, long familiarity with Aunt Lucy's habits made it easy for me to picture her. Middle-aged and slightly plump, at this hour she would be dressed for bed in an oversize T-shirt and loose-fitting pajama bottoms. Her glossy dark hair would be caught up in a braid and she would most likely be fiddling with its end as she spoke on the phone.

Like everyone else I'd talked with that day, my aunt asked me about finding the little girl and discovering human remains near Camp Cadiz. But Aunt Lucy was the only one who'd asked how I felt and how I was doing, and she worried aloud at the impact that another disappointment might have on Chad.

"He's such a dear, sweet boy," she said.

Aunt Lucy chattered on, unaware of the burst of laughter I smothered against my shoulder. Too easy for me to imagine Chad's reaction to such a glowing description. Undoubtedly, he would flush bright red and scowl. I smiled to myself as I thought of a new quip and awarded myself a point.

You might be a cop if…you practice your cold, hard stare in front of a mirror.

"Why don't you come by early tomorrow and have lunch

with Katie, Gran, and me?" Aunt Lucy continued. "It seems like forever since we've all just sat around the kitchen table and visited. Which, I suppose, is what happens when a family gets busy. What with your job and Katie and me running our feet off with preparations for that big wedding at the end of the month, Gran seems to be the only one with any leisure time. I told you, didn't I, that we ended up hiring more kitchen staff?"

Southern hospitality and a sweeping view of the Ohio had always drawn a steady trickle of paying guests to our family's historic hotel, but lately business was booming because of the food that Katie served in the antique-furnished dining room. And because of the beautiful pastries and cakes she created in the Cherokee Rose's modern, industrial kitchen. In the past few months, word of mouth had dramatically increased the number of wedding parties booking into the Cherokee Rose.

"I'm hoping we get a break in the weather by then," Aunt Lucy was saying. "The bride has her heart set on getting married in the back garden. Shade trees or not, her guests won't want to spend any time outside if it stays this hot. Of course, rain wouldn't be great, either. But with a little rear-ranging in the front parlor and dining room, we can bring the whole shebang inside on a day's notice. Oh, well... At least we can be sure the food will be fabulous. Which reminds me, Katie's experimenting with some new hors d'oeuvres for the occasion. I'm sure she'd love for you to sample them and tell her what you think."

"Sounds good," I said. "How's Katie doing?"

That was a question I always asked. Because I was always concerned.

Aunt Lucy replied with characteristic enthusiasm.

"At the moment, she's walking on air. Remember me telling you about the guest who insisted on touring the kitchen *and* meeting Katie? Well, it turns out he's a travel editor for the *St. Louis Post Dispatch*. They ran a story about us. Well, about Katie, really. He said she was the third generation of beautiful and charming innkeepers working at the Cherokee Rose. That her beauty, personality and European-inspired cuisine should quickly make the Cherokee Rose a *destination*. His only criticism was that Katie didn't spend enough time interacting with her guests."

Pleasure warmed Aunt Lucy's tone. But I knew her well enough that I heard the note of hesitation that crept into her voice just as it trailed off. It warned me that I wasn't going to like whatever she said next. And I was right. Her announcement stiffened my back, brought me upright from the pillows.

"Gran and I think he's right. We talked it over and decided there's no reason she shouldn't be spending more time playing hostess. Especially during special events like the big wedding that's coming up. She wants to do it, Brooke. She's earned the right. And it's not as if she'd be moving back into the hotel again."

Instead of moving back into the bedroom we'd once shared in our family's apartment on the hotel's first floor, Katie now lived in the brick coach house behind the Cherokee Rose. Used for decades as a honeymoon cottage, the tiny building was separated from the expansive flower gardens behind the Cherokee Rose by a six-foot-tall wrought-iron fence overgrown with jasmine vines. Her walk to work took minutes along a narrow, brick-paved alley. Katie had seemed content with her little home and her position as the Cherokee Rose's first formally trained chef. Until now.

I was upset enough that I broke with convention, specifically mentioning the Underground.

"But we agreed before Katie came home," I said, urgency

tightening my voice, "that it was too stressful—too risky—for her to be involved with the Underground ever again. And because the layout of the Cherokee Rose makes it impossible to separate regular guests from activities involving our *other* guests, we came up with our compromise. A place to live away from the hotel and a job that limited Katie's contact with *all* of the guests. Remember?"

My question was met with silence, a silence in which I easily recalled an alternative that I had offered a little more than six months earlier. When Katie had called and asked to come home. To stay. That's when I'd proposed to Gran and Aunt Lucy that we stop rescuing and sheltering abused women, that we shift that responsibility to other, equally competent members of the Underground. But Gran had been adamant.

"Absolutely not," Gran had said. "Your grandfather and I founded the Underground. I don't care how many volunteers and how many other safe houses we now have. The Tyler family *is* the Underground. And until I'm in my grave, the Cherokee Rose will remain at the center of the Underground network."

I took a breath, tried to reason with Aunt Lucy, although I knew that, ultimately, Gran would make the final decision. As she did with any issue that affected the Underground.

"It was a wise precaution then and it still is," I said. "We can't risk anything like Missy ever—"

Aunt Lucy cut me off.

"Gran and I both agree that Katie's long past that. If you spent more time with her, you'd know that she's a different person now. Stable. Responsible. Mature. She's worked through *her* problems. Maybe it's time you worked through yours. You can't go on not trusting people, pushing away anyone who gets too close to you."

After that, my own thoughts took up enough space that I

pretty much stopped listening to whatever else Aunt Lucy had
to say. Certainly, I stopped speaking. Except to say *goodbye*
and *see you tomorrow.*

Chapter 10

There's nothing worse than a headachy, cranky cop.

That's what I was the next morning, and I knew it. Anxious thoughts had chewed at the edges of my mind all night, triggering nightmares, disrupting sleep and offering little in the way of resolution.

I must have sounded as bad as I felt. At least to the practiced ear of someone who knew me well. When Chad called that morning, he immediately asked me what was wrong.

Reciting my list of woes wasn't an option. Especially because desperately missing Chad's comforting presence in bed when nightmares wrenched me awake would have topped the list.

The lie took only a moment.

"Nothing," I said. "Except this heat's beginning to get to me. Sure wish it'd rain."

"You and most of Hardin County," Chad said, laughing.

Then his tone turned serious. "Did you listen to this morning's weather report?"

I said I hadn't.

"Well, it looks like your wish just might come true. There's a front moving in from the northwest. They're predicting cooler air, possibly severe thunderstorms reaching our area within the next couple of days. Which is why I'm calling. I think we should search the ravine below the crime scene before the weather gets nasty."

He paused as if he was waiting for me to object.

I merely pointed out the obvious.

"There's been a lot of nasty weather around these parts over the last dozen years," I said mildly. "What do think we'll find down there after all this time?"

"Oh hell, Brooke," he said, "I know this doesn't make any sense. Crawling down into that ravine is probably pointless and definitely risky. In any other situation, I'd sit tight, wait for that damned official report, and then use it to narrow down our missing-persons lists. But I've got to do *something*. And I figure it can't hurt to look. Maybe we'll luck out. Stumble across my mother's wedding ring. Or my father's gun. Or just find some bit of evidence that points to someone else."

Like an asthma inhaler that's already been found, I thought. Of course, I didn't say that out loud. But I couldn't help thinking—hoping—that a search would produce evidence that proved the victim *was* Chad's mother. For Chad's sake. And because it would ease my worries about Katie's past *and* her future.

"Okay," I said slowly. "But not today, okay?"

Then I offered him a lie that was as close to the truth as I could make it. That strategy, I'd discovered, made my lies rest a lot easier on my conscience.

"Gran's got a doctor's appointment in Paducah—just a routine checkup—and I promised her and Aunt Lucy that I'd go along. I'm going off duty around noon. So can we do it tomorrow morning?"

"Sure," Chad said.

We agreed to meet at Camp Cadiz.

Minutes later, I left the house, climbed into my SUV and drove to Statler's. But not even strong coffee, a chocolate-iced cake doughnut and Ed's Hawaiian shirt—this one printed with hula girls and palm trees—were enough to improve my mood or cure my headache. Mostly because they didn't keep me from worrying about this afternoon's extraction. Or anticipating that sooner or later an unsuspecting guest would antagonize my sister. Or wondering why someone would take the time to entomb their victim in the trunk of a tree when a perfectly good ravine was just a step away.

I needed to concentrate on doing my job, I told myself. Another speed trap might be just the thing. I was in the mood to give out tickets, to be the one in control. Just let someone argue with me or try to give me a hard time. I'd show them who called the shots in my town.

That thought, and the narrow-eyed surge of anger that accompanied it, convinced me that giving out tickets was the last thing I needed to be doing. I was paid to serve and protect the residents of Maryville. That didn't include using my personal problems as an excuse to throw my weight around. Even if I did have a headache.

So I cruised along 146, staying within the posted speed limit, which was thirty-five in town. I drove that way past the ferry landing and past Maryville's three major intersections—Dunn Street, Main Street and Hill Street. All around me, drivers tapped their brakes as they glanced nervously at their speedometers, then carefully paced me.

On the west edge of town, I did a U-turn in the parking lot of the Antique Attic. As usual, the lights were off inside the old building and Larry's hand-lettered closed sign was leaning up against the interior plate-glass window. As a courtesy, the sign gave potential customers a phone number where the proprietor could be reached. But as I completed the turn, I wondered if even the promise of a sale would prompt Larry to risk missing the next battle in his ongoing war with his next-door neighbor, Marta Moye. At least they hadn't called 911 this morning, I thought as I tucked my SUV between an old grain wagon that was more rotted than wooden and a stack of used tires—ten dollars, your choice. Their mileage, I supposed, qualified them as antiques, too.

Minutes later, a Chevy truck—a yellow four-by-four with six-inch lifts, oversize mud tires and KC HiLites—tore past me, going about eighty. The license plate was obscured by dirt, and green cornstalks stuck out from the undercarriage and grillwork.

In my book, that qualified as begging for a ticket.

I hit the siren as I pulled out and floored the accelerator, following but not chasing.

How foolish are you going to be? I wondered as they kept going, slowing but not stopping.

As tempting as forcing the issue might be, I couldn't risk it. They might speed up again, might lose control of their truck. It would be better to let them think they'd gotten away.

I thumbed the switch to talk to county dispatch, to get some help. If I was lucky, Chad or another cop would be available to intercept them on the far side of town.

They pulled over before I made the call. And when I

walked over to the vehicle, I was treated to a truck full of shocked expressions on the faces of four teenagers.

Oh, yeah, I thought. Surprise, surprise. Those lights and sirens were for you. Don't you ever look in your rearview mirror? Is your music cranked up so loud that you can't hear sirens? Were you so busy talking that you missed seeing a police car with its lights flashing?

Minus the sarcastic edge, I asked the driver just that.

"Um, yes, ma'am," he said as a bright red flush spread up his neck to his cheeks and ears, then tinted the scalp beneath his blond crew cut.

Obviously embarrassed. And probably not actively delinquent, just thoughtless and bored. Which described most of the teenagers and some of the adults in town.

I wrote him a ticket and took his driver's license away.

All the while, his friends sat quietly. A few nervous giggles, male and female. But no snotty comments and no attempt to talk their way out of trouble. They were polite. Very polite.

Maybe they recognized cranky when they saw it.

I walked to the rear of the truck, pulled out a cornstalk that was trapped in the bumper, held it up as I asked whose field they'd torn up.

One of the girls volunteered the farmer's name, which made things easier.

I left them sitting in their truck while I called dispatch, requested the farmer's phone number, and then dialed it on the driver's cell phone. After I explained why I was calling, we chatted for few minutes. Then with the line still open, I walked back to the truck and handed the phone back.

"Talk to him," I said, using the stern, I'm-not-your-friend-or-your-social-worker scowl that I regularly practiced in front of the mirror. "Work out fair compensation for damages. Then pay him. I promise you, the traffic court judge will ask you about it. So be sure you do the right thing."

By midmorning, I'd had more than enough of traffic patrol. So I cruised into town on 146, swung left on Dunn Street and rounded a curve. Without warning, the road fell away from beneath the vehicle. Out past my white-knuckled grip on the steering wheel, the only view was a wide expanse of river a deadly distance below.

Then, within an adrenaline-driven heartbeat or two, the familiar illusion was gone. I no longer fought my instinctive reaction to slam on the brakes. The earth, in the form of a steep gravel road, still crunched solidly under all four tires of the SUV and I could see that the road angled acutely downward, then abruptly curved to the right. Easy enough, now, to notice and heed the series of warning signs and the stretch of reflector-emblazoned guardrail that alerted drivers to the sharp turns that the road made on the way down to the riverbank.

Dunn Street was a dangerous road. If the town's economy had been better, it would have been a closed road. But the town needed the tax revenues generated along the strip of riverfront where Dunn Street dead-ended and trouble began. Narrow, floating docks on the river and a weedy gravel lot at the base of the bluff provided ample customer parking for a maze of bars and restaurants built on permanently moored barges.

The local ministers held that Dunn Street was a road to damnation. From their pulpits, they condemned the street's loose women, drugs and plentiful booze. Certainly, there was no doubt that if you were looking for a good time, the strip on Dunn was the place to be. Especially on Friday and Saturday nights. Thanks to Dunn Street, Maryville had a reputation as a party town and drew people from a hundred-mile radius.

Dunn Street's best customers tended to be the jail's best customers, too. Court costs and fines added revenue to the town's coffers and helped pay my salary. The bars were open six days a week, from 4:00 p.m. until 2:00 a.m., though Friday and Saturday were the big nights for cash receipts, drunken brawls and city revenue. On Sundays, thanks mostly to pressure from Maryville's religious leaders, all the businesses on Dunn Street were closed.

At a spot where road, river and the base of the bluff intersected, Dunn Street ended at a pile of fallen rock, illegally dumped trash, discarded needles and rotting river debris. I made a U-turn, cruised back along the river, then took the steep bluff road back to 146. Along the way, I examined the guardrails and their footings for damage or vandalism. At the sharpest curve, near the top of the road, I left my engine running as I got out of the SUV to peer downward at the narrow ribbon of rocky shore and the rushing water below. I saw no twisted metal, no broken bodies, no evidence of a drunken or depressed driver crashing through the railing and plunging headlong into eternity.

After that, I detoured briefly to make a lazy loop through the two-block business district on Market Street, then back to 146. Near the west edge of town, a four-way stop marked the place where Hill Street crossed the highway. I turned right, and headed uphill—up Hill—past a block of modest brick houses. Chad's foster parents still lived in one of them.

As I called county dispatch to report that I was officially off duty until tomorrow morning, I rolled slowly past Maryville's grandest structure. A three-foot-tall wrought-iron fence separated it from a brick-paved sidewalk laid out in a herringbone pattern. At the midpoint of the property, an iron gate opened into a tall rose arbor, thickly overgrown with the hotel's namesake flower. A long flagstone walkway lead through the arbor and up to the Cherokee Rose's white-pillared front porch.

The massive redbrick structure had been built at the highest point along the ragged river bluffs and was visible for miles up and down the river. Early in its history, the Tyler family had welcomed the wealthy and famous to their hotel, offering river travelers an elegant place to stop and rest. Later, while their men were off doing battle with the Confederacy, Tyler women had invited in other, more desperate travelers to partake of the hotel's hospitality. They'd hung a patchwork quilt—now proudly displayed in the hotel's lobby—from one of the second-floor balconies. The carefully sewn pattern signaled weary runaways that the Cherokee Rose was a place of safety along their dangerous northward journey. Then, generations later, Gran began offering the hotel's hospitality—and our family's protection—to another kind of desperate traveler.

It was a good legacy, I reminded myself. A legacy worth protecting.

A quick look at the cars parked beside the kitchen door told me that all of my family members were at home. There was Gran's vintage brown Subaru, an economical little car whose backseat was always littered with birding books, binoculars and an assortment of boots and jackets. Next to it was Aunt Lucy's shiny gray Suburban, often used to transport visitors to and from the Cherokee Rose. Parked behind that was my sister's red Jeep.

I glanced at my watch, discovered I had a little more time before lunch, and didn't pull up to the front of the house.

Just past the Cherokee Rose, Hill Street angled suddenly downhill for a dozen yards and dead-ended at a barricade that kept cars from parking too near the ragged edge of the bluff.

Beyond the barricade, pale birch trees and a scattering of picnic benches invited visitors to linger for a moment and appreciate Maryville's most breathtaking view of the river.

That's exactly what I did.

But first, while I was still inside the SUV, I locked my service pistol in the glove compartment. Then I unbuttoned my shirt and stripped off layers until a sweaty white T-shirt and lacy white bra were the only clothes I wore above my tan uniform slacks. Once inside the Cherokee Rose, I planned to shower and change into the civvies I'd brought along with me. But in the meantime, I'd savor the simple pleasure of escaping the confinement of my bulletproof vest.

Despite the beauty of the little park, it had few visitors. Maybe because most tourists didn't know it was there and most of Maryville took the view of the river from the bluffs for granted. Something I never did.

I sat down in my usual spot on the grass near the edge and leaned back against the white paper-thin bark of one of the trees. As my eyes moved upriver and down, watching the barges and pleasure craft that dotted the water as far as I could see, I made an effort to relax and think of nothing in particular. I tipped my head back and closed my eyes, enjoying the warmth of the sunshine that broke through the branches above me and danced across my eyelids. The roaring engine of a barge filled the air, drowning out the sounds around me, making it easy for my mind to drift....

Chad's truck needed a muffler.

The big blue Dodge was his pride and joy, the kind of truck only a sixteen-year-old boy could love. It had a big four-eighty engine and oversize tires that were made for mud and off-roading. The truck was noisy enough that some folks believed Chad had installed a custom glass-pack muffler. But the fact was, the old muffler had simply rusted out. Which made the truck rumble and roar, drowning out the birds and making conversation practically impossible.

"Shut your eyes," Chad shouted. A necessity, even though he was in the driver's seat right beside me. "Shut them now, Brooke, before we get there."

I did as he said and also had the good sense to grab the handle mounted above the door frame and brace myself against the seat. The old Dodge jounced as he powered it through the shallow, weedy ditch that separated the road from the tree line. Then a quick correction brought it back parallel to the road. And he killed the engine.

Silence. And the ringing in my ears, already fading, was overlaid with the sound of the wind rustling through the tree branches.

"What is it that you want to show me?" I asked again.

"It's a surprise."

That's exactly what he'd said when he'd picked me up from the Cherokee Rose. He hadn't made any further explanation to Aunt Lucy when he'd apologized for taking me away from my chores, but had kept insisting that there was something he had to show me. Now. Please.

I was familiar enough with the roads around town that it hadn't taken me long to figure out where we were going. It had been more than a year since I'd been out here last. And for good reason. There was nothing pleasant about visiting the ugly turquoise single-wide that had stood uninhabited for years, a rotting reminder of things best forgotten. Nothing pleasant about watching Chad stand and stare and rub the scar on his cheek. As if the old wound were still raw and hurting. But I was his friend, so whenever he asked me to go with him, that was what I did.

Today, however, he seemed more than happy. And that surprised me. It was as if some wonderful secret was bubbling up inside him, demanding to be set free.

"Keep 'em closed," he commanded, "until I say open them."

He spanned my waist with his hands, lifted me down from the truck, and then slipped his arm around my shoulders to guide me. I could tell by the way the dappled light danced across my eyelids that we were walking through a thick stand of trees. Toward the old trailer.

We stopped when there was hot sunlight on my face again.

"Okay. Now you can take a look."

I opened my eyes.

Where the trailer had once stood, the ground was now cleared in all directions. Vines and scrub trees and brush and shadows were gone. In their place were rows of sunflowers planted to the distant tree line. All in bloom, their heads turned toward the sun. A field of glorious golden flowers.

Chad was smiling. Grinning. Almost laughing with pleasure.

"It's great, isn't it? I rented the land to a farmer down the road. Cheap, on the condition that he clear it. And this is what he planted. Isn't it beautiful, Brooke? I think my mamma would like it, don't you?"

A shadow blocked the sun.

"Hey, Brooke. Thought I'd find you here."

I reacted instinctively. Illogically. Even as my eyes flew open, I was grabbing for the gun I was certain still hung at my waist. Somehow, I'd forgotten to take it off. I'd gone off duty, but left the SIG-Sauer available and unguarded while I slept.

Then, a heartbeat later, I realized that I had fallen asleep. Now, fully awake, I knew without doubt that I'd secured my weapon inside the SUV. Because I was well trained and always careful. Because I knew what could happen when a gun fell into someone else's hands.

I relaxed my arm, looked up into my sister's face as I yawned and stretched.

"Sorry," Katie said. "I didn't mean to startle you. I noticed your squad, saw you sitting here and assumed you were watching the river. I remembered that this was always one of your favorite places."

"Still is," I said, smiling.

I glanced at my watch, realized that I hadn't been asleep for very long. But I felt refreshed and my headache was gone. With a sigh more internal than expressed, I decided I was as ready as I ever would be for lunch with my family. I braced one hand against the tree trunk to push myself into a standing position. But the weight of Katie's hand on my shoulder stopped me.

"Let's stay here for a minute," she said. "So we can talk privately."

I settled back against the tree, thinking that maybe I could avoid a nasty confrontation at lunch by talking with Katie now. By convincing her to accept the conditions she'd so readily agreed to when she'd returned to Maryville. At least until Gran, who was already talking about retiring, gave up her leadership of the Underground. Aunt Lucy, I was sure, would willingly reroute rescued women away from the Cherokee Rose. For Katie's sake.

Katie lowered herself to a patch of nearby grass, spent a moment smoothing her tailored skirt and the white chef's apron that covered it, and another moment concentrating on brushing back a few ash-blond tendrils that had escaped from her barrettes. Then, without warning, she flicked her hand against my hip, her fingers striking the place where my holster usually hung.

When our eyes met, hers—so much like our mother's—were troubled.

"Did you really think I'd grab your gun and shoot you?" she said.

Her accusation surprised me, and my face undoubtedly reflected that surprise. It had never occurred to me that my sister—my long-time protector—would ever deliberately hurt me. The only concern I'd ever had was that she might hurt someone else.

"Of course not," I blurted. "I'm a cop, and that was purely reflex."

Though she didn't look convinced, she shrugged dismissively, then looked out at the river. Not at all like the Katie I remembered from the past, who had often been reduced to tears or inspired to fury by an unintended slight.

No doubt the years away had been good for her, I thought. For the first time, I considered the possibility that Aunt Lucy was right. That Katie was not the only one wounded by childhood trauma. And I asked myself if my newest suspicions—based on finding the kind of inhaler that was prescribed to millions every year—had anything to do with evidence or instinct. Maybe it was another symptom of my chronic inability to trust those I loved.

"What do you want to talk about?" I asked into the lengthening silence.

Katie turned her head to look at me again.

"I want a chance to prove to you that I've changed," she said. "Aunt Lucy and Gran already believe it. That's why they've agreed to let me help out with the guests. So the only one I have left to convince is you."

I opened my mouth to offer my compromise, to ask her to give the situation just a little more time, to tell her that I thought she was doing a fine job at the Cherokee Rose. But she cut me off.

"No, let me finish," she said. "I want to do more than just help out with the regular guests. I want to be part of the Underground again. Just like you and Gran and Aunt Lucy. I'm a Tyler. I have that right."

I lifted the ball cap that was part of my uniform, briefly ran my fingers through my hair. Short, brown and curly. Not like Katie's hair, or our mother's. I wasn't like either of them. Or even much like Aunt Lucy. I took after Gran. Or, at least, I tried to. I did what needed to be done. And said what needed to be said.

"No, you don't," I said firmly. "I'm sorry, Katie. But you lost that right forever when you killed Missy Porter."

She recoiled as if I had slapped her and abruptly moved her attention from my face to the patch of heat-scorched lawn between us. She frowned as she curled her fingers into the grass and combed her short nails through it, raking out dead blades. Distressed, but still definitely under control.

"I want you on my side, but if you're not…" Her voice was calm as, once again, she shrugged dismissively. "My doctor said that it was up to me to make amends for what I did. So I've decided to devote the rest of my life to working for the Underground. But clearly, you have no intention of allowing me to do that. So maybe I should go to the police. The *real* police. And tell them everything about that night."

My reaction to her threat surprised me. Concern, yes. Though we'd been juveniles when the crime had been committed, I'd always worried about what a trial and its verdict would mean for Katie and for me. But in that moment, I discovered I was mostly relieved. Finally, I thought, the exhausting burden of her secret—our secret—would be lifted from my shoulders. I would be able to tell someone where Missy was and see to it that she was properly buried.

I tipped my head and looked into my sister's model-pretty face.

"Okay," I said slowly as I tried to figure out how to express my only reservation. "I'll go with you, confess to my part in it. But maybe we could say that we met Missy by chance and helped her run away from her husband. All on our own. Then you killed her because she reminded you of our mother. And I dumped the body to protect you. That way, we keep Gran, Aunt Lucy and the Underground out of it."

"Fuck Gran," Katie said very clearly, "and Aunt Lucy."

By now, the fingers on her right hand were repeatedly raking through the grass, almost as if they had a life and will of their own.

"You don't mean that," I said quietly, and I believed what I said. Katie adored Gran. She always had. And Aunt Lucy was more mother to us than Lydia Tyler had ever been. "I know you love them and would never do anything to hurt them."

She dug her fingers into the sod, yanked out a handful of grass, flung it away from her. The blades scattered in the breeze coming up from the river. Then she scrambled to her feet and stood over me. Her eyes narrowed, her face flushed red and her whispery voice became a snarl.

"You think you know everything, don't you? Gran's little *pet*. So smart and brave and *perfect*. But I know a secret that you'll never know."

I stared up at my sister, distressed at seeing jealousy I'd never realized was there. But mostly appalled that I'd been right all along. That despite her years away from Maryville, Katie remained a dangerously angry young woman. She'd just gotten better at hiding it.

The jealously made no sense to me. But I understood her anger, knew that its roots were twisted deep into the earliest years of our childhood. I understood her anger, had always felt somehow responsible for it. But now, most of all, I feared it. Feared that tomorrow or the day after or the day after that, Katie would lose control again and direct all her pent-up rage at another innocent victim.

At the moment, that rage was directed at me.

Perhaps it was my expression, but something made Katie realize that she'd gone too far. That I'd glimpsed the demons still possessing her. Her anger vanished as quickly as it had come.

"I'm so sorry, Brooke," she said urgently. "Please forgive me. I lied. I don't really have any secrets. I just want so badly to be a member of this family again. To do something worthwhile, just like you. More than anything, I want you, Gran and Aunt Lucy to trust me. Like you did before—" She shook her head, pushing away that thought of the past. "I would never go to the police. Never do anything to hurt the Underground. Or our family. Especially not you."

Her eyes filled with tears. She pulled the edge of the white apron she wore up to her face and, for a little while, she smothered anguished sobs in it.

As I had ever since I could remember, I ignored all my other concerns and focused my attention on my sister's breathing. I listened carefully, alert for gasping or wheezing or for any other sign that she might be having a potentially deadly asthma attack. From where I sat, I could clearly see the outline of her albuterol inhaler in her skirt pocket. A tiny metal cylinder with a jointed blue plastic sleeve. If I had to, I could help her use it.

But despite her tears, Katie's breathing remained normal. Her sobs turned to sniffles and, after a little while, she lifted her reddened face from her apron and carefully blotted her eyes. She spent a moment adjusting her tearstained apron back over her skirt. Only then did our eyes meet again.

She flashed me a shaky smile, stuck out her hand.

I hesitated for just a moment before grasping it.

Always stronger than she looked, Katie pulled me easily to my feet.

"Sisters forever?" she asked as she put her arms around me.

It was the way most of our childhood fights had ended. No matter who had won. With me reassuring her that, unlike our mother, I would never abandon her. And I never would.

"Sisters forever," I agreed as I returned my sister's embrace.

I patted her on the back as I held her tight. And I wished—oh, how I wished—that I could trust her as I had when we were young. But I couldn't help thinking about the secret she had claimed, couldn't help remembering that I had a tiny asthma inhaler locked inside by glove compartment. And even as I wondered what secret my sister had kept from me, I feared that I might already know.

Chapter 11

Southern Covenant Hospital was a regional medical center that drew patients from smaller clinics and hospitals in Kentucky, Illinois and Tennessee. Among other things, they offered specialized services for women. Thanks to a nurse who'd been with the Underground for more than two decades, Gran and Aunt Lucy and I were familiar with the hospital. But this extraction promised to be more dangerous than any other we'd undertaken there.

"This girl's in bad trouble," the nurse had told Aunt Lucy the day before. "Some of the worst trouble I've ever seen. She's tied in with a gangbanger. I almost didn't call you, Lucy, because I'm afraid that this extraction may be too dangerous for even the Tylers to manage."

When she'd phoned me, Aunt Lucy had quoted the nurse, then had repeated everything that she'd learned from her about the woman who needed rescue. Her name was Jackie

Townsend, and she'd been beaten, then dragged down a flight of concrete steps.

But that wasn't the story that her husband had told when he and Jackie had arrived in the emergency room. He'd claimed she'd tripped and fallen on the way to get a soft drink from the vending machine near the apartment building's laundry room. Once Jackie was in any condition to talk, she'd agreed with him.

"I'm just clumsy," she had mumbled through swollen lips. "Cain't hardly walk a straight line."

The police didn't buy it. But no witnesses had come forward to contradict anyone's story. Hector Townsend, one world-weary cop had confided to the nurse, wasn't the kind of man it was healthy to contradict.

Hector hardly left his wife's side, even posting himself by her door when the nurses shooed him out of her room. Sometimes, they'd interrupted him as he'd sat on the bedside chair, leaned forward so his head was on the pillow next to hers, holding her hand and whispering to her.

"We're praying together," Hector had explained. "And planning the future. Once Jackie's well, we're going to Vegas. For a second honeymoon. Maybe we'll make a baby while we're there."

Hector told anyone who was willing to listen how the accident was all his fault. Then he'd go on to explain that he'd left his precious Jackie alone just for a few minutes. To buy some smokes. And so hadn't been there to get her that cold Dr. Pepper that she'd suddenly craved. If only he'd been there…

The note that Jackie had finally slipped the nurse made it very clear that he *had* been there.

I was running away, but he caught me. And did this. He'll kill me if I try to leave again.

"You have to tell the police," the nurse had whispered.

Jackie's involuntary cry brought Hector immediately into the room. The nurse had palmed the note as she reached to readjust the blood-pressure cuff.

"Sorry, honey," she'd said. "I must have pinched a bit of skin."

When her husband left the room again, Jackie had added to the note. If he went to prison because of her, Hector had promised that his gang brothers would kill her. And she believed him.

Then Jackie scrawled a final line at the bottom of the scrap of paper.

Please, please help me.

The night before, after she'd told me about Jackie, Aunt Lucy had surprised me.

"You, Gran and I are a good team," she'd said. "But for a while now, you've been the one directing the extractions. Gran's decided to make it official, to put you in charge of extractions for this region. The board will have to vote on her recommendation, but I don't see any problem there. So if you agree…"

For a moment, I'd been shocked into speechlessness, unable to answer Aunt Lucy's implied question. Gran had never before relinquished control of any aspect of the Underground's operations. Not even to Aunt Lucy.

"Yes," I'd stuttered. "Of course."

"Okay, then," Aunt Lucy had said, sounding satisfied. "Now, about tomorrow. How do you want to handle things?"

This time, my brief silence had been filled with thinking.

"He sounds dangerously violent," I'd said finally. "Not someone we want to confront, especially in a hospital. He probably has a criminal record. I have a contact in the Paducah PD. I'll call in a favor, have Hector picked up tomorrow. For questioning. If we extract Jackie while he's away from the hospital, there's no risk to anyone."

Aunt Lucy had responded so quickly and so vehemently that I knew her reaction was pure reflex.

"No. We never involve the police."

"I *am* the police," I'd reminded her gently. "And so are some of our best volunteers. Besides, helping this woman find a safe place to live doesn't break any laws."

Aunt Lucy's voice had remained urgent.

"But we've broken other laws. Our people have threatened abusers, even blackmailed a few. Provided forged documents. Helped noncustodial parents hide their kids from molesters. If the Underground is exposed, our volunteers are betrayed. Those we've helped are put at risk. And if the police ever begin to suspect that Katie—"

And there it was, I'd thought. The chronic fear. Not just for the Underground and its operation, but the fear that Missy's murder might someday destroy everything that our family had built.

"Okay," I'd said. "No cops."

The six-floor hospital complex was a maze of structures that were heavy on glass, interconnecting walkways and modern lines. The women's center was on the second floor, connected to the multistory garage by one of the hospital's glass-enclosed pedestrian bridges.

I found a parking spot within a few rows of the bridge, near a bank of elevators and a flight of interior stairs. From the garage, Gran, Aunt Lucy and I walked across the bridge and into the hospital at the same time. But my manner and the distance I kept between me and them suggested to any observer that I wasn't with them.

Before we'd left the Cherokee Rose, I'd changed into a summery blouse and a loose-fitting cranberry-colored jumper. Hidden beneath the jumper was a pair of white shorts. Tucked inside the canvas backpack I'd slung over one shoulder were the keys to my SUV, my wallet and ID, a snack, two curly wigs and a gun. Not my grandfather's old revolver, which was hidden beneath a floorboard in Gran's bedroom. But my own service pistol. A weapon that, as an off-duty cop, I had every right to conceal and carry.

Midafternoon, and visiting hours were in full swing. Swarms of men, women and children flowed across the glass-enclosed bridge, their arms filled with balloons and gifts.

The pedestrian bridge ended in a sunny second-floor lobby. Carpeting and upholstered furniture in shades of periwinkle and pink created a welcoming, homelike atmosphere. The kiosk at the center of the lobby had been designed to offer a three-hundred-sixty-degree view to anyone sitting behind its circular counter. But coordinating colors, a clutter of glossy informational brochures and a fresh flower arrangement gave the impression that the staff—two blue-uniformed security officers and a perky young woman wearing a tag inscribed Volunteer and Mindy—were there to guide, not to guard.

As soon as we entered the lobby, I settled down onto an unoccupied bench, opened up my backpack, and pulled out a bottle of apple juice and a granola bar. I used the snack as an excuse to linger as Gran and Aunt Lucy walked on past the kiosk and made their way slowly down the corridor.

Actually, Gran shuffled and Aunt Lucy hobbled, their gaits intended to make their disguises even more believable.

Below the hem of Aunt Lucy's summery skirt was a shapely calf, a trim ankle and a sandaled foot with pink-polished toenails. But pink toenails were all that showed of her other leg. From the knee down, it was encased in a thick layer of bandages that were supported by a Velcro-and-steel-rod brace. A bit hot for the weather, Aunt Lucy had judged it while we'd still been in the Suburban.

Gran had transformed herself into a frail senior. She'd left her short graying hair unstyled and frizzy and had dressed in a faded floral shift that was a couple of sizes too large. It hung from her wiry frame, its hem uneven and well below her knees, her bent shoulders and shuffling gait adding decades to her age. Over the dress, she wore the kind of sweater that only a thin-blooded elderly woman would wear in hundred-degree weather. Among the contents of the well-worn overnight bag she carried was an old terry-cloth robe.

After about fifteen minutes, I got up from the bench, tossed my crumpled wrapper and empty juice bottle into a nearby trash bin, and walked swiftly down the corridor into the hospital.

Gran and Aunt Lucy were nowhere in sight, so I followed the wall-mounted signs to the room number the nurse had given us. The corridor was empty, so when I reached E2-114, I flattened myself against the wall so that I could peer into the tiny room unobserved by its two occupants.

A compact bathroom was just inside the door. Beyond that, the room's only bed was pushed almost against the window. A slight, young woman in a faded hospital gown was in the bed, which was cranked upward into a sitting position. I could see little of Jackie Townsend besides henna-red hair with chunky blond highlights and dark roots. Her face was turned away from the doorway and away from the man sitting in a chair between the bed and the door.

Hector Townsend was a short, burly man whose sleeveless, skintight Harley T-shirt did little to cover his tattoos, bull chest and the bulging muscles on his neck and arms. His eyes were closed, but his beefy, muscular legs—clad in scarred biker leathers—were stretched out so that his wife would have to step over them to go anywhere.

My God, I thought as I looked at him. Even if I had a nightstick and a gun, the guy would be intimidating. And I had no problem imagining him dragging his wisp of a wife down a flight stairs.

As I continued down the hall, I thought of my grandmother, who was seventy-one. And my aunt, who was brave but not particularly strong. If something went wrong, Hector Townsend was more than capable of killing them with his bare hands.

With that thought very much on my mind, I continued down the hall. I found Gran and Aunt Lucy at a spot where two corridors met. Aunt Lucy had leaned herself and her crutches against a stretch of wall between a row of vending machines and a bank of phones. Across from her was an elevator. Gran was talking on a house phone—describing, I was sure, the first part of our plan to the nurse who was our Underground contact. Aunt Lucy smiled at me, but seemed intent on Gran's half of the conversation.

I took a moment to step past them and glance up and down the other corridor. More patients' rooms and a locked utility closet were to my right. Men's and women's restrooms and a door labeled Stairs were to my left. I took a couple of steps, confirmed that the stairwell door was unlocked, and then returned to my grandmother and aunt. For a moment, I dug through Gran's overnight bag, confirming that it also held the tape, an indelible marker and sheets of eight-and-a-half-by-eleven card stock that I'd asked her to bring.

"Just pray that the easy way works," I heard Gran say as I closed the bag again. "Or we'll have to go to plan B."

Then she hung up the phone and turned to me. The reflection of the overhead lights glinted off her thick glasses as she pointed down the corridor in the direction of Jackie's room.

"The nurse'll be talking with them in just a minute."

"Okay. I'll trot on back there and listen in. If the strategy works and Hector leaves Jackie alone in the room, I'll get her dressed fast." I tugged briefly at the jumper I wore. "I'll drop this over her head, leave the way we came in, and get her into the car."

Gran and Aunt Lucy nodded.

"You and Gran leave through the front door and walk over to that fried chicken place on Twenty-seventh and Washington," I continued. "I'll park there and wait for you."

"And if he doesn't leave voluntarily?" Aunt Lucy asked.

"Like Gran said earlier, we go to plan B."

Hector didn't leave.

"Good news," the nurse said once she was back in Jackie's room. "The doctor says you can go home today."

I was eavesdropping just outside the door and heard the enthusiasm in Hector's reply. Whatever Jackie said was murmured so quietly that I couldn't make out her words. But I knew that she would be terrified by the prospect of going home with her husband. And perhaps devastated that, though she'd agreed to enter the Underground, no one had come to help her. For everyone's safety, the nurse hadn't dared tell Jackie that rescue was, very literally, just around the corner.

Then, as we'd agreed, the nurse suggested that Hector visit the business office to finish up paperwork. In the meantime, she would help his wife get dressed.

That was met by firm, but polite, refusal.

"Naw. But thanks anyway. Jackie doesn't like it if I leave her alone. Do you, honey pie? I'll just help her get dressed. Then we'll go downstairs and do that paperwork together."

The nurse put the alternate plan into action.

"No problem," she said. "As soon as Jackie's dressed, I'll bring a wheelchair in for her."

Hector objected vehemently enough that I suspected he planned on skipping out on the hospital bill.

"The doc said she's doing okay. You said he's released her. So we'll leave on our own."

A little steel crept into the nurse's voice.

"Hospital policy, Mr. Townsend. It'd be my job if Jackie walked out of here under her own steam. So you're stuck with me—and a wheelchair—at least as far as the waiting area for the business office."

From there, her tone implied, the issue of the wheelchair was the business office's problem. If Hector's intent was to leave without paying, she'd offered him the opportunity he needed. Once the nurse was gone, it would be easy enough for the couple to walk right out of the hospital.

The nurse winked at me as she left the room. She was a surprisingly petite woman with strawberry-blond hair, probably weighing no more than one-twenty and closer in age to Gran than Aunt Lucy. But I was confident that the force of her personality was more than enough to keep Hector in line. At least temporarily.

All she had to do was get him as far as the elevator.

I rejoined Gran and Aunt Lucy, and we quickly reviewed and modified a tactic that we'd used before.

A few minutes later, Gran was feeding quarters into the vending machine, intent on buying a large cup of very hot, extremely mediocre coffee. Aunt Lucy was standing upright, balancing on her crutches with her thickly swaddled lower leg lifted inches off the ground.

I had already walked around the corner carrying a neatly hand-lettered sign with tape doughnuts stuck to its back. Out of Order, it said. After the restroom's only occupant washed her hands and left, I stuck the sign to the door's exterior. Then I waited right outside the door, relying on my hearing and imagination to tell me what was going on just out of sight.

Soon, I knew, the nurse would help Jackie into the wheelchair and begin pushing her down the corridor in the direction of the elevator. She would steer the wheelchair close to the wall that was opposite the vending machine area, her position and pacing encouraging Hector to walk near the center of the corridor.

Not too far from the intersection of the corridors, Hector would encounter Aunt Lucy and Gran.

Frustrating to stay where I was, out of sight of the chaos that I knew was coming. I would have preferred to watch. Would have preferred knowing immediately if something was going wrong, if some unexpected circumstance was creating a situation more dangerous than this one already was.

But I had my own job to do. So I stood just outside of the restroom door and imagined the scene that would unfold the moment Hector walked past the little alcove containing the vending machines.

The nurse would say something to draw Hector's attention.

At that moment, Aunt Lucy would hobble past, heading along the corridor in the opposite direction. She'd teeter slightly on her crutches, then throw one wide to catch herself. And plant the crutch in front of Hector's moving feet.

Aunt Lucy would fall. And cry out loudly in pain and dismay. With luck, Hector would go down, too. But chances were, his balance and reaction time were better than that. Not that it really mattered. Because, right about then, Gran would step onto our impromptu stage.

Onlookers drawn by Aunt Lucy's cries would see the next accident coming. It would happen so quickly that they might be able to shout a warning, but wouldn't be able to stop it. Not if Gran had her way.

Frail and elderly, Gran would act oblivious to the unfolding chaos. Easy enough for onlookers to assume she was a little deaf. Certainly her thick glasses implied she didn't see very well. Her eyes and attention, anyway, would be fixed on her coffee cup. She'd be stirring it carefully as she shuffled forward into the corridor. And into the center of the melee.

Confused and disoriented by the drama erupting at her feet—a large man either falling or trying not to and a middle-aged woman flinging her crutches wide as she collapsed to the floor—Gran would panic. And fling the cup of hot coffee from her hands. If it landed where Gran wouldn't seem to be aiming it, hot liquid would cascade out in the vicinity of Hector's crotch.

If everything went according to plan.

I hated waiting, knowing that a moment of bad timing, some unanticipated circumstance, could turn opportunity into disaster. Then we'd be forced to rescue Jackie beyond the relative safety of the hospital. At her home or on the streets, places where Hector's violence would be unrestrained.

I heard a commotion just around the corner.

Let the games begin, I thought as a man—undoubtedly Hector—yelped with surprise.

Score one for Aunt Lucy.

A heartbeat later, Hector suddenly cut loose with a string of profanity, pain pushing his voice an octave higher.

Gran scores, I thought. And I allowed myself a smile.

Gran's voice and Aunt Lucy's mixed with Hector's, adding to the noise and confusion. An overlay of running footsteps and strangers' voices meant that others were rushing to help.

At this moment, I was sure that no one—not even Hector—would be paying attention to Jackie as she was pushed away from the fray by her attentive nurse.

The few people near me rushed around the corner, curiosity and desire to help emptying the corridor that I stood in. A good thing because soon, I knew, the ball would be in my court.

The nurse rounded the corner with the wheelchair.

"She'll help you," she said.

I grabbed Jackie's hand and, in my haste, nearly pulled her from the chair.

"Park it by the stairwell," I said quickly to the nurse. "Maybe it'll delay—"

Her quick nod told me I didn't need to explain further.

I turned my attention to Jackie, took her arm and guided her into the women's restroom. Pointed to the stall at the far end of the row.

"Hurry," I said. "In there."

I gave her an encouraging little push, pressed in behind her and shot the lock into place. As a defense against a well-placed shoulder or boot, I knew it was completely ineffective, no more a deterrent than the out of order sign that was still hanging on the restroom door. But the sign had done its job, clearing the room so that no one would witness our entrance.

And the lock might make Hector hesitate. Besides, maybe I'd misjudged the man. Perhaps he wasn't the kind of guy who would burst into a women's restroom, out of order or not.

Yeah, right, I told myself. When pigs fly.

Chapter 12

The toilet seat was down.

I flipped it upward to provide a stable surface.

"Step up here so that he can't see your feet," I said.

Jackie didn't waste time asking questions. She just nodded and put one foot up onto the porcelain rim of the stool.

After slipping my purse over a hook on the stall wall, I grabbed Jackie's arm to steady her, helped her climb up and told her to turn around so that she was facing the door. She braced her hands against the stall walls for balance, and I was pleased to see that they were tall enough to hide her.

Jackie was a skinny kid, not much older than nineteen or twenty. But it was too easy to tell that life hadn't been kind to her. The restroom's harsh fluorescent light illuminated her face, making her look paler than she already was. Badly dyed hair stuck out all over her head, accentuating the hollowed-out look of her eyes and cheeks. Her fine, almost delicate features were marred by the darker marks of bruises and the twisted path of dark, tiny stitches that marched from the corner of her right eye, across a swollen cheek, and down to a corner of her scabbed and swollen lips.

She was wearing black jeans and a skimpy black top. An outfit that Hector had helped her put on. Colors that he would most likely remember. Something that would work to my advantage.

I took a moment, no longer, to meet her too-large and very frightened brown eyes.

"Trust me, okay? It'll be fine."

I didn't know if she believed me, but she nodded.

"Good girl," I said.

I turned to face the stall door. And got ready for Hector's arrival.

I hiked up my jumper just long enough to undo the button and zipper on the white shorts I wore. Then, as the shorts fell around my ankles, I took the SIG-Sauer from my purse. Slid my right index finger through the trigger guard and my hand firmly around the butt of the gun. With my legs splayed forward, I slid back along the toilet until I was up against Jackie's feet.

Ready.

And just in time.

From outside in the hallway, Hector's loud, angry voice carried clearly into the confines of the stall.

"Where is she? What'd you do with Jackie?"

Though I couldn't hear the nurse's reply, I knew what she was supposed to say: "I left her right here, out of the way. Then I went to make sure you were okay."

Behind me, Jackie whimpered.

Quickly, I turned my head, looked up at her.

"Be quiet," I said urgently. "No matter what happens, you have to be quiet. Promise me."

She caught her lower lip between her teeth. Bit down hard. And nodded.

As Hector drew nearer the restroom door, I could hear the nurse's voice, too.

"Your wife wouldn't go in there, Mr. Townsend. It's out of order."

I held my breath, praying that Hector would agree. And move on. Once he was out of range, Gran would come into the restroom and give me the all clear. Then we'd slip away from the hospital, carefully detouring to avoid Hector.

Not all prayers are answered.

Hector came crashing into the restroom.

"Quit playing games, Jackie. I know you're here!" he bellowed.

He began opening stall doors, checking inside.

The nurse kept trying to reason with him.

"Mr. Townsend! This makes no sense. Your wife is probably waiting for you downstairs."

Hector ignored her. Kept checking. Despite the nurse's escalating threats, he reached the stall where we hid. I could hear his labored breathing on the other side of the door.

He rattled the lock. Called his wife's name again.

"Get lost, jerk," I shouted back, working to sound outraged rather than afraid. "I'm not Jackie. Whoever the hell *she* is."

Hector must have been from Missouri. The show-me state. He bent over and attempted to peer beneath the door.

I kicked at his face and shrieked as I pulled my legs—and the white shorts—back farther into the stall.

"Help!" I screamed at the top of my lungs. "Someone! Please! Help!"

All the while, I kept my gun aimed directly in front of me. If he attempted to break in, I would shoot him at point-blank range and claim self-defense. A not-unreasonable claim when a raging man has you trapped in the women's restroom. A realistic claim, in fact, should Hector find me hiding Jackie in the stall with me. No doubt, he *would* try to kill me.

I'd tell anyone who asked that Jackie had been in the stall next to me. That she'd crawled beneath the divider to escape her psycho husband. A female cop from Maryville would have a lot more credibility than a creep like Hector. He would, anyway, be too dead to speak on his own behalf.

I took a breath. Steadied my nerves and my aim. And waited.

That was when the nurse spoke again, her voice filled with outrage and authority.

"I'm calling security, Mr. Townsend!" the nurse said. "And I promise, you *will* be arrested."

There was a moment of quiet as, I supposed, Hector considered what to do next. Then he cursed, accused the nurse of incompetence and muttered something about suing the hospital. For what, I couldn't imagine. But, in the end, he made a decision that saved his life.

His footsteps retreated across the restroom.

The nurse followed in his wake, still threatening him.

Eventually, when I could no longer hear either of their voices, I exhaled. And relaxed. Just a little. I stepped forward in the stall and put my gun back in my purse. Then I turned to look up at Jackie. Smiled just a little, more from relief than anything else. And she giggled. Not quite hysterical, but darned close.

"It's going to be okay," I said. "But I think we'll stay right here for a couple more minutes, just to be sure that no one's coming back. Sound good to you?"

Her voice cracked, but she managed to answer. And almost smile.

"Yeah. Sounds good."

I bent to pull my shorts back on. After that, I stripped off my extra layer—the cranberry-colored jumper I was wearing. Which left me dressed in shorts and a blouse.

By then, my heart was almost beating normally.

I held out my hand to Jackie, helped her step down beside the toilet, and felt just secure enough to unlock the stall door. I snagged the purse as I left the stall. And I handed her the jumper.

"Put this on," I said.

She did as I said and didn't have to be told to slip off the black jeans that showed beneath the hem. Those, I stuffed in the trash.

Then I pulled out the wigs.

"Brunette or blond?"

"Blond," she said.

A moment later, she was transformed from biker punk to hometown girl. With bruises. But the simple change in appearance would make our escape easier. At a distance, Hector would be unlikely to spot his wife among the crowds of visitors to the hospital. And in the unlikely event that he'd managed to enlist anyone's help in finding his suddenly absent wife, she wouldn't look at all like he'd describe her.

We went back into the corridor, followed it around until we passed the kiosk, then continued, unaccosted, to the parking garage.

A few minutes later, Gran and Aunt Lucy joined us inside the Suburban.

Despite our success, Aunt Lucy looked grim and nearly exhausted. Not surprising. Though she'd gone on the Underground's rescues ever since *she* was sixteen, she faced each extraction with competence and resignation. As if they were nothing more than dangerous, unpleasant tasks that needed doing. For the sake of the women.

But Gran flashed me a grin that I could only describe as gleeful. As if, had she been unrestrained by age or convention, she would have been punching the air, whooping with joy and doing a victory dance.

I grinned back across two generations, recognizing my own feelings in my grandmother's expression. Not for the first time, I realized that she and I were of a kind. Certainly, our commitment was to the helpless and abused. But it was the challenge of outwitting—and defeating—human monsters that kept our work for the Underground interesting. And made us feel truly alive.

When we arrived at the Cherokee Rose, it was already dark.

Katie was on the front-porch swing, in a pool of yellowish light cast by the overhead bulb. Her workday was long over and she'd dressed for the warm, humid night in dark shorts and a pale green tank top. Her legs were curled up beneath her and a book was open on her lap. As I parked the Suburban, I saw her look up from her reading.

I expected her to go back into the house, to retreat to the kitchen or the private apartment where Aunt Lucy and Gran lived—where Katie and I had grown up—and avoid contact with anyone traveling along the Underground. But as Gran, Aunt Lucy and Jackie preceded me through the hotel's front gate, Katie hurried from the porch and along the flagstone path that bisected the yard.

She met us near the rose arbor. Pushing past Aunt Lucy and Gran, she reached out and grasped both of Jackie's hands, then pulled her in close for a hug.

"I'm so glad you're letting us help you," she murmured.

Her back was to Gran and Aunt Lucy. So they couldn't see the smug, almost vindictive smile that my sister shot me over Jackie's shoulder. It said, "I told you so," much louder than words.

After a moment, Katie released Jackie from her embrace, but kept a hold on one of her hands as she continued speaking.

"Your name's Jackie, isn't it? Well, Jackie, you'll be safe here. I promise. Are you hungry? Do you like chocolate cake? I just finished frosting one. But maybe something more nourishing first. Come on into the kitchen. You can tell me what you like to eat."

At first, Gran and Aunt Lucy looked surprised. But as Katie continued talking to Jackie, they began looking almost pleased. As if this were a moment they'd been waiting for. The moment our entire family was involved in the Underground.

Jackie, responding like a needy child to Katie's overt mothering, clung to Katie's side. Hand in hand, the two of them walked up the front steps and through the big double pillars that supported the porch.

Gran and Aunt Lucy followed them.

I stood where I was, watching mutely. Shocked as I saw how easily my concerns were dismissed. How easily the understanding we'd come to during lunch was forgotten. Now it was all too apparent that Katie was determined to get what she wanted. And neither Aunt Lucy nor Gran would stand in her way. Because they loved Katie, but more importantly, because they believed in second chances.

Aunt Lucy paused at the threshold of the big front door. She turned, looked over her shoulder and saw that I was still standing on the path.

"Come on, honey," she said. "Let's celebrate a job well done."

I shook my head and turned away, knowing there was nothing to celebrate. To protect those seeking refuge at the Cherokee Rose—to protect the Underground and those who ran it—I would have to prove to Aunt Lucy and Gran that my sister was still capable of violence. And I would have to do it quickly. Before someone like Missy came along.

But what if I was already too late? I asked myself as I had so often since first discovering the inhaler. What if I was many years too late?

As I walked back along the flagstone path—as Aunt Lucy continued calling my name—I prayed that Missy was my sister's only victim. For all of our sakes. But I also made the decision that I'd been trying so hard not to make. Because it would undoubtedly tear my family—and my life—to pieces.

If I uncovered proof that my sister had hidden her first crime in the trunk of an old tree, there'd be no cover-up. Not this time. No matter what impact that had on me, my family, or the Underground. I would not allow a serial killer to continue walking free. I would not give Katie an opportunity to kill again.

Fighting back tears, I walked beneath the rose arbor. And for the first time that I could remember, I was unmoved by the enduring beauty of the Cherokee roses that had flourished for many generations at the entrance to our family home. Ignoring the abundance of waxy white flowers surrounding me, I grasped the latch on the heavy front gate.

A stray rose tendril snagged my bare arm.

Thorns embedded themselves deep in my flesh.

Unthinking, unfeeling, I wrenched myself free.

Chapter 13

Later that night, I phoned my sister.

I waited late enough that I knew she'd be home, then dialed the number of the little coach house where she lived.

"How can I trust you after what you did tonight?" I said as soon as she answered.

Her voice was sweet and whispery, her response pure innocence. But she knew exactly what I was angry about.

"What did I do?" she asked, and then proceeded to answer her own question. "I welcomed a poor, scared woman to the Cherokee Rose. I took care of her. And she liked me, Brooke. Just as I knew she would. So why should you be upset? Gran and Aunt Lucy weren't."

Though I knew it wasn't necessary, I explained myself.

"At lunch, you told us that the hotel's guests didn't really interest you. All you wanted to do, you said, was to visit the dining room in your capacity as chef. Introduce yourself. Ask folks how they liked their food. Gran, Aunt Lucy and I agreed to that. *You* agreed to that."

I paused, giving her an opportunity to apologize for that evening's deliberate interaction with Jackie and the Underground. I wanted her to tell me that she'd made a mistake. That it wouldn't be repeated.

But the moment was filled with the silence I'd expected. Her lack of remorse strengthened my determination to follow through on the strategy I'd come up with during the long drive home. Even if Katie had nothing to do with the remains I'd found near Camp Cadiz, I had to expose the rage she kept so well hidden from Gran and Aunt Lucy. Before someone got hurt. I intended to make my sister angry. Irrationally angry. With the one person who could control her.

Me.

"You lied to us," I said.

My tone made it an accusation, which she dismissed.

"*That* was your fault," she said. "I was trying to make you happy. To do what you wanted. And I really thought that I could be patient for a while longer."

My sister's voice grew bitter.

"But you left me behind again. Like always. While you went with Gran and Aunt Lucy. On *Underground business*. No one had to tell me—I knew it was an extraction. So it's like I told you, Brooke, *before* lunch. I'm part of this family and I *will* be part of the Underground. You saw how happy I made Gran and Aunt Lucy tonight. You may not like it, but it's pretty clear that *you* can't stop me."

"Oh yes, I can," I said. "Because—"

Then it was my turn to lie. To myself, because I still believed that I could expose my sister's anger and not become its victim. And to Katie who, earlier that day, had unwittingly given me the means to provoke her.

"—because I know your secret."

She didn't call my bluff. Didn't demand that I tell her what, exactly, I knew. Or how, exactly, I'd found out. She didn't laugh at me or challenge me or deny having a secret.

What she did say made my blood run cold.

"If you tell," she whispered, "I'll kill you."

Then she hung up on me.

Soon after that, I tried to sleep.

A hopeless undertaking.

I tossed and turned, solving no problems, gaining no insight, but compounding my fears. A few hours passed, leaving me more exhausted than when I'd crawled into my bed. Leaving me at a point of frustration and tears, where life seemed hopeless and problems insurmountable.

Tears never solved anything. That's what Gran always said.

In my experience, she was right.

I resisted the urge to call Chad just to hear his voice. And pushed away a too vivid memory of the last night we'd spent together. The night he'd cuddled me in his arms, pressed his lips to the top of my head, gently wiped the tears from my cheeks. Asking no questions. Simply offering quiet comfort and a willingness to listen. Should I choose to speak. To tell him what was wrong.

I'd answered his love with my silence.

That thought chased me from my bed.

I wrapped myself in a sheet, grabbed my pillow, and padded through the dark and silent house, seeking the company of an old companion. Highball didn't stir when I settled down next to his bed and stroked my fingers through his thick, warm fur. And, though he was sleeping, I told him how I felt. As I had since I was a child.

I told him how frustrated and angry and hurt I was. How tired I was and how very lonely. How desperately I missed Chad. And loved my sister. And hated her. How I feared that another dreadful secret might be lurking in her past. And feared that Aunt Lucy and Gran had given her an opportunity to unleash violence in the future. But if I cried, they were silent tears. Unwitnessed and easily denied.

After a while, I leaned back against the kitchen door with one of my legs still touching the cushion where the old dog sprawled. I listened to the sounds of his deep, regular breathing.

At some point, I slept.

I dreamed that I searched alone through a forest and found a place where ancient trees pushed upward from stagnant water. Above me, dark-feathered turkey vultures gathered in the branches. They twisted their ruddy, cadaverous heads as they followed my movements with glittering eyes.

I walked carefully along the mud-slick shore, anxiously searching the water's surface, indifferent to the sinuous passage of snakes and the twisting larvae of unborn insects. I had hidden it well, I told myself.

Above me, I heard flapping and rustling, so I looked up into the trees. The birds were drawing closer, smiling down at me. I looked away from them, back out into the swamp. And saw what I had most feared. Bobbing just above the water was the roof of a passenger van, its corroded surface draped with duck weed and covered in slime.

I have to move it, I told myself.

My clothes fell away from me and, for a moment, I stood naked in the moonlight. Then I walked slowly into the water.

Above me, the birds screamed their approval.

Soon the brackish water covered my head, filled my mouth and nose and lungs. But that didn't matter because I knew I was among the dead. A forest of twisted human skeletons greeted me, their skulls and torsos impaled by the tree roots, their ivory hands and bony fingers floating loose and pointing the way.

She was still trapped inside the van. Where I had left her. But she'd shed her blanket and the crushing weight of the rocks I'd placed on her. She'd moved into the front seat, locked her hands around the steering wheel. And all around her, like holiday streamers, pale ribbons of waxen flesh floated gently on the current. Above the dark hole of her mouth, her colorless eyes were wide open, staring forward, trying in vain to find her way home.

When she saw me, she pushed the van door open. Caught my hand with bony fingers and urged me inside.

I followed willingly, took her place behind the wheel, touched my foot to the accelerator.

The car drifted forward into a narrow shaft of greenish light that penetrated the watery tomb. It skimmed along one of my passenger's rotting cheeks and exposed razor teeth lurking within the rictus of her smile.

The corpse wore my sister's face.

I panicked.

I pushed the door open, kicked outward, then upward. Away from the horror. Away from the danger. Back into the air.

Suddenly, I was breathing again.

I swam to the shore, lay there naked with my face in the mud. Gasping, crying, knowing that I had failed. I would go back, I told myself. Before it was too late. But some impulse made me roll over before I had strength enough to stand.

I looked up into a circle of rustling wings and cadaverous

faces. Up into beady, red-rimmed eyes that glittered with anticipation. Then broad wings blotted out the sky and pain lanced through my neck as they crowded forward. A heartbeat later, and the carrion eaters' hooked yellow beaks were tipped with bits of flesh and crimson.

I awakened with a crick in my neck and a scream on my lips.

A nasty night.

A morning that begged for buttered toast and comforting ritual.

Almost every morning, I made wheat toast for Highball and me. Butter on his. Butter and something sweet on mine. What had started as a girl's indulgence of a too-thin stray had evolved into a predictable moment for an adult at the start of almost every day.

In years past, I'd bring Highball in from his kennel in the barn before dropping his two slices of bread into a squatty aluminum toaster. He would pace the kitchen floor until, cued by the sound of the toast popping up, he would race to my side, tail wagging expectantly, watching intently as I slathered one piece of toast with butter, then put the other on top.

Now, as I had for many months, I dropped his toast sandwich into the dish beside his bed in the kitchen.

"There you go, Highball, baby."

He raised his head and tipped it to one side, as if digging through memory for the meaning of the familiar sounds. Old age was robbing him of memory and vitality. Failing eyesight had made him cautious. He waited, relying on his other senses to provide more information, to give him a reason to expend precious energy.

I counted the seconds until he registered the smell. One,

two, three. Four, five, six. Seven, eight, nine. Ten. Ten seconds before he sighed and slowly stood. He stretched, stepped away from his cushion and lowered his grizzled muzzle into the bowl. Eating was accompanied by the slow back and forth swing of a curly tail. Happiness, if not enthusiasm.

A week earlier, it had taken him only five seconds to remember the joys of buttered toast. A few weeks before that, only two. And earlier, in his prime, Highball could have located toast from several miles off.

I glanced at the percolator, noted that the coffee bubbling into the glass knob on its lid was nearly the proper shade of brown, and dropped a single piece of bread into the toaster for me.

Out in the yard, Possum began barking and howling, demanding my attention, demanding his breakfast. More than any of the other puppies I had looked at two years earlier, he'd had the best combination of instinct, intelligence and remarkable sense of smell. Possum had the potential to be better at his job than Highball ever was. He had a level of energy that Highball had never achieved and, for the promise of a tennis ball, would do whatever was asked of him. Highball's only goal in life was to please me and, for that reason alone, he had excelled at search-and-rescue.

Possum could never replace Highball as my companion.

Pity, more for myself than the elderly dog, was interrupted by the smell of smoke. I turned away from my contemplation of Highball and saw that the toaster was smoking. Fire, fueled by my toast, licked up the blue-and-white gingham curtains covering the nearby window.

I yanked the toaster's plug from the wall, then doused the growing flames with the liquid nearest at hand—the entire contents of my coffeepot. Then I followed up by yanking the still-smoldering curtains from the window, dropping them in the sink and soaking them with water.

When I was sure the fire was out, I looked at Highball.

In the old days, he would have been underfoot, excited by the smoke and activity, frantic to help or protect me.

He had returned to his cushion and was almost asleep.

After cleaning up the disaster in my kitchen, I didn't bother searching for an alternative to toast or making myself another pot of coffee. I pulled on jeans, hiking boots and a hot-pink T-shirt—not a fashion statement, but a color that would make it easy for Chad to see me when we were down in the ravine. Then I drove to Statler's seeking caffeine, carbohydrates, conversation and another tankful of gas.

The first thing I noticed when I pulled into the filling station was a colorful poster that completely blocked one of the filling station's big plate-glass windows. Hand-drawn palm trees, pink flamingos and stylized blue waves surrounded a cartoon drawing of a black man in an apron and a chef's hat. Beetle brows and a gold-toothed grin suggested the character was Ed. Emerging from his mouth was a comic-style text balloon.

The Missus Is On Vacation, it read. No Ham And Beans On Wednesday. Come On In For Ed's Special Jamaican Pork On A Bun.

When I pushed the door open, I discovered that my hot-pink shirt blended in nicely with the filling station's new decor. And amusement chased away the bleakest of my thoughts.

A Beach Boys tune was playing over the store's speaker system.

Throughout Statler's Fill-Up, pink flamingo yard ornaments roosted on all of the horizontal surfaces—floor, shelves, counter and tables. And a mounted swordfish—one that I recalled his missus wouldn't allow in the house—was hung in a place of honor above the beer cooler.

The counter area was furnished like a party-store version of a beachcomber's hut. An eight-foot-tall inflatable palm tree shaded the filled doughnut tray from the fluorescent lights overhead. A fisherman's net hung from the ceiling, weighed down by the catch of the day—shells, bits of driftwood and loops of colorful Mardi Gras beads. Obstructing the narrow cigarette shelves on the wall behind the counter was a bamboo-framed photograph, blown up to heroic proportions, of Ed standing on a beach.

But the store's decor paled by comparison to Ed's outfit. A parade of tiny pink flamingos marched along the hem of a lemon-yellow shirt. Below the shirt were brown surfer's shorts trimmed with stylized yellow and pink waves and palm trees. Ed's grizzled hair was covered with a hot-pink silk ball cap with a hooked brown bill that suggested a flamingo's beak.

I could practically see the laughter bubbling up inside Ed as the filling station's heavy glass door swung shut behind me. As he struggled to keep his laughter from escaping, his lips compressed, the edges of his mouth tipped down and his eyebrows slanted up over his dark eyes.

Traffic stops pretty much ensured that I was confronted daily by the absolutely ridiculous or the totally improbable. So I'd had plenty of practice keeping a straight face. I used that job skill now as I lifted my hand palm out and splayed my fingers in an exaggerated attempt to shield my eyes from the bright colors. Then I dropped my mirrored sunglasses back down on my nose and made a show of sniffing the air.

"Got some kind of head cold, Officer?" Ed asked, though he knew darn well I didn't.

"No, sir, I don't. I'm checking for the sweet smell of Mary Jane," I said, though I knew darn well *he* didn't.

One of Ed's mobile eyebrows crawled up his shiny black forehead, until it was stopped by his cap.

"Say what?"

"Y'know. M.J. Magic smoke. Mary and Johnny. Mexican locoweed. The kind of stuff beach bums and old hippies are known to smoke."

Ed grinned and his eyebrow relocated close to his eye.

"Oh, you mean pot. Well, why didn't you say so, Officer? What do you think makes my doughnuts so special?"

I slipped my sunglasses back into my breast pocket, picked up a doughnut and made a show of examining it carefully before I took a bite.

"I was certain that it was all that deep frying and sugar…"

"Definitely the deep frying," Ed retorted. "Give 'em time. They'll probably make that illegal, too."

Then Ed and I both laughed. His laughter deep and hearty. Mine closer than it had been in long time to a young woman's giggle. And though I didn't know what Ed's morning had been like, when we finally wound down to gasping and tears, I felt a heck of a lot better.

Ed took off his silly hat to wipe his eyes and then perched it on top of the cash register.

I filled my mug with coffee, then I leaned comfortably against the counter. As I sipped my coffee and nibbled on my doughnut, I looked at Ed's shirt a little more closely. That's when I realized that the flamingos were doing a bit more than marching. The busy pattern made their behavior subtle, but the birds were definitely engaging in X-rated activity. The shirt didn't violate any local decency ordinances, but it sure did push the limits of good taste.

Though I didn't have nearly the talent that Ed did, I let one of my eyebrows slide out of place, then waved my fingers in the direction of his shirt.

"The missus know you're wearing that outside your bedroom?"

He hooked his thumb in the direction of the sign on the window.

"She's out of town."

"So she doesn't know," I said flatly, making a real effort to keep laughter from creeping into my voice.

I was surprised that someone willing to wear that shirt didn't have thicker skin. But Ed rushed to explain.

"No, no. You don't understand. She's visiting up in Chicago this week, and I don't want to lose the Wednesday lunch crowd. So this here shirt is part of an in-store promotion. Just like in the big city."

"Seeing as how I'm local law enforcement, I'm compelled to ask. What, exactly, is that shirt promoting?"

"Jamaican jerked pork, of course," Ed said, managing to sound outraged.

Then, not surprisingly, he changed the subject.

"Gonna be mighty hot again. Not the day I'd choose to go scrambling down into a ravine. But worth it, I suppose, if you find something that helps you put a name to those old bones."

Then he answered the question he must have seen on my face.

"Chad came by last night, late, for gas and some chips. He mentioned you two were heading to Camp Cadiz today. Looking for clues. He told me you all figured the remains for around ten years old. Give or take a couple of years. And asked if I had any ideas about who that poor woman might be. I figure he wanted some place worthwhile to start in case it turns out that isn't his momma."

"What'd you tell him?" I asked, knowing that Chad would give me the information, but wanting an opportunity to hear it from Ed firsthand.

Ed shrugged.

"Not much. Except for his momma, no one else from these parts went missing around that time. And, after all these years, I sure couldn't recall any suspicious strangers passing through...."

But then Ed hesitated. He frowned and gave his head a quick little shake. As if he were chasing off some unwelcome thought. And then he changed the subject.

"You want some cold drinks or snacks to take along with you today?" he said. "Just like that doughnut and your coffee, they're on the house."

Without doubt, he was trying to distract me by baiting me into our usual argument. Why? I wondered immediately as suspicion chased away the lightheartedness that the flamingos had inspired.

The muscles across my shoulders and neck tensed and my eyes narrowed. In a flash, I saw Ed as nothing more than a reluctant informant. Not as a friend.

"This is a murder investigation," I said. "And if you're withholding information..."

I heard the echo of my own voice and noticed a flicker of shock—of alarm—cross Ed's face. That was when I realized how angry and frustrated I was, and admitted to myself that I'd carried those emotions into Statler's with me. They had little to do with Ed, who had always willingly told me anything I wanted to know. They had everything to do with Katie.

No matter who I was upset with, I scolded myself, I'd never before abused my authority or resorted to intimidation and hostile threats to solve a problem. That kind of behavior didn't suit my personality. And it sure didn't bolster my reputation as a fair-minded cop and respected hometown girl. Bottom line, it wasn't very effective policing.

In fact, it was piss-poor policing.

Something that Ed proved almost immediately.

Within a moment of his first reaction, he'd pressed his lips together into a tight, straight line. Now he was looking at me across the counter and shaking his head. But the look in his eyes made it clear that this was less a refusal to talk and more an expression of irritation. And disappointment. As if I had no reason to speak to him that way.

And I didn't.

I made the effort, moderated my tone.

"Come on, Ed. We've been friends for a long time. We've always leveled with each other. So if you know anything, I'd really appreciate…"

I allowed my voice to trail off, let my expression convey my apology.

"It was nothing as important as what you and Chad have been asking about," he said. Then he added, with some heat, "And it doesn't have anything to do with it, either."

"Okay," I said, making it a concession.

He looked away, out through the big plate-glass window, toward the row of gas pumps between the station and the street.

"Chad asking about folks going missing reminded me of someone I saw around these parts a while back. And a promise I made myself. But the person I saw wasn't missing at all. Or a stranger. She was just passing through."

Obviously, he still wasn't ready to tell me who he was talking about.

"When was that?" I asked.

Absolutely nothing was going on outside, but Ed continued to focus in that direction as he answered my question.

"A couple, three years after Chad's momma died. It was my wife's birthday. I don't remember which birthday exactly, but I do remember I played her birthdate in the lottery and won five hundred dollars. It's the most I've ever won."

That was certainly within the time frame Chad and I were investigating, I thought. But I made a point of looking vaguely dissatisfied with what he'd just told me. Which I was.

"Give me a name, Ed," I said gently. "If it's nothing, it can't hurt to tell me. And if it's something, I really need to know."

Ed shifted his eyes, this time looking down at the bright fabric he wore. He spent a minute fingering the hem of his shirt, just below the last coconut-shell button. A place where two flamingos were obviously doing the wild thing. But his eyes seemed to be on the floor rather than on the birds' activity.

Finally, he raised his eyes to mine.

"I don't want you thinking I'm some busybody gossip who takes joy in spreading poison. That habit is bad enough in a woman, but intolerable in a man. Anyway, that's what I told my missus last night. Which got us to arguing over the very thing we're talking about now. She's prob'ly gonna be a lot happier with me when I tell her that I went along with her advice. Even though I said last night I wouldn't."

My expression reflected patience that I didn't feel.

Okay, I thought. You've obviously made the decision. Now just spit out the information. Of course, I didn't say that. I just ate the last bit of my doughnut, washed it down with a little more coffee, and waited.

He spent a little time rearranging the doughnuts that were still on the tray, probably rearranging his thoughts at the same time. When our eyes met again, I saw nothing but concern in his expression.

"I wasn't trying to keep information from you, Brooke. It's just that talking about what I saw so many years ago would be nothing more than airing dirty laundry. People's mouths flapping loose in this town have caused enough hurt as it is. Especially for you and Katie. But my missus told me you had a right to know, especially now that you're all grown-up. She said you might be thinking she was dead."

"My mother."

I said the words flatly. Knowing he could be talking about no one else.

He nodded, sighed.

"Nine, maybe ten years ago, she drove into town. And I figure she drove right back out. 'Cause I would of heard if she'd stopped to see her girls."

Why, I thought suddenly with all the bottled-up anguish from childhood, hadn't she come to see me? And Katie? Didn't she love us?

The cop in me answered the victim. The only reason our mother would have come into town was to get money. Because that's all that addicts care about.

I continued facing Ed, deliberately not giving myself the privacy I'd always needed when I cried. I was a professional, I told myself. I needed to do my job. And I wasn't going to let the very mention of my mother reduce me to tears.

Certainly, though, I didn't look happy.

Neither did Ed.

His usually smooth forehead was wrinkled; his mobile eyebrows slanted downward, away from the middle of his forehead, and his mouth was pulled down into a frown. But he didn't offer me useless words of sympathy. He just waited, quietly, giving me a little time to think. Which I managed to do with something resembling detachment.

Lydia Tyler had left town at sixteen. And I doubted Ed had had more than a passing acquaintance with her. Decades had passed before he'd seen her again.

I asked the obvious question.

"Are you sure it was her?"

He nodded.

"She'd changed, for sure. Real skinny, for one thing. Wearing lots of makeup, a skimpy halter top, and a short black skirt. She looked like a—"

He caught himself. Whatever my mother looked like, Ed wasn't about to tell her little girl about it. Even if she was grown-up now. And a cop.

But I had long ago figured out that any fond memories I had of my mother weren't memories at all. They were from photos in old family scrapbooks and Aunt Lucy talking about her sister. Unlike Gran, who never spoke of Lydia, Aunt Lucy told us about all about their childhood together and how pretty and smart our mother was. Mostly, she reminded us that, even though our mother couldn't take care of us, she still loved us. And always would. Those lies, Katie had believed far longer than I.

The only real memory I had of my mother was of her walking away. Beautiful and leggy in her high-heeled sandals and thigh-length dress. With her hips swinging and ash-blond hair brushing her bare shoulders. I remembered that the sweet smell of her perfume had lingered in her wake, and that she'd had a couple of twenty-dollar bills clutched tightly in her hand.

That day, she hadn't locked us in the closet as she usually did. Hadn't patted us each on the cheek or given us a candy bar or told us to be good. And quiet. She'd simply turned her back. And left us with the man who'd given her the money.

It didn't take a cop to realize that—even back then—Lydia Tyler had supported her drug habit in whatever way she could.

"—well, not at all like a teenager," Ed was saying. "So she probably figured I wouldn't recognize her. But no matter how much she'd changed, she couldn't hide the fact that she was a Tyler woman. She wasn't beautiful anymore, but she still had that look. Like all the rest of you have. Kind of self-contained. Real private. No offense, Brooke, but a body could know you for years and not really know you."

I didn't say anything. What could I say? Tell him that he was right, that for generations Tyler women had made secrecy their life's work? And for good reason? My silence most likely reinforced his view of my character.

"So anyway," he continued, "as changed as she was from the child I remembered, I looked at her real close. And I knew. Lydia Tyler. When she and Lucy were kids, folks'd always comment on how different the girls looked from each other. Kind of like you and Katie."

"Was there anyone with her, Ed?"

He shook his head.

"No. Looked like she was traveling alone."

I'm not sure if it was personal need or professional curiosity that prompted my next question. Maybe I hoped to hear something, anything, positive about my mother. Maybe I was just confirming what any cop would have already suspected.

"Did she pay you for the gas?"

If it was possible, his eyebrows sagged even farther. But he kept his eyes straightforwardly on my face, and I had no doubt that he was telling me the truth.

"Yeah. But then she lifted a carton of cigarettes and a six-pack of beer on her way out the door. I didn't call the cops, because of who she was. And, back then, response time was…" He shrugged. "Well, you know. Besides, I didn't want to make trouble for your family."

A few minutes later, I carried that thought, my coffee mug, and some ugly feelings out to the SUV with me.

Chapter 14

I was damned tired of family secrets.

That was what I told myself as I drove to Camp Cadiz.

I was tired of pretending that Katie's life and mine went back no farther than the day we first walked up the steps of the Cherokee Rose. Tired of the persistent guilt that came with covering up Missy's death. Tired, already, of worrying about whatever secret Katie was so angrily protecting. I was even tired of the very worthwhile secrecy of the Underground.

Some secrets could never be told.

But I couldn't think of one good reason to continue tolerating secrets about my mother. Why, I asked myself, had I spent most of my life supporting the deception? Never asking questions, but pretending to believe the fairy tales my family spun about her and keeping every awful thing I'd learned about her to myself?

My response was quick and easy from long practice. I'd

done it for Katie's sake, of course. And to avoid hurting Gran and Aunt Lucy, who'd been so kind to us.

The truth, however, was harder to face.

I'd kept those secrets for my own sake.

I was twenty-four, I reminded myself. A member of the Underground. And a cop. For years, I'd made life-and-death decisions for myself and others. On the job and off, I regularly confronted and controlled dangerous situations. I'd never thought of myself as brave, but certainly I was determined.

Then why should it be so difficult for me to face my childhood fears?

I made a decision as I turned off 146 onto a winding road that would take me deep into the center of the Shawnee National Forest. Followed up on it before I could change my mind. At not quite six-thirty in the morning, I used my cell phone to call the Cherokee Rose. Knowing that Katie and Gran would be busy with breakfast preparations. And that Aunt Lucy would be at the front desk in the empty lobby, using the quiet of early morning to work on the hotel's accounts. That she would answer the phone.

When Aunt Lucy heard my voice—my simple "Hello"—she began talking immediately, chattering nervously. As she rushed to tell me that everything was all right, she said more about an Underground operation than she usually did over the phone. A clear indication, at least, that no one was within earshot.

"We've already found a place for Jackie down in Tucson," she said. "She told me she likes animals and—just by chance—there was a job available in a vet's office. Our folks are already working on her new IDs. So it's just a matter of arranging transportation. With luck, that'll only take a few days. In the meantime, Jackie will be spending most of her time in her room, resting and recuperating."

That, I supposed, was meant to be reassuring. To make me feel better about Katie's new involvement with the Underground. But my lingering anger over that made it easier for me to ask the questions that I should have asked years earlier.

"I need some information about my mother," I said without preamble, and I felt no guilt over the hard edge in my voice.

"Okay," Aunt Lucy said slowly.

"Was she an addict before she left Maryville? Is that what landed her in prison?"

"So you knew," Aunt Lucy said, sighing softly. "I'd always wondered. You always seemed to hear—and know—so much. And your eyes... I remember the first time I saw them. So dark and beautiful, but so very sad. And you tried to act so tough. Only five years old, but determined to take care of your sister." She paused for a breath, then added, "In that regard, not much has changed, has it?"

I wanted to ask my questions, to get the answers I needed, and then to stop thinking about my mother. So I ignored that emotionally charged question.

When I didn't answer, Aunt Lucy's voice became more businesslike.

"Lydia had drug problems before she ran away. That was one of the reasons she left. Gran wanted her in rehab. She'd been in and out of prison."

Aunt Lucy hesitated.

"For what?"

"Why, Brooke? Does it really matter?"

I was tired of secrets, I reminded myself. So I didn't back down. But I did pull my SUV onto the grassy shoulder at the side of the road because I'd begun speeding dangerously along a hilly, winding road.

"She's *my* mother," I said firmly. "And I'm asking. So, yes, it matters."

Easy enough to hear the resignation in my aunt's voice.

"She went to jail for exactly what you'd expect. Possession. Prostitution. Petty theft."

"But you still gave her money," I said flatly.

That surprised her.

"You didn't tell Katie about any of this?" she asked urgently. "She'd be devastated—"

"I never told anyone," I cut in, offended by the suggestion.

"Of course not," Aunt Lucy said.

She said it as if my keeping a secret was something she could always take for granted. And I realized that it was.

"I don't think Gran ever suspected, either," she continued. "If she had, she would have tried to stop me from sending money. Gran always said that Lydia was a user, and maybe she was right. But I loved my sister, so I helped her whenever I could."

"Was money all she was after when she visited town? Back when I was fourteen or fifteen?"

That inspired enough silence that I anticipated Aunt Lucy would try to lie to me. As she had when we were children.

She didn't.

"You were fifteen," she said with certainty. "You, Katie and Gran had been gone only a matter of minutes—shopping, I think—when she knocked at the side door. She told me she'd been on her way to Nashville with a friend, but they'd fought and he'd taken off with all her money. So she needed my help to get clean. To start a new life. I figured that was a lie, like so many others. But I gave her the money anyway. And then she drove away."

No, I thought, as I stared out through my windshield and watched a passing car kick up a layer of dust. There had to be more to it than that. She couldn't have asked for money and just left. Not without seeing us. Not without at least *asking* about us.

I blurted out a question—an accusation—I had never intended.

"Why did you send her away? Were you afraid that she'd want me and Katie to go with her?"

Even to my own ears, my voice sounded like that of a hurt, angry child. But I wanted my aunt to admit that she'd ordered my mother to leave. That she'd forbidden her to see us and maybe even threatened to call the police. Because it was easier to be angry with Aunt Lucy than to know with certainty that my mother didn't love me.

"I'm sorry, honey," Aunt Lucy said. "I asked her to stay. I even showed her your pictures. Yours and Katie's. I told her that you both still loved her. And would forgive her. That I'd help her stand up to our mother. But all she wanted was money. I gave her every extra dollar I had. And then I told her that this was the last time, that I had to save for college for you and Katie. She must have believed me, Brooke, because I never heard from her again."

By the time I said goodbye to my aunt, I was running late. But I lingered a while longer, parked at the side of the road, shedding the tears that I needed to shed and telling myself that it was foolish to be upset by the past actions of a virtual stranger. Especially someone whose maternal instincts—assuming that she'd ever had them—had long ago been replaced by the compulsions of an addict. It didn't really matter, I assured myself, that my mother had passed through town nine years earlier and hadn't sought me out. I'd accomplished what I'd intended by talking to Aunt Lucy and cleared away the secrecy surrounding my mother's actions. The best thing to do now was to forget all about Lydia Tyler.

When I turned into the rutted parking lot at Camp Cadiz, I wasn't surprised to find that Chad was already there. He'd pulled his personal vehicle—a red, three-quarter-ton Chevy pickup—into the very spot where I'd once parked a boxy blue van. Back when I was sixteen and was just learning to believe in human monsters.

As I slid from my SUV, Chad climbed down from his truck. Like the hot pink I wore, he'd also chosen a T-shirt that would be easy to see among the rocks and foliage of the forest. It was a brilliant orange, emblazoned in dark blue with the University of Illinois logo and the words Fighting Illini. But it wasn't the way the shirt's color clashed with his copper hair that drew my attention and made my breath catch in my throat. It was how the fabric stretched across Chad's broad shoulders and muscular chest. The way it tucked into the waist of his soft, worn jeans, drawing my eyes downward…

Abruptly, I focused my attention on lowering the tailgate and leaning into the back of my SUV. Oh God, I thought, how long would it take before the very sight of him didn't make me ache?

I didn't look his way again until the scrunch of his footsteps on the gravel ended next to me. Before glancing back over my shoulder and flashing him a smile, I took a deep breath and then another. And I hoped he'd attribute the flush that I could feel still warming my face to the outside temperature, which was already creeping in the direction of ninety. With the humidity already at more than seventy percent, the forecast predicted that by midafternoon Maryville residents would feel as if the thermometer were well over three digits.

A thunderstorm, I thought, would be a welcome relief.

Chad immediately pitched in to help me unload our gear

and add it to the lightweight backpack, canteen and metal detector he'd brought with him. Climbing harnesses for both of us. Nylon rope. Binoculars. A canteen for me. And my backpack, filled with ready-for-anything supplies that included toilet paper and wet wipes, an all-in-one tool, a first-aid kit and the inevitable crime-scene tape and evidence bags. Chad, I knew from experience, would have packed an assortment of supplies very similar to mine and some kind of snack for us both.

"Sorry I was late. Been waiting long?" I asked as we slung on our backpacks.

He shook his head.

"Fifteen minutes at the most. Figured that you'd gotten hung up admiring Ed's tropical paradise. His wife should know better than to leave him home alone."

Though he was chuckling, now that my attention was focused on the details of his face, it was easy enough to see that his thoughts while he'd been waiting hadn't been happy ones. The line of old scar tissue along his jaw was stark white against the irritated redness of his cheek.

As if to confirm my observation, he raised his hand to his face again. But this time, his anxious fingers drifted toward the new, much smaller wound on his cheek. The one framed by adhesive residue and bridged by several no-longer-white butterfly closures.

I grabbed his wrist and stopped the movement. Gave his hand a quick shake before releasing it.

"Sorry," he muttered. "It itches."

"Yeah. I bet it does. But leave it alone. I did a darn good job patching that cheek, and I'd be pissed if it got infected."

"Wouldn't want that."

I couldn't tell from his voice whether he meant pissing me

off or infecting the cheek, but he'd taken that moment to rub his fingers over his eyes, so I couldn't read his expression, either.

He looks tired, I thought as our eyes met again. As if the past several nights hadn't brought him much sleep, either. Though I still wasn't optimistic, I hoped that we'd find evidence in the ravine proving that the remains belonged to his mother. Chad would sleep better knowing that.

So would I.

We followed the River-to-River Trail from Camp Cadiz, with the two of us walking single file and steadily, but not quickly. Conserving our energy for the more difficult terrain at the bottom of the ravine.

For a time, Chad took the lead, and I couldn't help but notice how confidently he moved through the forest. Long practice, I thought, remembering all the time we'd spent outdoors together hiking and camping. As childhood friends. As adult lovers. And though I knew that the reason for going into the forest was serious, for this little bit of time I indulged myself. I pushed away anxious thoughts about the past and future, focusing only on the pleasant and familiar present. On the sight of a man who was undeniably sexy in tight jeans. And on life as it might have been.

Halfway across the footbridge, Chad paused. He leaned on the railing, looking up the ravine toward our crime scene.

I joined him and spent a moment peering downward.

Fallen trees, many of them mature, were wedged across the narrow ravine. Some of them had roots that—like a child's loose tooth—clung tenaciously to the embankment or to one of the more substantial ledges. Those trees were still green and leafy. But most were dead or dying, their leaves a withered, tattered brown.

At some point either rockfall or rotting would send them

tumbling to the bottom of the ravine, more than forty feet below the bridge where Chad and I stood. There, hundreds of years' worth of rotting trees and the water from a meandering stream supported the abundant vegetation that softened the edges of all but most recent rockfall.

"See the stream down there?" Chad asked. "That's the dividing line between federal land on the Camp Cadiz side of the ravine and county land on the opposite side. Nearer the crime scene, Maryville jurisdiction intersects with the county's. No landmark there, just an arbitrary line on the map."

I nodded, acknowledging the information as I kept looking downward. Today, there was more sandy, rock-strewn stream bed than there was stream. But heavy rains could change the meandering ribbon of water into a torrent that could sweep away whole trees. And as we left the bridge, I thought—not for the first time—that Chad and I were embarking on a fool's mission.

It was just past 8:00 a.m. when we left the marked trail and began hiking parallel to the ravine.

I took a turn walking in front and watching for hazards.

The strip of land nearest the ravine was relatively clear of plants, enabling us to avoid much of the tangled undergrowth and jutting rock formations that had made searching for Tina so difficult. But the same erosion that swept away so much of the forest's lush growth had created crumbling edges, deep fissures and sinkholes, often camouflaged by thin layers of soil, vegetation and forest debris.

As we walked, a dank breeze occasionally scrambled up from the stony depths of the ravine, providing welcome moments of relief. But it wasn't enough to offset the humidity and steadily rising temperature, which made the air heavy and difficult to breathe. Before long, perspiration was trickling down my forehead and the clothing beneath my backpack was damp and itchy.

I called out a warning to Chad, and we carefully skirted a spot where a narrow tower of limestone had sheered away from the face of the ravine. The rockfall had created an abrupt drop-off along the edge where we were walking and added tons of jagged rubble to the dangerous tangle of debris forty feet below us.

Even Possum would be feeling this heat, I thought to myself as we moved away from the shade of the tree canopy and back along the ravine's edge. I was glad I hadn't been tempted to bring him with us. Though I had the equipment to lower him down into the ravine with me, and Possum—like Highball—could negotiate the trails better than any human, today Chad and I were searching for objects, not people. Unless we were looking for tennis balls, I thought with a smile, Possum wouldn't be any help in this kind of evidence search.

By necessity, our route was a meandering one, sometimes angling sharply away from the ravine and into the surer footing of the deeper forest. The last time Chad and I had passed this way, we'd been going in the opposite direction, carrying equipment back to the crime technician's van. Then, we'd stopped along the way to remove the temporary trail markers that Chad had placed for the technicians' safety. It was a strategy intended to discourage the curious or the ghoulish from visiting the murder site.

Now I noticed that much of our path was marked by plant life that had been broken or trampled underfoot on our previous visits. Easy enough, I feared, for someone to follow our trail straight to the crime scene. But then I told myself not to worry. That the weather predicted for tomorrow would take care of the problem. Rain and wind would cover any sign that we'd come this way and make the "easy" route along the edge of the ravine discouragingly slick.

Something about that thought made me stop in my tracks.

Chad, who was walking close behind me, misinterpreted my reason for stopping.

"By my reckoning, we're just minutes away from the scene," he said once he was beside me. "Probably as good a time as any to take a breather."

He took a couple dozen steps away from the precipice, stopping in a small clearing beneath a clump of pines. There, with an audible sigh, he slipped the gear he carried from his back, dropping it to the soft, needle-covered ground. After rolling his shoulders and stretching, he sat down. With his backpack supporting his back, he stretched out his long legs in front of him, twisted the top off his canteen and took a long swig.

Almost absentmindedly, I followed his example. I dropped down beside him and, with my canteen in my hands, supported my elbows on my knees. As fresh air cooled the damp patch between my shoulder blades, I looked back in the direction we'd just come. I put my canteen to my lips, took tiny sips, and let the cool water trickle slowly down my throat as I tried to tease the edges of a thought into something more substantial.

Undoubtedly, this was the most direct way to get to the scene. No other marked trails or access roads were nearby, so any other approach meant hiking for many miles through the deepest part of the forest. Chad and I had encountered—and avoided—any number of natural hazards just to get safely to our resting spot. And we had a lot of advantages. Our overall fitness. Years of experience trekking in the forest. Sturdy hiking boots. Familiarity with this route. Dry weather. And daylight.

"What are you thinking, Brooke?" Chad said.

I shook my head, briefly postponing my reply as I tried to sort through a tangle of facts and emotions. None of them happy.

I put my canteen down beside my pack and shifted so that I was facing Chad. Within an easy arm's length of him. In his clear, green eyes and relaxed expression, I saw nothing more than friendship and trust. And maybe a little curiosity.

Hope, I thought bleakly, had blinded us both to the obvious.

"Would you hike along this ravine at night?" I said.

He shook his head immediately.

"No way. Too dangerous. You'd have to be crazy, suicidal, or a pretty gal determined to find a lost kid."

The beginning of a smile conveyed the teasing compliment he'd intended. But, almost immediately, his smile wobbled and disappeared as insight ravaged any thoughts he might have had about finally putting his long-lost mother to rest.

Then I explained my reasoning. Because, though it made my heart ache to hurt him further, we were investigating a crime. Assuming that another investigator saw things exactly the way I did ran contrary to everything I'd been taught about law enforcement.

I delivered the information as gently as I could.

"At night, even in good weather, *no one* could have made it as far as the crime scene. Not without falling. The night your mother died, it was storming. And your father was drunk. He couldn't have negotiated this trail, Chad. Especially not if your mother was fighting him. And she would have been, wouldn't she?"

Chad nodded. Began scraping his fingernails along his cheek. But his expression remained almost emotionless and his voice was cool. Very detached.

I wondered how he managed it.

"You think we have a daylight killer," he said flatly.

"Yeah. Or someone who disposed of the body in the forest during the day."

"No. That'd be too risky. And too much work," he said, echoing the conclusion I'd reached the night I'd found the remains. "Odds are, our victim died right there."

By then, he was struggling to keep his voice steady.

"Thank you," he said, "for seeing this. For telling me. This is your first murder investigation, but you're thinking clearly. Professionally. I'm the one who let it get personal, let my emotions—"

That's when his voice cracked. And he turned away. So I couldn't see his face. But the way he was dragging his fisted fingers back and forth along his jaw made it easy enough to guess at his expression.

"I tried to keep my perspective, but I just kept thinking how it was my fault that she died, that she's lost," he continued. "The only person my daddy ever really wanted dead was me. His bastard son. That night, I think his hate just spilled over on my momma."

He looked back at me, his eyes bright with the threat of tears.

"I shouldn't have let her push me from that truck. I should've hung on. Should've stayed to protect her."

And then you would have died for sure, I thought. But I didn't tell him that because, at some level, I was certain that he already knew. That he understood he'd only been a boy back then. Not a man with big fists or a tough cop with a gun and the power of the law behind him. But his words proved that, at least at this moment, he was feeling a child's helplessness. And guilt.

I knew exactly how that felt. And how much it hurt.

Without thinking, I leaned forward, gathered him in close,

closing the inches that separated us from each other. I held him as I often had in the past, during the other times he'd had to face old loss and newly shattered hope.

My fingers smoothed the short copper hair at the back of his head, stroked his broad shoulders, patted his back. I comforted him as if he were weeping, though he didn't cry or even make a sound. Because I knew that cops—especially big male cops from small towns—were always afraid that someone might guess they weren't nearly as tough as they seemed.

I don't know when comforting and being comforted demanded more than mere holding. But in the space between one heartbeat and the next, the limits so carefully maintained between friends were forgotten as lovers became desperate to reunite.

Impossible to know whose lips were the first to seek the other's, whose hands moved from caressing cheeks and face and hair to seeking more intimate warmth. But he was the one who unclipped my bra, who held my breasts cupped in his warm, callused hands. And I was the one who tugged his shirt from his waistband and skimmed my hands upward beneath it, following the contours of the muscles that wrapped his ribs, relishing the softness of the hair on his chest as it slid through my fingers and tickled my palm.

And whether his fingers slipped beneath the waist of my jeans before mine sought the zipper on his… Who was to know?

What mattered was that the days and nights of loneliness and longing were coming to an end. That Chad was back with me where he belonged. He pushed my willing body down onto a bed of soft pine needles and his lips moved against my bare skin, following the path of his hands.

As my eyes slitted with pleasure and my thoughts focused

inward, the canopy above me blurred into a kaleidoscope of green and shadows and dappled sunlight.

Shadows tore through the pattern. Black wings fluttered in the trees above us. Angry birds screamed out a warning.

Carrion birds. That was the image that flashed to mind.

Carrion birds with yellow beaks tipped in blood.

Caught off guard by a living nightmare, my eyes flew wide open, and my body tensed as I fought the impulse to panic. A cry, almost stifled, escaped my lips.

It was not a sound of satisfaction.

Chad lifted his head. Looked anxiously down at me.

I don't know what he saw in my face. And for my part, I couldn't put a name to the emotions I saw slide across his. But he tugged my shirt back down over my breasts and shifted away from me.

The crows continued flapping and cawing out an alarm, alerting each other to some threat to their flock.

Between Chad and me there was silence.

As we sat up, we were careful not to touch each other, careful not to meet each other's eyes.

I wrapped my arms around myself, fighting my body's reaction to frustrated desire. But if Chad hadn't called a halt to our lovemaking, I knew that I would have. Months earlier, I'd had a good reason for sending him from my bed and insisting that we had no future together as lovers. Nothing about that had changed. Except that, in recent days, the situation seemed even worse. Yet knowing all that, I'd still stepped over the line I'd drawn for myself. And for Chad.

As I cursed myself for being a weak, self-indulgent fool, Chad's hand moved to his right cheek again. But this time his fingers deliberately sought the bandage protecting the wound on his cheek. In it, he seemed to find inspiration.

He spat out a bitter accusation.

"If I hadn't stopped, what exactly was that going to be? More first aid? A little sympathy sex for the ex-boyfriend?"

That's when I looked straightforwardly into his angry green eyes. I'd hurt him, I thought, and not just today. If he now despised me, I deserved it. But I had to tell him the truth. At least, about this.

"It was more than that," I said softly. "Not at all as trivial as you're making it out to be. But, yes, it was a mistake. My mistake. And I'm sorry."

It was troubling that he forgave me so quickly. That his next words carried no hint of rebuke. Or inquiry. Just resignation.

"I don't understand...about us," he said.

For the briefest moment, he extended his hand, almost touched my face. Then he curled his fingers back into a fist, dropped his arm to his side. Quickly, he rose to his feet and turned away as he spent a minute or two buttoning, zipping and tucking.

Just as well. Because I spent that time dashing away tears I didn't want him to see.

He turned back in my direction when his clothing was neat again.

"Can we still be friends?" he asked almost brusquely.

I nodded, managed a shaky smile.

And I wasn't lying to him. At least not about today or even tomorrow. But I knew now that our friendship was doomed. Had finally admitted to myself what I'd been so determined to deny. Chad and I would never stop wanting to be more than just friends. More that just lovers.

Only I understood why that was impossible.

Chapter 15

We hiked to the crime scene.

For a moment we stood silently in front of the big cotton-wood tree, our eyes drawn to the vine-shrouded split in its massive trunk. Chad's hand crept up to the scar on his cheek, his expression signaling that his thoughts were on what he hadn't found there. My thoughts were likely as bleak as Chad's as I considered what *had* been found. A murdered woman's remains and a corroded inhaler. And I feared that Katie's mind held more answers than this scene—or the forensics report—would be likely to provide.

"Do you still want to do this?" I asked.

Chad dropped his hand, shrugged.

"Why not?" he said. "We've come this far. And who knows? We might just find something relevant."

I thought, Why not? And then I said, "Okay. Let's get to it."

After that, whatever else was on our minds became secondary as we focused on familiar technical issues. The first was finding a safe place to descend. With the big cottonwood tree as our starting point, we walked in opposite directions along the edge of the ravine, peering downward.

A few minutes of searching, and Chad called from a dozen yards away.

"How about here?"

Here turned out to be a near-perpendicular drop of about forty feet down an irregular rock face with no jutting ledges or branches or tangles of bush. But heaped up against the base of the wall was a ten-foot-tall pile of rocky debris.

"Looks good," I said, "except for the riprap at the bottom."

Chad dug a boot heel into the soil near the edge, creating a mini-avalanche of dirt, plants and pebbles.

"Thick enough here that the rock's not exposed. So we won't have to worry about our ropes fraying. We can keep looking, Brooke, but I'm not sure we're going to find much better."

I had to agree.

Rapping is deceptively simple. *Deceptively* being the key word. That's what Chad and I'd learned during our earliest climbing forays back in high school. And that was now very much on my mind as we prepared for the climb down into the ravine. Chad, I noticed, was also checking every element of the system twice. It was a good idea in any event. A great idea given how much stress we'd both been under lately. Exhausted, anxious minds tended to make simple—and deadly—mistakes.

We'd climbed together so often that we worked efficiently, each of us concentrating on our specific tasks. Because he was stronger, Chad secured the two-bolt anchor to the trunk of a healthy tree that grew well back from the drop-off. Then he passed our rope through the rappel point he'd created.

While he did that, I strapped on my helmet and buckled on my climbing harness. At the front of my harness was a strong nylon belay loop. Using a locking carabiner, I clipped the small hole of a figure-eight device onto the loop. Then I threaded the rope that Chad handed me through and around the larger hole on the device. Finally, I used an autoblock to back up the rappel I'd created. If for any reason I lost my grip on the rope, the autoblock would keep me from sliding downward, out of control.

I checked my rigging one more time, backed up to the very edge of the precipice, then grinned at Chad. Who always managed to look his most worried at this point in the process.

You know you're a cop if...you're compulsive about over-protecting the ones you love. And because the unbidden quip hurt rather than amused, I awarded myself no points. Instead, I touched a couple of fingers to my helmet and flipped him a quick salute.

"See ya," I said, my voice cheerful.

Then I pushed off.

Into midair and falling.

Into a moment of absolute exhilaration.

I felt my harness catch my weight and leaned back into it, keeping my torso upright and my legs perpendicular to the wall. As if I were in an easy chair and my legs were resting on an ottoman. But I kept my knees slightly bent and my feet apart as I touched my boots to the vertical rock face.

With one hand on the autoblock so that it would slide and the other on the rope below to provide a bit of extra braking, I pushed away from the wall again and slid downward. Several repetitions later and my feet touched the pile of rubble. After that, I used the support of my rope and harness to offset the unpredictable movement of sliding rock beneath my feet.

And then I was down.

Chad lowered the awkward metal detector down on a separate length of rope. Then, several uneventful minutes later, he was in the ravine beside me, stripping off his helmet and harness.

For almost an hour, we concentrated on the area directly below the cottonwood tree and the pair of ledges that the state's crime-scene technicians had processed. Using binoculars, Chad and I took turns examining the ravine wall, looking for anything that might have snagged on roots or rocks or nearby branches.

When that perspective produced nothing, we moved outward from the base of the bluff in a semicircle, toward the stream at the center of the ravine. Much of that time I spent half-bent over or kneeling, looking for bits of out-of-the-ordinary debris—smooth bits of bone, ragged scraps of clothing or any suggestion of a man-made object—among the vegetation and rocks.

For a time, Chad joined me in that kind of search. Then he used the metal detector, watching a small screen mounted near the handle as he slowly swept the instrument back and forth, holding it just inches above the relatively smooth surfaces along the stream bed and between rockfalls and rotted trunks.

Our search yielded an inch-long piece of bone that, to our untrained eyes, could have been human but might as easily have been animal. And a badly corroded horseshoe—big enough, I guessed, for a draft horse—that we both judged interesting but irrelevant.

After taking a break, we began working our way downstream, in the direction of the footbridge. We'd decided to search for several hundred feet along both sides of the stream, then double back to take one last look at the terrain. After that, we'd climb back up our ropes. A process I never particularly looked forward to. Jugging was considerably more work than rapping. And a lot less fun.

The flip of a coin had given me the federal side of the ravine.

I took off my boots and socks, rolled up my jeans, and waded into the rocky stream, walking carefully so I wouldn't slip on the slick rocks, but still enjoying the rush of cool water over my feet. Five strides in, and the water was just below my calves. Another few strides and I was back in shallow water, then a couple more long steps and I was high and dry on a pebble-strewn shore.

On my side of the stream, the distance between the water and the wall of the ravine was little more than twenty feet. And, looking downstream, I could see that it remained that way for quite a distance. So I went to stand at a rough midpoint between stream and bluff. Once there, I turned slowly in place, stopping to visually examine the ground ten feet behind me, ten feet to each side and, finally, ten feet in front of me. After that, I detoured from my spot to check behind anything within the makeshift grid that had obstructed my view. Then I returned to my starting point and walked forward twenty feet.

I repeated that process again.

And again.

I'd searched forward for more than one hundred feet when I stopped to rest. I lifted the ball cap that I'd traded for my safety helmet, ran my fingers through my damp curls and took a drink from my canteen.

I turned in Chad's direction, caught his eye.

"Anything?" I yelled, noticing a slight echo.

"Nothing," he hollered back. And that word, too, bounced off the rock walls, repeating itself.

I waved to acknowledge news that was not surprising, then put my cap back on my head and refocused on my search pattern. I'd already run my eyes over the entire section, but there was one spot that needed a closer look before I moved on to the next grid. A logjam created by previous years' flooding had isolated one of the curves in the stream from the flow of fresh water, creating a stagnant pool.

I had turned my attention to the side of the logjam away from the pond when, out of the corner of my eye, I saw Chad stop. Abruptly, he bent forward. Then he dropped to one knee. And shouted my name.

Without a second thought, I jogged in his direction, paralleling a stubby section of tree trunk, then crossing the slight mound of a nearby sandbar. The soles of my boots scrunched against the pebbly, uneven surface.

That's when the ground beneath my right foot gave way. When I felt as much as heard a wet, hollow sound, like rotted sticks breaking.

My foot encountered an uneven surface about a dozen inches down.

Surprised, struggling to remain upright, I cried out once. Loudly.

I stood teetering for a moment, managed to find my balance. Then I looked down to see what I'd stumbled into.

My right foot was surrounded by a jagged cage of bones.

Then the smell hit me.

I gagged, yanked my foot away from the dark sludge oozing up over the toe of my boot. Pulled away a couple of broken ribs, one of them tangled in a piece of rotting fabric. With a row of buttons still attached.

I don't know how long I stood there, just staring. Noticing that blackened flesh still clung to the torso. That splintered bits of bone showed white at the ends of the ribs that I'd shattered. How everything else was blackened and decaying.

Just like Missy would be.

I shut my eyes.

A mistake.

That made it even easier to recall her bloodied face and single, staring blue eye. Made it even easier to remember the way the ends of her bullet-shattered ribs had ground together when I'd unbuckled her seat belt and pushed her down in the well in front of her seat. Covered her with a blanket. So that no one would see her as I drove…

I pushed those thoughts away, opened my eyes. But my head was already throbbing and my face seemed to be on fire. And no matter how shallowly I breathed, I couldn't avoid the clinging, putrid smell.

Bile rose in my throat and I gagged again.

I didn't want to contaminate the crime scene.

I turned, staggered back to the logjam, managed to make it to the far end of the stumpy log. Stood there, staring at a beetle crawling along the rough bark, holding my breath, pressing my lips shut, willing myself not to vomit.

And then my best friend was there behind me, his hands cool against my neck and shoulders, his voice soothing.

"No shame in being sick," he said. "Sooner or later, every cop sees something that makes him puke. Lucky if it only happens once in your career. Don't fight it. Just get it over with."

He supported me as I retched violently, painfully onto the ground.

We worked around natural obstacles, pushing the sturdy wire stems of tiny orange flags into the ground, making the body a bull's-eye at the center of an irregular circle.

When we were finished, I stood looking back at the body from the downstream side. Realized that, from this angle, I might have recognized a human form beneath a crusty layer of earth. Or noticed the triangle of tattered fabric that the sand hadn't completely covered and recognized it as the corner of a man's trousers. Unfortunately, what I now saw most clearly was the terrible damage my misplaced footstep had caused.

I sighed.

"Sure messed up that crime scene," I said.

Chad put his hand on my shoulder, gave it a little squeeze before releasing it.

"You *found* the crime scene, rookie," he said, smiling. "Don't be greedy."

Minutes later, we crossed the stream to deal with what Chad had found, the discovery that had prompted him to call out my name so urgently. The bits of spine he'd discovered near the mouth of a fox's den prompted us to search for a few minutes longer. It took a much larger circle of flags to mark the scattered remains of a body that hadn't been buried beneath a layer of sand. That'd had no protection from the teeth of small carnivores.

"Two," I said, thinking out loud.

"Three if you count the first victim," Chad corrected. "We should go back, call in. We've got a hell of a lot more here than a simple murder."

I nodded, agreeing with him. But then I said: "Let's walk for another hundred feet, see what's there."

"Greedy," Chad repeated, then softened that judgment with his smile. "Which side of the stream do you want?"

I lifted my chin in the direction of the opposite ravine wall.

"I'll go back there," I said, mostly because I wanted an

excuse to wash my boots and the cuffs of my jeans in the stream again. And then I had another, unrelated thought. "The Feds are going to be involved in this one, aren't they?"

Chad nodded, sighing heavily.

Because of Hardin County's odd mix of jurisdictions, it wasn't at all unusual for FBI field agents to work with deputies investigating crimes that took place in the forest. I'd never heard Chad complain about it, so didn't understand his obvious lack of enthusiasm.

"I thought you liked working with those guys."

"Those guys, yes," he said. "But we both have the same gut feeling about what we're going to find out here, don't we? If we're right, this will be a headline-getter—one of those cases that's too high-profile to be left to mere field agents. And it's been my experience that those big-city bureaucrats don't play well with others."

Twenty feet was all it took for me to confirm our gut feelings. Twenty feet and a sun-bleached skull hanging almost upside down in a fallen tree. Impaled on a jutting branch a few feet from the ground. A veil of browning leaves and other debris from the flooding that had put it there framed the jawless skull.

The branch entered through the right eye socket and exited through a slightly smaller man-made hole. The opposite route, I thought, than the bullet had taken. Strands of dried grass and tattered bits of fabric hung from the other eye socket. As I watched, a tiny yellow finch darted into that opening, intent on feeding a demanding chorus of nestlings inside the dome.

No shouting was needed over this one.

I simply planted a flag, crossed the stream and caught up with Chad.

It was difficult to know when the huge section of ravine wall had collapsed, but the tumble of jagged rock—easily double Chad's height at its peak—cut the width of the ravine by more than a third. From the base of that rock pile, Chad spotted what looked like little more than a heap of dirty rags.

I was lighter and more sure-footed than he was so, despite his objections, I climbed up solo to take a closer look. Stretched as far as I could to shove my fingers into a narrow gap between rocks, found a narrow ledge where I could step up with my right boot, then levered myself upward. Found a place to wedge my left boot, stretched to find the next handhold, and moved upward again. Until I was just able to look across the top of the rock mound.

I looked into a face long dead. One that still sported a fringe of curly, close-cropped beard and a parchment face with a third eye in the center of the forehead.

"Got another one," I called down to Chad, amazed at how quickly the macabre had become almost commonplace. "If the bullet hadn't killed him, the fall certainly would have."

Once back on the ground, I joined Chad in tying bright loops of crime-scene tape around a few large rocks. A reminder that another victim had been discovered here. As we worked, we did a head count. Literally.

"There was a head on the one back by the cave," Chad observed. "You found a skull in the tree."

"And the bearded guy up there."

"The one by the sandbar? Do you think the body's intact?"

Briefly, I thought about the shape and length of the mound on either side of the exposed rib cage.

"Yeah, I suspect it is."

"Four victims for sure, then," Chad murmured, tying off a

final knot in the ribbon of plastic. "Five counting the Jane Doe on the ledge."

As our eyes met, I nodded, agreeing.

"All within a few hundred yards of each other," I said.

If I hadn't been looking right at him just then, I doubt I would have seen the flash of emotion, quickly hidden. But in that moment, I saw a reflection of my own feelings. Unexpected feelings that had nothing to do with love or lust.

You know you're a cop if...discovering a killing field excites you.

Chapter 16

An old skeleton didn't get much attention.

Four more victims found in the same area of the forest did. Especially when their remains were discovered in multiple jurisdictions. Most especially when two turned up on federal land.

Within a few hours of Chad's call to dispatch, representatives from all of those jurisdictions held a joint press conference. Me, still in blue jeans and a grubby pink shirt, representing the Maryville PD. Chad's politically savvy boss speaking for Hardin County but having Chad—in his jeans and grubby *orange* shirt—stand by his side. Joining us was a middle-aged man in a city suit and a Harvard haircut who looked more like a Beltway politician than the FBI agent he was. When he'd arrived at Camp Cadiz from Chicago, he'd taken just enough time to be briefed by a field agent—and to learn that two more bodies had just been discovered—before organizing a press conference.

Guarded barricades had been set up to limit access to Camp Cadiz and the forest beyond. One such barricade and several uniformed county deputies confined the press—its cars and satellite trucks and camera operators and reporters—to a corner of the gravel lot. As we approached the press area, reporters with microphones in their hands and camera operators hanging over their shoulders swarmed like locusts. They pressed themselves against the wooden barricade, leaning hungrily forward, shouting questions.

A tall man near the front of the crowd craned his head to look at the laminated ID hanging around the FBI agent's neck.

"Agent…Franklin! What's the body count so far?"

Agent Franklin, with an air of long experience, didn't answer. Instead, he planted himself about six feet from the reporters on the police side of the barricade. Then he gestured for the county sheriff—a beefy middle-aged man with a comb-over hairdo—to stand beside him. Once Chad and I joined the lineup, Agent Franklin lifted a hand. His frown and the force of his personality quieted the babble of voices.

Only then did he speak.

"This investigation is in its earliest stages so it would be premature for me to comment on specifics. Except to say that, at this point, we have recovered a total of seven bodies in a very limited area where federal, Hardin County, and—"

Here he hesitated.

"Maryville," I murmured.

"—Maryville jurisdictions intersect. The state of Illinois is also providing invaluable technical assistance in this endeavor. So this will be a cooperative, multi-agency investigation."

That sounded good. But *cooperative,* I'd quickly realized, didn't leave me with much. Small-town cops were rarely viewed as equal partners. And a rookie female cop from a one-

person department was doubly cursed. Even my expertise in
search and rescue was trumped by the arrival of a large, well-
equipped and tightly organized state-police team. Bottom
line, I had no leverage. Because I'd insisted, I was still at the
scene, still formally "in the loop." But I didn't delude myself.
I wasn't needed for what Agent Franklin referred to as a "full-
fledged investigation." And if I spoke, the odds were against
anyone listening.

Under different circumstances, I would have complained
bitterly to Chad. But his situation was worse than mine. He
had already been informed by his boss, the county sheriff, that
right after the press conference he was to take the rest of the
afternoon off and return to his regular patrol duties the next
day. The sheriff's explanation for Chad's banishment was
amazingly straightforward. He was an elected official, and no
matter how competent Chad was—no matter how much the
sheriff liked him personally—this case was too important to
the outcome of his upcoming reelection bid to be left in the
hands of a young deputy.

As the FBI spokesman spent a bit of time talking about the
Bureau's success rate on cases just like these and made
another mention of the value of interdepartmental cooperation, the sheriff ran his fingers over his balding dome to re-
plaster long strands of very black hair back into place and then
ran those same fingers beneath his nose to neaten his salt-and-
pepper mustache.

"And now Jake Hargrove, sheriff of Hardin County, will
make some comments."

At that introduction, Sheriff Hargrove straightened his
shoulders and puffed out his burly chest. Then, very deliberately, he stepped forward just enough to put Agent Franklin
behind his left shoulder. And smiled for the cameras.

"First, I want to congratulate Hardin County deputy Chad Robinson and Maryville police officer Brooke Tyler for the fine work they've done. Their initiative brought these murders to light. Deputy Robinson characterizes the kind of dedicated officer who protects and serves the citizens of Hardin County. And I know that all the fine folks who live in Maryville are particularly proud of this feisty little hometown gal of theirs."

That's when he reached over and put his arm around my shoulders to pull me in closer to him. He held that pose long enough to give the still photographers from the local newspapers a good shot of the two of us. I smiled into the cameras, knowing darned well that the sheriff was using me to cultivate my town's voters. But I was all too aware that continued goodwill between my department and the county was essential. Which, I supposed, made me just as political as the sheriff.

Released from the sheriff's avuncular embrace, I stepped back out of the limelight as he kept speaking.

"I also want to take this opportunity to assure local residents that they're in absolutely no danger. I can't compromise an ongoing investigation, but I can say that early indications suggest some kind of a connection with organized crime."

That statement earned him a repressive glare from Agent Franklin. But the sheriff had his back to Agent Franklin, so he continued heedlessly on.

"The murders sure have the look of mob executions."

At that point, Agent Franklin pushed forward.

"The sheriff and I have a lot of work to do," he said smoothly. "So we'll take a few questions before wrapping this up."

That's when, much to my surprise and—I was certain— the sheriff and Agent Franklin's dismay, a female reporter turned the press's attention to me.

"Hey, Brooke," she said, "aren't you the one with the search dogs?"

I nodded. "I am."

"You and your dog discovered a skeleton out here a few days ago, didn't you? While you were looking for a lost toddler?"

I nodded again, adding that the child had been found safely and returned to her parents.

Another reporter chimed in, a thin guy with an aggressive chin.

"Hey, I remember you!"

In that moment, I remembered him, too. Remembered how he'd shoved his microphone into my face, demanding to know how I felt about finding a little boy's body. As if my tears hadn't said it all.

"Didn't you find a murdered kid right around here, too? About a year ago? Are all these murders somehow connected?"

Well, all the victims are dead, I thought sarcastically. But I kept my face bland and my voice neutral when I answered.

"The child's body was discovered near a residential area, there was a history of domestic abuse, and the boy's father confessed to his murder. So no, I don't think they're related."

Then Agent Franklin announced that the interviews were done and that the next official news conference would be tomorrow morning at nine.

I turned my back on the camera and walked back across the length of Camp Cadiz, knowing that I'd only answered half the reporter's question. I, too, wondered how—and if— the murder I'd uncovered days earlier was tied into the bodies in the ravine.

Mowed areas of grass marked each of the campsites at Camp Cadiz. Beyond the outhouse, on the far side of the campground, were two adjacent campsites. That was where the human remains brought up from the ravine were laid out on plastic tarps. A stand of trees and the stone foundation of an old Civilian Conservation Corps building shielded the makeshift morgue area from the curious eyes of the press and a gathering crowd of spectators. Not surprisingly, word of the murders—like every other piece of bad news that surfaced in Hardin County—had spread quickly.

Though it was hours from sunset and the afternoon sun beat down on the unshaded field, battery-powered light stands already ringed the grassy morgue area. Similar lights were also among the equipment that had been lowered down into the ravine along with a small army of crime-scene techs and forensic investigators. With the resources of the FBI driving it, this investigation wasn't going to be interrupted by sunset. Or limited by lack of equipment or personnel.

The weather, I thought, was the only element they couldn't control. I'd mentioned that to the first investigators arriving on the scene. Mentioned how quickly the shallow stream could be turned into a raging torrent. The kind of torrent that had already scattered body parts down the length of the ravine. Since then, a portable weather radio had arrived on the scene. Now periodic National Weather Service announcements echoed across the campground, reinforcing my warning, spurring the investigation into high gear. Severe thunderstorms were predicted for tomorrow afternoon. Flooding was likely in low-lying areas. And nothing, I thought, was lower-lying than the bottom of the ravine.

The perimeter of the morgue area was marked with crime-scene tape. A single opening, on the side nearest the River-to-River Trail, was monitored by a woman dressed in a short-sleeved blouse and khaki slacks with a badge and ID hanging from a cord around her neck. She was also in charge of a nearby bulletin board on which a blown-up section of Chad's topographical map had been mounted. Bright colored pushpins, each with a number, dotted the map, indicating where remains had been found. The pushpins were keyed to numbered plastic triangles placed on a corner of each of the tarps.

I looked over the double row of tarps then back at the map, my eyes lingering on a lemon-yellow pushpin. Number one. There was no corresponding tarp for that pin because the remains that Possum and I had found were already at the state's forensics lab. Thinking back to that night, I now wondered about Possum's reaction. When he'd whined and tucked his tail down, he probably hadn't been reacting just to the remains on the ledge, but to the odor of decaying bodies wafting up from the depths of the ravine. Overlaying the scent of a little girl who was very much alive. And still Possum had managed to stay on task and find Tina.

I moved slowly around the perimeter of the morgue area, pausing often to watch what was going on while trying to stay out of the way of the people who scurried back and forth despite the heat. Only one edge of the campsite was shaded by trees, so the technicians worked in the beating afternoon sun. And most of them were dressed for air-conditioned labs.

As I stood nearby, several grubby searchers arrived with more remains. After consulting briefly with them, the woman in the khaki slacks pointed to the next empty sheet. She added pin number fourteen to the board. A police photographer documented the fourteenth body just as he had every new addition to the sheets.

Other workers—some wearing lab coats, some in civilian clothing, and all wearing latex gloves—bent over particular piles. A few concentrated on the bits of clothing and personal effects salvaged from the kill sites and placed in bags that were also numbered. Most were carefully arranging bones, creating incomplete jigsaw skeletons with a few ribs and a jaw bone and a shattered hand. Or a femur, a pelvis and bits of spine. Or matching forearms, one with a fingerless hand still attached.

The collections on each tarp, I knew, had been found in geographic proximity to each other. But it would take DNA testing to match all the pieces that had been scattered over longer distances by scavengers and the stream.

Every intact skull I saw had a ragged hole at the back of the head.

"Execution style," I overheard a nearby county cop say. "Stand 'em up or kneel 'em on the edge. Put the gun up near their head. Then—" he pointed at one of the skulls with his right index finger and jerked his thumb upward "—bang. A quick push and you're done."

That, I thought, explained the sheriff's off-the-cuff comment to the media. He probably figured the ravine for a dryland equivalent of a pair of cement overshoes. Certainly, the Shawnee National Forest could be as impenetrable as the deepest lake. And a bullet to the brain was just as permanent as drowning.

I looked back down at the remains nearest my feet. A single item on a corner sheet. It was the cap of a skull, the bone still half covered with skin, soil clumping the hair, making the color impossible to determine. And on the sheet beside that, a pair of femurs, their heads tucked in next to the hip sockets they fit in, looked almost porous and polished clean.

I waylaid one of the FBI technicians, a younger guy with a pleasant face whom I'd noticed earlier. Then, he'd been standing off to one side, staring over the bodies laid out before him, looking more than a little overwhelmed. Now, he was moving efficiently along the perimeter, dividing his attention between two incessantly squawking walkie-talkies.

I managed to catch him in a moment when he wasn't talking into either.

"This has been done over a lot of years, hasn't it?" I said.

He hesitated as he searched for my ID, then noticed the Maryville PD badge I'd retrieved from my SUV and clipped to my waist.

"Oh, you're the one who got this circus started. You and your partner."

No point in telling him that Chad wasn't my partner.

"Yeah," I said. "Sorry about that."

"You should be," he said, suddenly grinning. "To answer your question *unofficially,* some of these bodies may have been down there for twenty years or more. But a couple of them—like number six over there—are a lot more recent. Maybe just a few months old."

One of the walkie-talkies crackled to life, demanding his attention.

I mouthed a "thank you," carefully kept the relief I felt from showing in my expression, and left him to his work.

These murders, I thought, had nothing to do with my sister, nothing to do with the secret that had prompted her to threaten me. This place was someone's killing field—someone's dumping ground—when Katie and I had still been children. Maybe even before we'd been born. And it was too much of a coincidence to believe that the remains I'd found on the ledge were unrelated to the bodies down in the ravine. As the search progressed, I was confident that other victims would be discovered along the edge of the ravine.

I continued my walk around the perimeter. Looking. Listening to the conversations around me. Gathering information

I feared that "cooperation" through official channels would be much slower to provide.

A tall, thin man with wire-framed glasses and wispy hair had been moving from one set of remains to the next, squatting down close to each sheet to look carefully at them. Sometimes turning a skull over to examine it or using calipers or a tape to measure a rib or a piece of spine or a bone from an arm or leg.

An intact rib cage and spinal cord with a bit of clothing still clinging to it seemed to catch his attention for a moment.

"Scoliosis," he murmured.

Then he moved on to the adjacent sheet. Number nine.

Behind him, a young woman carrying a clipboard made another quick note, as she did whenever he spoke.

Another time, he pointed to the forearm with the partial hand still attached.

"See that. Teeth marks. Gnawed the fingers right off."

The young woman nodded, looked a little green and took another note as she moved away from sheet number eleven.

The last set of remains they examined brought them close to me.

"Odd," he said as he stood.

That softly spoken word focused the young woman's attention—and mine—on him. He spoke to her as a teacher would to a student, and I wondered if that didn't define their relationship.

"Consider the numbers you've recorded and what we've seen," he said. "Skulls with relatively large external occipital protuberances. Long bones that are, overall, quite large and robust. Femoral shaft circumferences consistently exceeding eighty millimeters. Every femoral head we've measured is well over forty-five millimeters. What does that tell you?"

It certainly told me nothing.

The young woman seemed stumped, too. She glanced down at her clipboard as if the answer was there.

"No, don't look at your notes," her older colleague snapped. "Look around you. And think!"

Apparently unoffended by—or simply used to—his tone, she took a little time to work it out. The tall man stood quietly, not looking nearly as impatient as he had sounded, a slight smile playing across his features as he watched her.

Pride, I thought. And maybe a little affection.

Abruptly, the young woman lifted her head.

"Well?" he said, soliciting her opinion.

When she spoke, she sounded awestruck.

"Males," she said. "All of these victims are men."

I waited to shake my head until I had moved past the teacher and student. And in my mind, I scolded them for jumping to conclusions. What you have now might be all male, but the ground search is still in its earliest stages. Maybe the remains you've examined so far belong only to men, but one victim is definitely a woman, I thought. Which means the continuing search will probably turn up at least a few more female victims. And more victims who are buried along the ravine, not in it.

In the time it took me to walk completely around the perimeter, three more numbered pushpins were added to the map and three more plastic sheets were filled with soil-encrusted remains.

Even I could see they were male.

Chapter 17

I went home before dusk.

There was no point in staying and watching the makeshift morgue expand one tarp at a time when there was nothing I could do there. Unlike the others at the scene, I had a town to take care of. No matter that I'd already had a grueling day and would have preferred to spend the evening sitting on the back porch and pitching balls to my dogs. It was Friday and, within a few hours, the action at the bars on Dunn Street would be in full swing. It was my job to make sure nothing swung too far out of control.

But first, I needed a shower, clean clothes and maybe a decent meal. One involving fresh vegetables and protein. After that, I figured, I'd be pretty much ready for whatever life threw at me.

Before leaving my SUV I took my holstered gun and the inhaler from my glove compartment. Temporarily, I hitched my gun belt around my waist and tucked the evidence bag into my pocket. Then I crossed the yard to the kennel area, spent a moment fiddling with the latch on Possum's dog-food bin, and scooped out a heaping portion of kibbles as he bounced and barked with anticipation.

"Sorry, bud," I said as I dumped the food into his dish. "No playtime tonight."

Whatever canine disappointment Possum might have felt was lost in tail-wagging enthusiasm over his food. He didn't even notice when I let Highball out of his kennel and walked in the direction of the house. Highball followed me across the yard, wagging his tail happily as I detoured briefly to my garden—a quartet of staked tomato plants that flourished on heat, humidity and neglect. After a quick inspection convinced Highball that the ripe tomato I pulled from the vine was not a tennis ball, he trotted to the back door and waited.

Briefly, I disrupted our routine by taking my boots off before letting us inside. Despite my trips back and forth through the stream—and though the smell I detected on my boots was now mostly in my imagination—a dog like Highball should have perceived the odor of decomposition still clinging to the rough leather. And he would have, even a few months earlier. But Highball simply sat patiently at my feet. Old and oblivious.

I felt a familiar twinge of sadness as I pushed open the door and watched him go directly to the empty food dish beside his cushion. He stared eagerly at it as I dumped my gun belt, car keys, the tomato and the contents of my pockets onto the kitchen counter next to the phone. Then I went to the pantry, measured out his kibbles and supplemented that meal with a can of soft food especially formulated for elderly dogs.

As Highball pushed his gray muzzle happily into his dish, I patted him.

"You're a good boy," I murmured. "A very good dog."

After that, I poured myself a big glass of water from the tap, took several gulps, quickly rubbed the back of my arm across my eyes, and refocused my attention on the present. Away from the inevitable day in the near future when I would have to bury my old companion.

As I did every evening when I returned home, I made sure pen and paper were handy, then hit the flashing message button on the answering machine.

The first was from Katie. Whispery, sincere.

"I hope you like your surprise."

The answering machine announced that the message had been left at 12:42. I didn't know what she was talking about. Not understanding the message upped my anxiety and, along with it, the acid level in my stomach.

Before playing the next message, I went to the fridge intending to cut myself a slice of cheese. And discovered the surprise. Katie had made me a cake. The kind usually reserved for the hotel's guests on special occasions. Single serving, tiny and perfect, it was encased in a paper-thin layer of marzipan and sprinkled with something that made it glitter like an ornament. This cake was decorated with miniature roses. Yellow Cherokee roses.

Nice, I thought. It didn't solve any problems, but it reminded me how sweet and thoughtful my sister could be. How hard she was trying to do the right thing. And the gesture gave me hope.

I picked up the cake, carried it back to the kitchen counter, and took a bite as I listened to the next message. Inside the marzipan wrapper, the cake was yellow with ribbons of dark chocolate dividing three uniformly thin layers.

On the answering machine, the next caller was Aunt Lucy.

Her voice was calm and pleasant even though her message was all business. As was typical when we spoke about the Underground, Aunt Lucy's message was deliberately vague. But it conveyed a wealth of information.

"I'm going out of town this afternoon, honey. To meet an old friend for dinner. I'll be back before midnight. Thought you'd be pleased."

She'd called at 2:00 p.m.

Though I didn't envy Aunt Lucy the long drive to rendez-vous with another Underground volunteer, I was happy for Jackie. Pleased she was on her way to a new life. Mostly, though, I was thrilled that she was well away from the Cherokee Rose. Now only regular guests remained for Katie to interact with, and I had a little more time to resolve the issue of her involvement with the Underground.

Maybe, I thought as I took another bite of Katie's lovely cake, there was some middle ground. Maybe Katie could be convinced to focus on some other aspect of the Underground, one that didn't involve direct contact with abused women. Like finances. Despite private donations, demand for services were a constant drain on Underground resources. My sister was clever, good with money and investments. She could really make a difference.

As I hit Erase, the phone rang again. Before I could review the last message.

"Oh, good. You're still home."

The relief that I heard in my grandmother's voice was completely out of character. And absolutely alarming.

"What's wrong?" I blurted, abandoning the last bit of cake on the counter.

"Our special guest checked out earlier, but I saw her husband a few minutes ago."

I had no doubt that Gran was talking about Hector Townsend.

My first thought was that Jackie'd had a moment of doubt. Beatings destroyed a woman's confidence, often making her believe she couldn't survive apart from the very person who mistreated her. So sometimes, no matter how vigilant we tried to be, women traveling along the Underground contacted their abusers. Told them where they were. Jackie, I feared, had done just that. Called Hector to come get her, then changed her mind again. And escaped with Aunt Lucy. Leaving Gran to deal with an enraged, possessive and physically powerful man who could easily recognize her from the hospital. Might assault her to get information. Or just to get revenge.

"I'm on my way," I said as I grabbed for my gun. "If he trespasses, call 911. Tell them you're Officer Tyler's grand-mother and a man is threaten—"

"No. Brooke. Honey. Listen to me!" Gran said urgently. "I was running errands and saw him drive his motorcycle off the ferry. He was headed up Route 146, so he's probably long gone. But I decided it was a good idea to tell Katie about him and to have her work late tonight. Until Lucy comes back home. And I want you to keep your eyes open, too. You're the police, so I'm sure you can handle any trouble he makes."

"Of course I can, Gran," I said as I moved my fingers away from my gun belt and let out the breath I hadn't realized I was holding.

Though I hadn't taken the job in Maryville just to protect the Underground, there were certainly advantages to my position. If I saw Hector tonight—and it seemed to me the bars on Dunn Street would be a magnet for someone like him—I'd find a way to discourage him from remaining in town. Arrest him, if need be.

"I saw the evening news," Gran was saying. "And I'm

proud of you. Finding all those people who were executed out there. Anyway, as busy as you've been with that, I wasn't sure I'd even catch you at home."

And that explained the relief in Gran's voice, I thought. She hadn't expected to reach me so easily. Cell-phone reception out at Camp Cadiz was nonexistent, and routing an emergency call through dispatch required an explanation—some good excuse for using official channels for personal business. Claiming a family emergency risked calling attention to the other activities taking place at the Cherokee Rose.

"So just do your job," she said. "Oh, by the way, I moved that antique of your grandfather's downstairs."

I knew exactly what she meant. Knew that she'd rolled back the rug beside her bed, lifted one of the floorboards, and unwrapped the revolver from the piece of old patchwork quilt that protected it. After eight years in the darkness.

"You cleaned it up, didn't you?"

She laughed at that.

"Don't worry, honey. It's nicely polished. And now it's in the safe behind the counter, so if anyone ever tries to rob us…"

Armed robbery. That was the excuse that we always held at the ready. Just in case we were confronted by someone like Hector. It was an explanation that law enforcement would readily accept. A strategy that we'd been careful enough—and fortunate enough—never to have used.

But I'd never had any trouble imagining my Gran acting in such an extreme emergency. Now, as I continued speaking on the phone with her, I could see her taking my grandfather's gun from the safe. I pictured her as I often had, her sinewy arms extended, pale eyes focused and intent through her thick lenses, arthritic hands unwavering. Gran would face an intruder courageously, without regard for her own welfare.

Just the way *her* great-grandmother had faced down a posse while a group of runaway slaves had hidden just yards away.

If the need arose, Gran was more than capable of pulling the trigger.

I'd hung up the phone, pushed the answering machine button again, and was about to take the last bite of cake when I heard the third message.

My sister's voice again. Still whispery.

Now furious.

"I saw the way everyone was smiling at you on TV. If you tell them, I swear—"

The message and the threat cut off as Katie slammed down the phone.

The answering machine beeped—3:20 p.m. Some station, I realized, had broken into their regular programming and broadcast a segment of the news conference. And I knew there was a small TV in the kitchen of the Cherokee Rose. Katie liked to leave it on as she worked.

Suddenly, I lost my appetite for the cake my sister had made especially for me. I dropped it into the garbage, wiped my fingers on my jeans. Spurred by a half-spoken threat I didn't fully understand, my anxiety—my suspicions— returned in a rush. But now they made less sense than ever.

Katie couldn't have been involved, I told myself. Not in all those murders. They'd taken place over decades. She'd been too young....

But what about just one murder? The one that didn't fit the pattern?

Once more, the inhaler that I'd found—the inhaler that now shared the kitchen counter with my gun, car keys and a ripe tomato—took on significance.

I punched Chad's number on the speed dial. Not because I wanted to hear a friendly voice or because my sister's threats made me feel abandoned and alone. I called him because I needed a professional's perspective. At least, that's what I told myself.

Two rings and a few minutes of small talk later, I gave him an update on the crime scene. Twenty-one bodies for sure. Another half-dozen tarps filled with random bits of clothing and miscellaneous body parts. Search efforts so far limited to the bottom of the ravine.

Then I told him that all the recovered bodies seemed to be male.

"Weird," he said, which pretty much summed up my feelings. "I wonder how our Jane Doe fits in?"

My question exactly, I thought.

"I dunno," I said. "Maybe she doesn't."

Then I spoke my next thoughts out loud. And though Chad had no way of knowing it, I was telling him why—at least, in this instance—I thought it was unlikely that Katie had committed murder. Despite the secret she thought I knew. Despite her threats. Despite the inhaler.

"It'd be a coincidence, wouldn't it, if someone else killed our Jane Doe?" I said. "And then, by chance, hid the body along the same stretch of ravine where at least twenty other people were executed?"

"One hell of a coincidence," Chad said with enough passion that I believed him. "Even if all the other victims *are* men."

Then he stopped speaking abruptly, as if he was thinking over the words he'd just said or chasing some wisp of a thought.

I knew him well enough that I waited, not interrupting. And though pacing was an obvious remedy for the impatience I felt, I used the time instead to tuck the bagged inhaler into a roasting pan I rarely used. By the time I stepped back down from my kitchen stool, Chad was talking to me again.

"Maybe it has do with the fact that she *is* female. So she was executed, just like the men. With a bullet through the brain. But, unlike the men, her body wasn't just shoved into the ravine like so much garbage. The place was remote and the odds were against finding her, so our killer could simply have left her out in the open. But someone made sure that the body wasn't exposed to the weather or scavengers. I bet, at the time, the inside of that old tree looked pretty secure. In an odd sort of way, our Jane Doe was buried. Or, at least, *placed* somewhere permanent. Undisturbed. Out of respect, maybe. Or love."

And that, I thought, let Katie off the hook.

I put my gun away as I always did unless I was wearing it or cleaning it. No matter that I lived alone and wasn't expecting company. Too many people—among them, Katie—had keys to my house. So I locked it into the gun box in my bedroom and then I showered.

For the second time in the past several days, I stripped and dumped my filthy clothes in a plastic bag, isolating them from a hamper full of more conventionally dirty clothing. Once again, I ran the shower hot, scrubbing away—at least from my flesh—all residue of the day's activities, the day's discoveries. And then as I stood in the shower, I checked for ticks, running my hands through my hair, below my breasts, over my entire body. Alert for anything that felt like a freckle, but hadn't been there when I'd showered that morning.

Finally clean, but far from refreshed, I turned off the shower and dried myself off. Then I wrapped the towel around me, intending to step across the hallway into my bedroom. To get dressed.

I made it out of the bathroom.

Two steps down the hall.

Four steps from my bedroom door.

That was when the kitchen door flew open, its flimsy latch torn away by the force of a shoulder against the door.

He lurched forward into the room, surveyed the kitchen.

Hector Townsend. Wearing tight jeans, leather chaps and heavy boots. The bulging muscles on his upper torso exposed by a black, sleeveless athletic shirt.

"Jackie!" Hector roared. "I know you're here. One of your new friends called me. Told me how to get here. You can't trust them. Come on out. I promise I'll take care of you!"

I flattened myself against the wall, knowing that even the most casual glance down the hall would betray my position. Then I took a step sideways, toward the bedroom.

The floor creaked.

And he saw me.

"Where's Jackie?" he bellowed as I dove for my bedroom door.

Hector's heavy footsteps stormed down the hall.

I slid across my bed, losing my towel as I stretched out, grabbing for the gun box on the lower shelf of my night stand.

My fingers touched it.

I keyed in the three-digit number.

Almost had it open.

Too late.

Hector grabbed my feet, dragged me back away from the edge of the bed. And then he was on top of me. Crushing me. Scrabbling upward over my body to grab my hands, capture my wrists.

He was a big man. Massive.

I knew I couldn't fight him. Not from this position.

I went limp instead.

That's when he rolled me over. Held my arms over my head as he straddled my hips. Pinning me to the bed.

I prayed for an opening. Any opening.

He used his free hand to slap me. Hard.

"Where's Jackie?"

I tasted blood in my mouth. From the inside of my cheek. And I recalled too vividly how Jackie's face had looked when he'd finished with her.

I tried to buy myself some time.

"Please," I cried, "I don't know any Jackie."

The grip of his massive left hand around my wrists tightened. He slapped me again with his right, then curled his fingers into a fist that he swept just inches from my face. Threatening.

Then he thought of something better.

He shifted slightly, settling his mass onto my thighs.

"I know you're hiding her," he said.

He spread his fingers wide, dragged his hand downward past my breasts, down across my belly.

"I've really missed Jackie," he said. "Understand, bitch?"

I ignored the movement of his hand.

Stared up into his violent, evil face.

Then I turned my head, closed my eyes, blinding myself to this human monster as I fought the hysteria that was making it difficult to think.

No matter what was happening, I had to think clearly.

Just like Gran had taught me.

That's when I heard the high-pitched whine, the sound of Highball's nails against the uncarpeted floor of the hallway. He was pacing, agitated by a human behavior he didn't understand.

I made it clear to him.

I screamed, long and loud.

One of Highball's paws scraped across my trapped legs as

he leaped onto the bed. He lunged for Hector's arm, bit down hard. And held on.

Hector yelled out. Surprised. Terrified. Swung himself off of the bed. Off of me. Moved toward the door as he attempted to escape Highball's teeth.

I grabbed my gun.

Aimed past my now-empty bed just as Hector shook my dog loose.

Highball landed in a heap on the floor, then sprung back onto all four feet. Growling. Circling in close. Limping, but intent on keeping a predator at bay.

Hector lifted his booted foot, a prelude to kicking my dog.

"Freeze!" I shouted to get Hector's attention.

He glanced away from Highball, saw the gun, realized that I was a greater threat than the dog. He put his foot down, then stood very still, moving only to follow my unspoken command. The quick upward movement of the tip of my gun prompted him to raise his hands above his head. After that, the only thing that moved was his chest, which heaved up and down, and the thin line of blood that dribbled slowly from the bite mark on his bare shoulder.

Only then did I call Highball over to my side, where he stood with his soft, furry shoulder pressed against my leg. Obedient to my command, but still growling deep in his throat, his tawny-brown eyes fixed on Hector.

I used my free hand to pat my dog's head as I considered what to do with the man in front of me. Arresting him, charging him with assault and attempted rape, facing him in court...all of that risked exposing the Underground.

Then I thought about shooting him. Point blank.

If I dialed 911, county would respond to my call. My cheek was bruised. As were my wrists. And the back door was broken in. No one would question my decision to defend myself against a rapist. One who targeted a woman living alone in an isolated area, but hadn't counted on going up against a cop. And her dog.

A tempting solution.

Not a viable one.

I would have unhesitatingly killed Hector to defend Jackie's life. Or my own. But Jackie was long gone. And I wasn't a murderer.

That narrowed the options to one.

With Highball as an escort, I walked Hector through the house at gunpoint, angry enough that I didn't much care that I was still naked. Besides, I didn't think Hector would stand idly by as I threw on some clothes. I made him open every closet, look under every piece of furniture.

"She's long gone," I said finally. "So get over it."

Then I took him to the back door.

"If I ever see you again, you're a dead man. Understand?"

He nodded.

I gave him a quick prod with my gun, encouraging him in the direction of the motorcycle I hadn't heard because I'd been showering.

He ran across the yard, not looking back. Threw a leather-clad leg over his bike. The engine roared to life and gravel scattered as he sped away.

Now shivering from reaction, I stepped back inside. Pushed a kitchen chair beneath the doorknob to secure the back door. Then I knelt down beside my protector, laid my gun down on the kitchen floor and gave him a hug.

I checked him for injuries.

Just bumps and bruises, I thought when I was done. Just like me.

With Highball close at my heels and my gun back in my hand, I walked back down the hall. From now on, I thought, I'd have to watch my back. And keep my gun close at hand. Even in my own home. My own bathroom. Because Hector didn't strike me as the type who'd just give up.

Neither did my sister.

Jackie didn't know where I lived. She had no reason to send her abusive husband to my house. But I'd made myself a target for Katie. For Katie's rage. And I'd become its latest victim.

Easy enough to imagine her wheedling a phone number from Jackie just before she left. All Katie had to do was tell Jackie that she was sending Hector on a wild-goose chase.

A chase that had landed him at her sister's door.

Had she intended that he murder me? I wondered. Or had she simply intended his visit—his violence—to warn me away from something she thought I knew?

I took another shower, this time with my gun on top of the toilet tank. And Highball sprawled across the doorway. Then I put on my uniform and held an ice pack to my bruised cheek as I ate a bologna sandwich stacked with a tomato for dinner.

I went to deal with the drunk-and-disorderlies on Dunn Street.

A situation I was well equipped to control.

At 2:00 a.m., I drove back home.

I let Possum run loose, knowing he wouldn't leave the yard while Highball and I were inside the house. Knowing that he would raise an alarm if anyone approached.

Insecurity prompted me to dress for bed in sweatpants and a once-maroon T-shirt that had faded to pink. Then, after popping a couple of aspirins to tone down my aching jaw and wrists, I dragged Highball's cushion into the bedroom, tucking it between my bed and the doorway. Once he'd gotten

over the excitement of being invited to sleep in the bedroom—
a rare treat indeed—he settled happily onto his cushion.

Then I tucked myself into bed and settled my head against
the pillows.

Exhausted, I shut my eyes. Drifted.

Back into a locked closet.

Just as the bare bulb burned out.

Impossible now to see the spider that was slowly lowering
itself toward us. Supporting all but two of its spindly legs on
a thin strand of web.

Those two legs, I knew, were searching the darkness.
For children.

Katie's hand was tight around mine as we sat huddled
together.

"Sh-h-h-h," she whispered. "Be quiet."

Hector's footsteps. In the room beyond the closet.

If he found us, he'd do to me what a stranger had done to
Katie.

Then I felt the wisp of sticky web fall against my face. And
tiny, dry legs rasping across my cheek.

I couldn't help myself.

I screamed.

Hector wrenched the closet door open, grabbed my wrists.

And I screamed again.

I jolted awake in a quiet room, its peace broken only by the
snoring of an old dog on the floor next to the bed. Woke up to
the realization that my screams only echoed inside my head.

For a moment, I lay very still, longing for the presence of
Chad's warm body beside me. Remembering how many times
I'd awakened from a nightmare and found myself within the
protective circle of his arms. Found comfort there no matter

what horrors the too-familiar closet had revealed on that particular night.

With a quick shake of my head, I rolled over and dangled my hand off the side of the bed, locating Highball with my searching fingers. Disturbed his sleep by stroking my hand over his thick coat. By telling him that I was a grown-up. That I didn't need anyone besides him to protect me.

Not Katie.

Not even Chad.

After that, I checked that my loaded gun was still within easy reach, settled my head back down on the pillow, and closed my eyes.

I didn't object when, a few minutes later, Highball crawled into bed with me.

Chapter 18

The next morning, the clock radio didn't awaken me with music or even the throaty drawl of the fellow who did the farm commodities report. Instead, I was pulled from sleep by a meteorologist explaining that a cold front, approaching from the west, was on a collision course with the warm, humid air that had plagued our region for weeks.

"And you all know what that means for Hardin County," he said, his voice much too cheery for 5:30 a.m. "Severe weather coming our way, folks. Strong thunderstorms. Some with hail and damaging winds. And the possibility of tornadoes." He lingered over the last phrase, investing it with the kind of orgasmic anticipation that only a weather junkie could manage. "So keep it here on Classic Country. Ninety-five-point-seven FM. Your station for up-to-the-minute weather."

Though I worked on Saturday, I didn't usually go on duty until noon—compensation for the late evenings I spent patrolling Dunn Street. But this morning, like every other morning, Possum's barking from outside and Highball's pacing by the kitchen door made sleeping in an impossibility. Possum was simply hungry for breakfast. But with Highball, it was a little more than that. The old dog needed to go out and, from experience, I knew that I had about ten minutes from the time he began pacing to the moment an accident flooded the linoleum floor.

With that very much on my mind, I hurried out of bed and I went to take care of my dogs.

Minutes later, I was sitting at my kitchen table, still in my sweats and faded T-shirt, eating toast that I'd scorched in the broiler. Feeling—as Gran was fond of saying—like I'd been rode hard and put up wet. A folksy way of describing sore and utterly exhausted.

As a remedy, I'd turned on the radio in the kitchen, hoping for some blood-stirring, toe-tapping music. Something that would energize me and lighten my mood. But today, I quickly discovered, the customary ten-in-a-row music format had been modified. Thanks, in large part, to Chad and me.

"The official body count is now at twenty-five," the DJ was saying, managing to sound as if he were reporting the winning score at a Friday night high-school football game. "Oh, and someone's just slipped me a note…. Okay, folks, the sheriff's office has just called and asked us to remind you all that the road to Camp Cadiz is closed to through-traffic. So don't waste your gas heading over that way. Why don't you give me a call instead? Let me know what you think of all this. Our number here is…"

The DJ spun a Garth Brooks tune about a guy in love with rodeo as he waited for the inevitable flood of phone calls from people eager to gossip publicly. I took a bite of toast, tried to convince myself that the layer of marmalade was enough to disguise the bitter, burned taste of the bread, then followed up with a sip of black coffee.

Breakfast of champions, I thought. *You know you're a cop if...* Then my mind sheered away from the game and the stab of loneliness it inspired to refocus on talk radio.

The song ended, the DJ plugged a car dealership in Harrisburg owned by a pure-hearted, straight-talking hometown boy, and the calls streamed in. The sheriff's theory that the killings were mob connected seemed now to be public knowledge. But that didn't slow speculation about a resident serial killer stalking the streets of some small town in southern Illinois. A place like Maryville, the current caller was saying.

"It's like I was saying just yesterday, when I called in to the regular afternoon talk show," he said. "This is why we have to continue fighting for our constitutional right to bear arms. You never know who the enemy might be, when some criminal will invade your home, threaten your family..."

Yeah, I thought cynically, let's put a loaded gun under every citizen's pillow. That way, in a moment of fear or anger or stupidity, you can kill a loved one or someone you don't love anymore or the unlucky cop responding to your 911 call.

Striking a balance between a reasonable level of self-protection and an unreasonable risk to those around you was a topic Chad and I had debated more than once as we'd shared breakfast. And I wondered, now that someone had actually invaded my home—and been stopped because I had a gun and a dog—if my opinion hadn't shifted ever so slightly to Chad's point of view.

I ended that thought with a last bite of toast and a refill on my coffee. Then another caller was on the line. She began telling the DJ and a county's worth of listeners about rumors she'd heard about a secret organization that had been operated out of Maryville for years and taking women—

My God!

I inhaled my coffee, began choking and fought to listen to the caller's shrill voice as I tried to clear my airways, thinking that the moment we'd always feared had arrived. The Underground would be publicly exposed.

"—and shipping them to a secret laboratory in Roswell, New Mexico."

Oxygen and relief arrived at about the same time.

I was merely sputtering when the DJ—who was now as fascinated by the caller as I had been moments earlier—asked a question.

"What do they do with them?"

"They've got genetic material they've saved from when the flying saucer crashed. The women are going to be incubators for half-alien beings—"

The call abruptly disconnected, but not before the shrill voice cracked, dropped a couple of octaves, and was suddenly, clearly revealed as belonging to an adolescent male. You could hear his buddies' laughter in the background.

I laughed, too. Relief, I suspected, was making the whole incident seem funnier than it was. Laughter, unfortunately, inspired a bit more choking and sputtering.

The station cut to music, which lasted about as long as it took me to clear the breakfast dishes by tossing the paper plate in the trash and washing the knife I'd used to spread marmalade. When the tune ended, the meteorologist came on again, this time announcing that the National Weather Service out of Lincoln had just placed Hardin County—and, in fact, the station's entire listening area—under a severe thunderstorm watch. That meant, he reminded listeners, that conditions were favorable for storms to develop. The front that was now heading our way, he reminded everyone cheerfully, had battered a couple of towns in Missouri with baseball-sized hail. And had spawned a couple of category-two tornadoes in Iowa.

Lovely, I thought as the Dixie Chicks began singing something about a guy named Earl. Just lovely.

I spent a few minutes washing counters that were already clean, then threw on a load of laundry, ran a damp mop over my kitchen floor, and went outside—with my gun at my waist—to clean the kennel area. All in an effort to keep busy and not think too closely about anything that might hurt. And to avoid a tendency to search shadows and corners for an attacker I knew was no longer there.

Finally, I gave up on killing my extra hours of free time.

I put on my uniform as I considered where my on-duty time was best spent. I certainly wasn't needed at the crime scene, where activity would be in full swing. Then I took a good look at the sky. Thick masses of clouds were already gathering to the west on the distant horizon. Bright white and shaded with gray, they boiled upward against the hazy blue sky, dwarfing the dark green forest below them.

I drove into town.

I headed directly for the marina on Dunn Street, knowing that boat owners—always among the first to react to threatening weather—would soon be speeding down the hazardous roadway, intent on making sure their boats were secure. Familiarity breeds contempt, I thought, especially in drivers with other things on their minds. Like checking their boat's anchorage and mooring lines. Not worth risking your life. But folks often didn't consider that until it was too late.

As I turned onto the first sharp curve, my worst fears were

validated by a squeal of brakes and the sound of an impact echoing upward from somewhere on the road in front me. The usual terrifying moment of optical illusion, when my vehicle seemed destined to plunge into the Ohio, passed unnoticed. Now illusion was secondary to the urgency of reaching someone who had just crashed into—or through—the guardrail farther down the winding road.

I rounded the next curve and was abruptly confronted by the scene.

My God. I recognized the car—a polished yellow Cadillac. And its driver—my old friend, Larry Hayes. But my exclamation was as much a prayer of thanksgiving as an expression of shock. The skid marks and the trail of debris painted an ugly—but amazingly, not a deadly—picture.

He'd obviously lost control of his car, but couldn't have been going much faster than the speed limit posted at the top of the roadway. The heavy old car had been deflected by the railing rather than ripping right through it. A streak of yellow paint on the railing clearly showed that first point of impact. Skid marks betrayed the path the car took as it left the railing, careening back across the road, and then smashing a fender against a solid wall of limestone. That impact, I suspected, had buckled the hood, but hadn't stopped the car. It kept moving, finally ending up broadside across the center of the road with the driver's side facing oncoming traffic.

That was a mighty poor place to be.

A potentially fatal spot if a speeding, careless driver had been the next one around that curve. The first car would have been T-boned and Larry probably killed. To prevent just that, I parked my taller vehicle on the curve, knowing that the flashing lights would be seen soon enough to warn the next vehicle on the road to slow down and stop.

Larry's passenger was already out of the car.

Marta Moye. His next-door neighbor. Blood was smeared on her right arm, which hung limply at her side, and stained the floral dress she wore. But she wasn't thinking about her own injuries. Apparently realizing how vulnerable the driver was, she was attempting to help Larry from the car one-handed. Not a great idea.

She turned her head briefly in the direction my SUV.

I opened my door, braced a foot on the running board, stuck my head out above the roof, and waved her away from her own vehicle.

"Leave him be," I shouted. "I'll be right there."

The wind was loud enough that I doubted she could hear me, but the combination of my gestures, the imminent arrival of help and the condition of her arm seemed to be enough to make her stop tugging at him.

I ducked back into the squad car long enough to thumb my mike button, requesting immediate medical assistance and a tow truck. The tow truck, I knew, would probably arrive within minutes. Medical assistance was more problematic.

The fire station, which housed several chartreuse-painted fire trucks and a boxy emergency rescue vehicle, was just blocks away. But Maryville's firefighters and first responders were all volunteers. They had to leave homes or jobs, get to the fire house, load into the appropriate vehicle, then drive to the accident site. Sometimes that could take twenty minutes. A long time for someone who was badly injured.

I grabbed my first-aid box and jogged down to the curve. My relatively brief stint as Maryville's entire police force rather than my years of search-and-rescue work had provided most of my practical medical experience. Mostly because drunken brawlers occasionally moved from using fists to slashing at each other with sharp objects like beer bottles and knives.

When the paramedics arrived at an accident scene, they'd stabilize the victim but usually wouldn't transport. That was handled by an ambulance dispatched from the nearest hospital, which was north of us in Harrisburg. With sirens, a heavy foot, and a bit of foolhardiness, their drivers could usually make it to Maryville in thirty minutes.

But for the next several minutes, I was the entire response team.

As I slipped on latex gloves, I took a quick look at Larry. Determined that he was conscious and not actively bleeding. In fact, he was coherent enough to start telling me how to do my job. Which mostly involved insisting that I tend to Marta first.

Marta, of course, insisted that I treat Larry first. Because she loved him. And, I half suspected, as a matter of principle. If Larry said one thing, she was obliged to say another.

Of course, my own experience dictated whom I would treat first. And that was Marta because I knew that her normal complexion was not the color of spoiled milk. And I could see that the blood on her dress was from a spot on her forearm where a jagged spur of bone had punctured the flesh. But the blood was oozing, not gushing. A good thing. And she seemed alert and not in too much distress. Physically, at least.

Shock, I thought, was often a blessing at this point. It did a good job of blocking pain receptors.

"Support your arm this way," I said, showing her how to use her uninjured arm to cradle the broken one.

Then I guided her a few steps to the side of the road where another section of guardrail and six feet of bristling, wind-swept scrub separated her from the drop-off. I hung on to her as she settled down onto the pavement and leaned back against the railing.

That was when, much to my surprise, a Yorkshire terrier came darting out of a nearby patch of weeds. Landed squarely in its owner's lap and began bouncing on its short hind legs, intent on reaching her face.

"Oh, Peanut," Marta wailed as she leaned forward to accommodate the little dog's tongue. "You bad, bad dog."

But she didn't sound at all angry.

I pushed Peanut aside long enough to cover Marta's wound with a large piece of gauze bandage, using only enough tape to keep the wind and the dog from tearing the sterile covering away. The gauze would keep the wound clean, but mostly it would shield it from the woman's view, which would keep her calmer.

Then I went to help Larry.

He still had his seat belt on and was leaning back against his seat, his head supported by the headrest. His face, which had undoubtedly struck the steering wheel, was bloodied and I suspected he'd broken his nose.

Still, he managed a smile when I opened the car door and bent over him.

"Hey there, Brooke," he said, and his voice was nasal and weak. "How's Marta?"

I smiled back, tried to keep my voice lighthearted as I wrapped a cervical support around his neck.

"She'll have that arm in cast for a while," I said. "But she's gonna be okay. Glad to see that you two are back together."

Briefly, he tried to shake his head, then realized that the collar was designed to prevent such a movement.

"Dog's fault," he said. "He ran off this morning. She kept calling him. Top of her lungs. Peanut. Darling Peanut. I had to

help, just to quiet her down. Last time he ran off, he ended up
down here. So that's where we headed. Darned dog waited until
we were almost around the curve, darted right in front of us.
Barking his fool head off. I swerved to keep from hitting him."

As I secured his broken ankle against further injury, Larry
continued talking. A good distraction from the pain. He told
me what a feisty old gal Marta was. And how he didn't even
remember what had started their feud.

"Maybe I should marry her," he said.

"I'm all for it," I said, smiling. "It'd sure cut down on
911 calls."

Larry managed to chuckle.

"That should hold you until the paramedics arrive," I said
a few minutes later, satisfied that I'd done all I could for him.

If he was lucky, I thought, a mild case of whiplash would
be the only neck or back injury he'd sustained. But I wasn't
taking any chances. There was no reason to move him, so I
just told him to stay put.

"Just be patient," I added. "Help's on the way."

"Mmm," Larry said.

That's when he shut his eyes.

I checked his pulse as he began mumbling about fixing a
broken fence. And dancing. And a pretty pink dress. And
please shut that damned dog out of the bedroom.

Shock, I feared, was making him irrational.

A diagnosis he confirmed by opening his eyes, looking
around wildly and struggling up from his seat.

"Marta!" he cried out. "Where's Marta?"

I put my arm across his body, restraining him.

"She's fine, Larry," I said, keeping my voice calm. "She's
sitting by the side of the road."

"I have to go to her," he said.

Once he stepped down on his shattered ankle, no doubt he'd abandon that plan. But I couldn't allow him to embark on such a voyage of discovery.

When I didn't let him out of the car, he glared at me. Outraged.

"Darn it, Brooke. Let me loose. I have to tell Marta that I love her."

I invested my voice with confidence.

"She already knows that, Larry," I said firmly. "She's known it for a long time."

Amazingly, he sagged back against his seat.

"Is she okay?"

I smiled as I glanced back over my shoulder at Marta, who was still sitting quietly by the side of the road. With Peanut now curled in her lap.

"Yeah," I said. "She's just fine."

Chapter 19

The fire department arrived faster than I could have hoped. The ambulance from Harrisburg showed up ten minutes later.

By the time the tow truck had hauled off Larry's yellow car and I'd opened Dunn Street to traffic again, a tornado watch was in effect for the entire county. Overhead, the sky had grown overcast. On the horizon, the clouds were closer and darker than they'd been an hour earlier.

As I pulled back onto 146, I saw one of Maryville's volunteer weather spotters speed past me on her way to the edge of town. Breaking the law for all the right reasons. She and a handful of others were scattering to predetermined areas—places from which they could see the weather coming. If a tornado was spotted, they'd radio its location and direction of travel to the local ESDA office. That information would be transmitted to emergency services all over Hardin County.

I, too, kept one eye on the horizon as I continued to cruise the streets.

A good part of Maryville's population was also glancing at the sky as they pulled flapping laundry from their clotheslines or parked vehicles inside garages or called children closer to the house. On Main Street, the post office and Maryville's other businesses—a tanning salon that also rented videos, an insurance office, a barbershop and a pizza place— were rolling up the maroon-and-yellow striped canvas awnings that shaded their front windows and were supposed to give the business district an old-fashioned look.

By ten, the sky to the west suggested the hour before sunset. Not the tranquil beauty of a pastel horizon, but the ominous threat of darkness. Wind gusts whipped through the streets, sending small branches and trash cans and debris tumbling. A solid wall of storm clouds—lashed by internal lightning and raging winds—gradually blotted out the sun, obscuring the daytime sky. Bathing Maryville in a premature, green-tinged twilight.

I swung onto 146 again. Just past the intersection of Main Street, a wading pool blew across the highway. I slammed on my brakes as it skittered right in front of me. The pool ended up in the oncoming lane, facedown on the pavement, and the few drivers who were still on the main road swerved onto the far shoulder to avoid it. By now, everyone had their headlights on, and I prayed they were heading for shelter.

I pulled onto the shoulder on my side of the road, jumped from the squad car and ran onto the highway. Grabbed the pool by an edge and dragged it out of the road. Then I stood for a moment—fighting the wind for possession of the bright blue plastic pool with smiling dolphins dancing around an octopus—deciding how to get rid of the thing. After a bit of thought, I walked a dozen feet to the nearest fenced yard and tossed the pool into it. The wind gusted again and the kiddy pool began tumbling but was promptly caught by four feet of chain link.

I brushed off my hands and then, on impulse, looked up toward the top of Hill Street. There, on the highest bluff in town, was the Cherokee Rose. The hotel's redbrick walls stood out against the boiling clouds; its slate roof practically glowed in the odd light, and the tall oaks that surrounded it whipped madly in the wind. Suddenly and for no particular reason, I saw my family home not as strong and unassailable, but as particularly vulnerable.

Back in my squad car, I used my cell phone to call my family.

Katie answered, her voice whispery, but not breathless.

"Are Gran and Aunt Lucy inside with you?" I asked without preamble.

"Yes, they're right here. And so are the guests. But you needn't worry...."

Belligerence in her voice. But at the moment, I had other things on my mind besides my sister's potential for homicide and malice.

"Katie, listen to me. If the sirens go off, I want you to make sure that everyone gets down into the basement. All the guests. You, Aunt Lucy and Gran. Don't let anyone give you an excuse for staying upstairs. Take the flashlight and the little radio on the counter in the broom closet downstairs with you. If the power goes out, remember Gran won't be able to see very well. Take care of everyone, okay? I know you can do it."

The belligerence fled her voice, and all I heard was eagerness to help.

"Okay, Brooke. You don't have to worry. And I'll tuck my

inhaler into my pocket right now, so you won't have to worry about that, either."

Sometimes my sister surprised me. Pleasantly.

My radio crackled to life as dispatch announced that the tornado watch had been upgraded to a tornado warning for the entire county. A tornado had touched down northwest of Maryville and was moving southeast at thirty miles per hour.

The siren positioned near the center of town went off.

I could hear its echo through the phone.

"Go now, Katie," I said urgently.

"I love you, Brooke," she blurted before disconnecting.

I didn't believe her.

The radio on my dashboard crackled to life.

Not dispatch, but Chad's voice.

"Looks like Maryville's right in the path," he said. "I'm heading your way to help."

And though I hadn't felt afraid, that call—the promise of his presence—made me feel safer.

Maryville's weather spotters, I knew, would soon be seeking shelter out of the path of the storm. And so would I. As soon as I finished my loop, made sure everyone in my town was safely indoors. Then I'd park my vehicle and take shelter inside the fire station, which also served as the ESDA office. From there, we'd coordinate the storm cleanup and any rescues.

I pulled into the parking lot at Statler's Fill-Up, intending to turn around and head back into town. The wind was making driving even the SUV difficult; the rain was nearly blinding, and it had begun hailing bits of ice about the size of quarters.

That's when I saw Ed. Though he was obviously soaked, he was ignoring the rain and wind and ice as he struggled to close the front door. The wind had forced it back against its hinges and the heavy metal handle was threatening to smash into the big plate-glass window where Ed's Jamaican-themed poster was hung.

I pulled up just beneath the wide metal canopy that sheltered the pumps and jumped from my SUV.

"Get the hell inside, Ed!" I yelled. "Now!"

Above us, the canopy was vibrating with the force of the wind.

Ed shook his head as rain streamed down his dark face.

"I turned off the pumps. But I gotta get this door closed. If it breaks my window, everything inside'll be ruined."

I took a quick look at the sky. Realized there was no time for patience. Or talk.

I pointed. Glanced back at Ed. Saw his eyes widen.

We ran inside. Me in front, Ed fast on my heels.

Behind us, it was as dark as an hour past sunset.

Inside, the overhead lights flickered. And the thought flashed through my mind that a tornado didn't really sound at all like a train. More like a growling, ravaging beast about to consume us all.

Wind roared through the doorway, knocking me off my feet.

I slid along the slick, wet linoleum floor.

Ed threw himself sideways to avoid stepping on me.

The lights went out, pitching us into darkness.

The roar became deafening.

Then the building shuddered—something I felt rather than heard.

The front windows seemed to implode.

Suddenly, the wind was inside with us. All around us.

I wrapped my arms over my head as stinging glass and pieces of debris peppered my body.

I think I screamed.

* * *

And then it was over.

I lifted my head cautiously. Not that I really expected anything more to happen. But when it feels as if you've just lived through the end of world, caution seems appropriate.

The sky, still overcast, suggested twilight rather than full dark. The rain, still falling, wasn't driven by an impossible wind. And it was cool. The temperature had dropped at least twenty degrees in a matter of minutes.

Inside Statler's, it was also dark, cool and rainy.

Because there was no roof anymore. Only rafters and sky where a roof had once been.

I stood, letting the debris that covered me fall away from my body. As I moved, I checked each limb and joint carefully. Slow, methodical movements that reflected a brain moving in slow motion, too. And I asked myself—more as a matter of academic interest than focused concern—if it was shock or a miracle that left me feeling no pain.

A miracle, I decided.

I turned slowly, looking around me.

Enclosed within the two remaining walls of the little building was a demolition scene. Random bricks and beams. Twisted framework and broken tiles. Collapsed shelves. Piles of merchandise. Hot-pink flamingos. A cash register. And a plastic palm tree, still amazingly inflated.

In front of the station—separated from me by yards of rubble, a ragged four-foot section of brick wall and little else—was my SUV. The gas pumps were still solidly connected to the ground. But there was sky where a metal canopy had once offered shelter.

I took a step forward.

Then full consciousness—full awareness—returned with a snap. I'd used my arms to cover my head, and my right forearm throbbed with the impact of some heavy object that I now recalled had struck it. My back—my whole body—ached from falling and from being pummeled with debris. And, though my vest had protected my back, I felt the sting of dozens of cuts and scratches on my arms and legs.

Almost as quickly as I realized I'd been hurt, I dismissed the injuries as minor. And irrelevant.

Ed, I thought urgently. Where's Ed?

"Ed!" I called.

And then I called his name again as I began climbing through the rubble between me and where I remembered last seeing him. He'd stumbled over me, thrown himself to the right. Into an area where collapsing roof and collapsing walls now intersected.

"Ed!"

There was a noise somewhere in front of me. One that seemed unrelated to wind or rain.

I scrambled forward.

Then I heard him.

"I need a little help here, Brooke."

A familiar voice, but oddly calm.

For an instant, I flashed back to a time he'd been teaching me and his daughter how to make fried chicken. He'd gotten distracted, bumped the heavy iron skillet and drenched his hand with hot grease. I knew that it hurt. But he'd just smiled, told us it was no big deal. And managed not to frighten two little girls.

I was frightened now.

Ignoring the pain lancing through my back, I began shifting rubble. Throwing aside chunks of shattered roof and wall inter-mixed with merchandise from the automotive section. Cases of oil. Gallon jugs of coolant and wiper fluid, some intact, many popped like balloons. Smaller bottles of brake and transmission fluid. Finally I spotted the sleeve of a Hawaiian shirt beneath a raggedly torn piece of steel shelving. Shelving that had probably saved his life. I grasped it by one edge, dragged it away from him. Exposing a dirt-encrusted profile and kinky hair clotted with debris. A sky-blue shirt with monkeys and banana trees. Brown Bermuda shorts. And blood.

Too much blood. A crimson pool around his legs.

"Don't move," I said.

He either didn't hear me or simply ignored me. Rolled onto his back as I was kneeling down beside him.

The change in position sent blood spurting upward from a deep gash on his leg. Spurting in rhythm with his heart.

I clamped my hands just above the wound, pressed down.

The flow of blood slowed.

By now, the sky had lightened and it was merely drizzling. That made it easier to see as I ran my eyes along Ed's body, looking for other injuries. I found nothing obvious, but wasn't particularly reassured by the cursory exam.

It was the best I could do.

My search ended at Ed's face.

The rain was carving dark paths through his dusty mask. He was blinking, clearing it from his eyes as he turned his head slightly, taking in the devastation all around him.

He managed a smile just wide enough to expose a sliver of gold tooth.

"Like I said, we shoulda closed that front door."

I forced myself to smile back.

"Yep, you were sure right about that," I said.

Then I looked down at the wound again, at the amount of blood still welling up and spilling over Ed's leg.

If I didn't get us help soon, he was going to bleed to death.

With one of my hands still applying pressure to his leg, I stripped off my uniform shirt, exposing the vest and white T-shirt beneath it. After yanking my badge and nameplate from the uniform's breast pocket, I used both of my hands to roll the shirt and bind it around Ed's leg. Two spurts of blood later, and I had the ends of the shirt twisted together. Tightened them until the pressure slowed the bleeding to a trickle.

Arterial blood flows slower when it has to work its way uphill. With that in mind and my hands now free, I grabbed a board that had once been part of the counter, slid it beneath Ed's injured leg and used a case of motor oil to create an incline.

"I'm going to get us some help," I said. "I'll just be a minute or two."

I couldn't have moved any faster than I did when I scrambled out of what had once been a building. As I forced my way through the rubble, the radio in my SUV periodically crackled to life. Broadcasting the dispatcher's familiar voice demanding that I report in.

The storm had sent a two-by-four through my rear window and—though there were no trees in Ed's lot—a heavy branch had taken out my Mars lights on its way to crushing my hood.

I leaned in on the passenger side, grabbed the microphone and called for immediate medical assistance. Gave dispatch the address.

Then I went back to Ed's side.

Chad was the first on the scene.

Briefly, I wondered if the priority he'd placed on this particular emergency call was personal or professional. And then I realized I didn't care. What I cared about was that he was here. Ready to help me as he always was.

He pulled his dark blue squad car in next to mine.

"Brooke!" he shouted.

His voice bordered on frantic.

"In here," I yelled back.

I almost lifted a very bloody hand to wave to him.

Then I thought better of it.

He was scared enough already.

I'd ruined another uniform.

"What's this?" Chad was saying. "Maybe the fourth or fifth this year? Gotta be a record of some kind. Don't you think so, Ed?"

Chad continued babbling about my uniforms—listing all the creative ways I'd managed to destroy them—as he pulled a dry, waterproof blanket up beneath Ed's chin, then carefully tucked it around his body. Slowing the hypothermia that the combination of soaking rain, cooling temperatures and blood loss made inevitable.

Ed's flicker of a smile encouraged the nonsensical patter, signaling Chad that this effort to capture Ed's drifting attention was working.

"So you see," he continued, "Brooke's gotta start blaming other people. The way I figure it, though, you're only responsible for ruining fifty percent of her uniform."

"Didn't ask for a big bandage," Ed murmured, alert enough to play along. But his voice was terrifyingly weak.

Chad shook his head.

I slid my hand beneath the blanket, captured Ed's wrist and took his pulse.

"I'm not talking about the shirt she tied around your leg. That'll clean up fine. But the trousers, Ed. Oh, my. Those are torn pretty badly. From crawling around your property."

A sweep of Chad's hand took in our surroundings.

"So it's only fair you provide compensation. She's a cop, so I'm thinking doughnuts are the perfect payoff."

"The chocolate-iced ones," I chimed in as I let go of Ed's wrist.

I frowned, shook my head briefly to let Chad know I wasn't happy with the result.

He covered his obvious concern with a nod.

"So, Ed, how many do you think she'll have to eat before you two are even?"

"Dozens."

The word was barely audible.

"That's what I'm thinking, too," Chad said, and then began working some silly word problem aloud for Ed's benefit.

How much longer could he hang on? I wondered as I half listened to something about the cost of half a uniform divided by the value of a doughnut. How much longer could the paramedics take?

Five more minutes, dispatch had promised the last time I'd called.

Downed trees and power lines across the roadways—not casualties—were slowing response time. Maryville had survived mostly intact. From what I was hearing on the radio, the tornado's path had clipped only the extreme northeastern edge of town—mostly farm fields and forest—then fallen apart at the river. Statler's and the used-car dealership, it seemed to me, had taken the brunt of the storm's wrath.

What Chad had seen as he'd driven into town then doubled back to help me, confirmed that.

"Just down 146, there are cars strewn everywhere. And what looks like the entire damn roof from their building," he'd told me earlier. "The road was pretty much impassable, so I wound my way through side streets to get here. Fortunately, all the folks at the dealership evacuated before the weather hit."

Which made them a darn sight smarter than Ed and me, I thought as I looked at my watch again. Seven minutes. Three more minutes, I decided, and Chad and I would risk loading Ed into a squad car and driving to meet the ambulance.

I heard a siren in the distance.

Chad lifted his head in response to the same sound and smiled. This time—for the first time since he'd arrived at the scene—the smile was genuine.

"Hear that, Ed?" he said. "They'll be here soon. Hang in there, man."

I prayed that Chad was right, that the siren was actually headed our way. But if I had doubts, I left them unspoken.

Ed didn't speak, either.

A quick glance at his face convinced me that his silence was unconsciousness, not lack of faith.

But Ed proved to be a lot tougher than I thought.

Though his eyes remained closed, he slowly lifted his hand a few inches. And flashed us a thumbs-up.

Chapter 20

I left before the paramedics arrived.

Even as the sound of the siren drew closer, the dispatcher's voice was broadcasting in stereo over both squad-car radios. An armed robbery in progress.

The address was the Cherokee Rose.

Chad wasn't the kind of man who needed to play macho games. He didn't spend a moment arguing that I shouldn't do my job. Or insisting that I should wait until he could protect me.

"Go!" he said almost before the call ended. "Your family. Your jurisdiction. Call for other backup if you need it. I'll take care of Ed and follow you as fast as I can."

I crawled back over the rubble, ran to my SUV.

After yanking the two-by-four loose from my shattered rear window, I tossed the disabled bar of Mars lights to the ground, dragged aside the branch that had crushed my hood, and climbed in. Ignoring the cracks that snaked across the windshield, I said a quick prayer as I turned the key in the ignition. Blessedly, the engine roared to life.

As I raced through the streets, taking detours around obstructed roads, I wondered if the call was actually a robbery or if Hector had somehow found his way to the hotel. Because—unlike my house—there was no reason to believe that Katie had told him how to get to the Cherokee Rose.

Maybe he'd remained in Maryville despite my warning. Perhaps he'd seen Gran or Aunt Lucy and had recognized them from the hospital. And had followed them home.

My fault.

I'd let a violent man go loose the night before because I was more concerned about the risk to the Underground than the risk to my family.

I should have killed him when I'd had the chance.

Within a block of the Cherokee Rose, the wind had knocked down a massive old oak. The tree and the power lines that it had dragged down with it blocked the entire street and the adjacent sidewalks. And here, near the top of the bluff, there were no alternate routes, no alleyways, no quick detours around obstructions.

I got out of my SUV, clambered over a picket fence and angled across a yard that was filled with another fallen tree. Following a leg of the "shortcut" that Chad and I had often taken between our houses, I pulled myself up and over a privacy fence. That put me into the front yard of the hotel's nearest neighbor, still half a block away from the Cherokee Rose. Then I jogged to the front corner of that yard to skirt a snapping, spitting power line that was draped across the sidewalk and road. Finally, I pushed my way through a thick privet hedge—a maneuver that had been easier when I was smaller and the hedge was younger. Back out on the sidewalk, I headed uphill, jogging the remaining distance to the Cherokee Rose.

As I approached, I could see a crowd gathered on the sidewalk in front of the hotel. Trapped, for all intents and purposes, at the top of the bluff. I recognized our nearby neighbors and the kitchen staff. Figured that the strangers were probably guests. They all stood in clumps of two or three or four, in proximity to the people they knew, not moving from their little groups.

Except for Aunt Lucy and Katie.

The two of them were circulating. Patting shoulders, giving quick hugs, chatting with people in one group, then another.

Keeping everyone calm.

Gran wasn't anywhere to be seen.

Aunt Lucy was the first to see me approaching. She said something to Katie, who nodded and stayed with the crowd. Then Aunt Lucy ran down the street to meet me.

Her eyes widened and her mouth formed an *O* as she drew closer. She was shocked, I supposed, by my appearance. Which was undoubtedly shocking.

I was stripped down to my Kevlar vest, a once-white T-shirt and torn uniform pants. My bare arms were covered with dozens of scratches, the newest of them inflicted by the hedge. And though, back at Statler's, I'd wiped my hands and the worst of my cuts with antiseptic from the first-aid kit, I was soaked with equal parts blood and rain.

"I'm fine," I said before she could ask. "What's going on?"

I grabbed her arm, and as we walked quickly back in the direction of the Cherokee Rose, we talked quietly so that our voices wouldn't carry up the hill.

Aunt Lucy's face was tense with worry, but her voice remained calm.

"I don't know how he found us, but Hector got into the hotel while we were in the basement waiting out the tornado. We were just walking the guests back upstairs— had gotten as far as the kitchen—when we heard him on the second floor. Kicking his way into every guest room, yelling for Jackie. So Katie and I rushed everyone out here. And called 911."

"And Gran?"

Only then did Aunt Lucy sound upset.

"I tried to make her come with us. Even grabbed her arm and tried to drag her outside. But she refused and pushed me away. She said I was to send you in when you got here. Said something about being wrong about last night."

I shook my head, thinking that Gran had actually been right. Hector *had* returned to Maryville the night before. And I'd encountered him, just as she'd feared. Just not in town.

No one—not even Gran—could have foreseen that he'd find his way to the Cherokee Rose today. And only I could have prevented it. But I'd let him walk away. With a stern warning, I thought bitterly. I'd done a better job of deterring a car full of kids who'd off-roaded through a cornfield and then sped through the center of town than I'd done deterring Hector.

"She was opening the safe as we left, Brooke," Aunt Lucy was saying. "Getting her gun out. I think she was going upstairs after him."

I would have predicted nothing less of my Gran.

Still, I was horrified.

I went into my family home with my gun drawn.

Loud voices—one male, one female—drifted down the center staircase. I couldn't quite make out the words, but I was familiar enough with the acoustics of the old building to know that Gran and Hector were inside one of the guest rooms. With the door into the hallway open.

I bounded up the carpeted stairs, taking them two at a time as Katie and I had done so often in play. Once in the second-floor hallway, it was easy enough to hear the conversation clearly. It carried from a room near the middle of the hall.

Hector's deep voice was angry and outraged.

"You told me she was here!"

Gran's retort was just as angry. Just as outraged.

"I lied! Just like you did when you promised to love and protect Jackie!"

By then, I was creeping through the hall, knowing that the sound of footsteps in the hallway echoed into open guest rooms. I knew that from playing endless games of hide-and-seek with Katie and Chad.

"You tell me where she is or I'll—"

Gran laughed.

"Or you'll what? I'm the one with the gun. Both of them, in fact. How does it feel, having a woman get the best of you?"

That's when I realized that she was holding him at gunpoint, waiting for me. He hadn't hurt her, wasn't brutalizing her. Going into my childhood home, I'd known only too well what Hector was capable of. But now, though I kept moving as quickly as I could, I no longer feared for my grandmother's safety. And as appalled as I was that she'd gone after Hector on her own, I couldn't help admiring her toughness. I was proud of my Gran and her willingness to confront a problem, then deal with it.

I was just steps away from the door. But I didn't call out for fear that I'd distract Gran and inadvertently give Hector an opening to exploit.

Gran murmured something so quietly I couldn't make it out.

Hector's response was a shout.

"Bitch!"

He must have flung himself at Gran.

The sound of a gunshot overlaid her cry of surprise and pain.

I heard a hand strike flesh.

That's when I reached the doorway. In time to see Gran on the floor. Definitely dazed. Her glasses were askew and the left side of her face was reddened from the impact of Hector's hand. But she was conscious. And alive. She'd fallen against a nightstand and now sat with her back against it. Almost upright. On the wall nearby, the stray bullet had torn through one of my great-grandmother's oil paintings—a view of the hotel when the Cherokee roses were in full bloom.

And Hector—

He'd tossed my grandfather's old revolver into a far corner of the room and was backing away from Gran, now back in possession of the gun she'd taken from him. He held the cheap Saturday-night special gangsta-style, sideways in front of him. And had it aimed at my grandmother.

He stopped a few feet from the door.

"Last chance, old woman," he said. "Tell me where my wife is."

My very proper Gran replied, very clearly, "Fuck you!"

He would have pulled the trigger.

Except I was behind him by then.

In one movement, I stepped forward and pressed my gun barrel against his neck. At a point just beneath his ear. A place where a bullet would be instantly lethal.

"Drop the gun, asshole," I said quietly. "I'm a cop and you're under arrest."

He'd almost killed my Gran.

I wanted nothing more than an excuse to pull the trigger.

Hector must have heard his own death in my voice. He let the gun fall from his fingers.

I was almost disappointed.

With my free hand, I reached for my cuffs. And only then realized that I'd lost them in the rubble at Statler's or hung them up as I'd crashed through the privet hedge.

"Get your hands behind your head, lock your fingers and keep them there," I said.

Hector listened and obeyed.

As a precaution, I decided to kick his gun beneath the bed. To keep him from being tempted by the proximity or the sight of it. But it was difficult to manage the angle and keep Hector covered at the same time. I succeeded only in pushing Hector's gun closer to Gran.

She was already back on her feet, had hung on to a corner of the nightstand as she'd pulled herself upright. Now her glasses were in place and her eyes were more focused. But she was trembling, and she looked very frail.

She bent over and picked up the gun before I could stop her. Stood with it pointing at the floor. And stared at Hector. Still a bruised and battered elderly woman, but now potentially very dangerous.

No cop likes to see a gun in a scared civilian's hands. Even if that civilian is their grandmother. He'd terrified her, I thought. Made her feel vulnerable. Probably for the first time in her life. So I acted accordingly, kept my voice soothing and my eyes on Hector.

"It's okay, Gran. I'll take care of this."

"Yesterday, you said that you could do the job. Handle any trouble he made."

"I am handling it," I said, reacting to the accusation in her voice. "I came as fast as I could. And now I'm arresting him, Gran. He'll go to jail."

She shook her head.

"There's only one way to protect women from men like these," she said. "I thought you understood that. That's why I gave you your chance last night. So you could prove that you're strong enough to take over for me. That you can do things the way they need to get done."

I stared at her, horrified. Thinking of how close Hector had come to raping me the night before. And knowing now that Gran—not Katie—had sent him after me.

"He's just like them. Those men you found," she continued. "They were the worst of the abusers. So I dealt with them. Just like I expected you to deal with Hector."

I choked out a single word.

"How?"

She smiled. Unpleasantly.

"It was difficult the first time, but I got better at it with practice. And I figured out to ask for money. To help us with our work. I phoned each of them, promised to show them where their women were hiding. For a price. They could have said no. Accepted that their wives—their lovers—were bound for a better life. Away from them. But they didn't."

She sounded reasonable. So terribly reasonable.

Hector shifted his weight, and I jabbed him in the spine with my gun. Just to let him know that I still knew he was there. Knew, and wondered why Gran was talking so freely in front of him. But I wasn't going to stop her. I had to find out what she'd done.

"I'd meet them somewhere public. Lately, at one of those big outlet malls. And I'd tell them to leave their cars parked, so they wouldn't be recognized. Then I'd drive them to Camp Cadiz. I'll show you where she's hiding—that's what I'd say.

There's an old cabin not far from here. In the woods. So they'd follow me. And I'd cast them into hell for their sins."

She was still holding Hector's gun at her side.

In the hallway, I heard running footsteps. And Katie and Aunt Lucy's urgent voices. But my attention was already consumed by Gran and Hector. Of the two, I feared that she was the more dangerous.

I had to stop her before she killed anyone else.

"Let me help you, Gran," I said, struggling to emulate Aunt Lucy's unflappable calm. "Give me the gun, okay?"

"When you found them, I thought it was a sign," she said. "I thought you were ready. You were supposed to kill him. And find a safe place to discard his body. Just like you did with Missy. But you let me down, Brooke. I can see now that you're weak, too. Just like your mother and Lucy. Just like Katie."

Behind me, in the hallway, Aunt Lucy gasped.

I ignored the sound.

Because Gran had lifted her gun. Pointed it at Hector.

Her hands weren't trembling any longer.

"For the Underground," she whispered.

Gran's finger tensed on the trigger.

That's when Hector threw himself against me. Using the same strategy that had saved his life minutes earlier.

The impact drove me to the floor.

He landed on top of me, his elbow in my stomach. Knocking the breath out of me. Then he rolled aside and made a grab for my gun.

I couldn't breathe, but I could still shoot.

My bullet hit him in the head.

But the bullet that Gran had meant for him sped, unimpeded, across the room.

Through the open doorway.

Katie made an odd, moaning noise when it struck her in the chest.

For a heartbeat, she stood, eyes widening with surprise. And then her legs folded beneath her.

Gran screamed. An agonized scream.

I crawled, still gasping, to my sister.

Blood spread outward from the hole in her chest.

Aunt Lucy was already on her knees, pressing her hands against the wound. Trying to stop the flow of blood. For a moment, she turned her face toward me. And in it I saw the hopelessness I already felt.

My grandmother was just standing there, staring at us.

"Call an ambulance," Aunt Lucy said. "Hurry!"

Gran went to make the call, but I knew they'd never reach us in time.

"We heard the shot," Aunt Lucy said to me. "Katie ran in to help you. And I followed her."

"You see," Katie whispered breathlessly. "I *am* brave."

"Yes, I know you are," I said as I cradled her head in my lap. "You've always been brave. Ever since you were little. When you saved me."

She smiled at that. Pale, pink foam dribbled from the corners of her mouth. And I knew that this time the blood filling her lungs—not her asthma—was robbing her of oxygen.

"I know you kept the secret," she gasped. "You didn't tell anyone that Gran killed Momma. So I'll tell you another secret. One that even Gran doesn't know. She said just to leave her. Out in the woods. But I was brave then, too. I went back all by myself. I found a good place for her."

And the stress, I realized, had triggered an asthma attack. She must have used her inhaler and then lost it. Next to our mother's body.

Katie died in my arms.

Aunt Lucy was sobbing, huddled in beside me, when Gran walked from the bedroom. She stood in front of us with the gun that had killed my sister still in her hand, dangling again at her side.

"It was an accident," she said softly. "I never meant—"

Aunt Lucy lifted her head, her voice making her next words an accusation.

"And Lydia?"

"I did what I had to," Gran said, and the old defiance—the old strength—returned to her voice and stiffened her back. "She said you hadn't given her enough money. That she needed at least ten thousand dollars or she'd take the girls away from us. Because that's what she thought they could earn for her once they were properly broken in."

I hadn't known I could hurt so much inside.

Hadn't thought I could hurt any more that I already did.

I was wrong.

"Katie overheard me talking with Lydia. Arranging a meeting. And she followed me. Saw what happened. But she understood that I had to do it. Lydia was a terrible mother who didn't care about her children. She had to be punished."

I recognized the words. Remembered that Katie had said something much like that the night she'd murdered Missy. A year after she'd witnessed our mother's murder.

That was when I decided that our family legacy—a legacy of lies and murder—would end here.

As gently as I could, I shifted my sister's body onto the carpet. Then I stood, stepped forward and took the gun from my grandmother.

She didn't resist, didn't even seem to notice.

"I'm arresting you for murder," I said.

That was when Gran laid her sinewy hands on my arm. Grasped me with her strong fingers.

"You'll destroy the Underground," she said urgently. "Think about the women, Brooke. The women will suffer."

I shook my head, though I knew that she was right. But I also knew that my grandmother was insane. I prayed that a good lawyer could prove just that. And perhaps save her life.

"I don't have a choice," I said.

"I'll give you one," Gran said. She released my arm as she turned her attention to my aunt. "You're a good girl, Lucy. And Brooke is still young. You help her make the decisions she needs to. In the meantime, I'm going to take a walk in the park. The breeze on the bluff will be lovely right now. And the view of the river always makes me feel so peaceful."

Then Gran turned her back on us. On the gun I held. On her daughter. On her granddaughters.

I took a step forward, knowing what she intended.

Aunt Lucy stopped me.

"Let her go, Brooke," she said in a voice that was rough with tears. "Let her go."

Gran held her head high as she walked down the long hall. And she kept talking, giving us directions. Guiding the Underground.

"Katie's death was an accident," she said, "caused by a stupid, arrogant old woman. Your Gran thought that your prisoner was escaping. Thought that you couldn't do your job. So she picked up the gun you'd made him drop and she tried to help you. By pulling the trigger. But you didn't need an old woman's help to stop a dangerous man. A man who was beating your Gran, trying to make her tell where the hotel's cash was hidden. You shot him. Because you're strong enough to do the right thing."

At the top of the stairs, she turned toward us again. Just for a moment. And then she gave her last directions to the new leadership of the Underground.

"Brooke, that old gun of your grandfather's has been used plenty. I think it's time it was retired. Somewhere no one will ever find it again. Understand?"

I nodded.

"Yes, ma'am," I said.

"And, Lucy, you take down that old painting of my grand-mother's. Put your foot through it before you shove it up in the attic. There's another old picture up there that's about the same size and almost as ugly. It'll look real nice in that spot. Maybe, when things settle down, Brooke can fix that old hole in the wall."

My aunt, who was now standing beside me, sobbed. And nodded.

Gran turned away.

"Forgive me," was the last thing she said to us.

The investigation went quickly. And Maryville gossip was kinder than usual. Even the most malicious could find little about the events at the Cherokee Rose Hotel that were anything besides tragic.

The day after the funeral, I invited Chad to dinner. Because he was my friend. Because he'd stood by my side through the investigation and had held me as the coffins were lowered into their graves.

I'd gone into the kitchen to put a chicken in the oven.

He'd remained outside, celebrating the fall-like weather by chucking tennis balls to Possum.

I heard him laughing, and the pure joy of that sound drew me to the window.

Highball was napping on a sunny patch of grass, oblivious to the game that was taking place. Possum was barking enthusiastically, bouncing in front of Chad, encouraging him to throw the tennis ball again. Chad pitched it into the meadow and the young dog ran after it, putting his nose down and zigzagging to track it through the grass. Then he pounced on it, barked with pleasure and carried the ball back to Chad.

And the whole process began again.

I turned away from the window. Back to dinner preparations and the bleak thoughts that had plagued me through the night and that I'd carried into the day.

There were two new graves in the town cemetery.

Thirty-seven male bodies had been removed from the ravine, their deaths now being officially investigated as mob hits. As was the death of the single female victim.

A victim who only Aunt Lucy and I knew was also my mother.

She would be buried somewhere at state expense, in an unmarked grave. No more accessible to me in death than she had been in life. She would never be more than a scrap of childhood memory, a woman whose strengths I had never glimpsed, whose weaknesses I would never understand.

Which left Missy.

For sake of the Underground, she would have to remain where I had left her. Unburied, but not unmourned. And never forgotten.

"Forgive me," I murmured, echoing Gran's words. "It's the best I can do."

That was when I forgave myself.

And gave myself permission to be happy.

I opened the back door and called out to Chad.

My dearest friend. An irreplaceable companion.

I wanted nothing more than to grab his hand, to laugh with him as we ran through the house together. To tease him as he followed me into a warm shower and then murmur lovingly as his soap-slick hands moved over my body. I wanted him back. Wanted to reestablish the intimate bond we'd once shared and that I so desperately missed.

But that would have to wait.

Because the truth needed to come first.

I sat him down at the kitchen table.

"I want to tell you a story," I said. "About human monsters. And people who fight them."

I ignored the confusion I saw in his face. Began my story with two little girls left alone with a stranger. Ended it with one of those girls all grown-up and finally willing to take a chance.

A woman ready to trust the man she loved.

Epilogue

Bright lights glowed against the gently falling snow. From the young woman's vantage point at the window of the rest stop on I-57, the procession of taillights disappearing in the distance reminded her of a string of red Christmas lights. Christmas, she thought with a smile as she softly rubbed her protruding abdomen. They would both be safe by Christmas. She stood for a while longer, watching the lights, ignoring the ache in her back and the soreness of her feet.

At least, she thought, that kind of hurt was normal for a pregnant woman. Not like the other—

She shook her head, not wanting to think about that. Instead, she walked carefully across the linoleum floor, now slick with melting snow, and settled onto the bench near the entrance to the women's room. For a fruitless minute, she attempted to re-arrange the oversized, faded red flannel shirt she wore as a jacket so that it covered most of her belly. She gave up when the shirt covered all but a triangle of her double-knit maternity top. Its faded floral print was in shades of lilac-and-pink, and it was loose enough to hide the roll of fabric and the large safety pin that rested on the swell of her belly and kept the stretched-out pink sweatpants from dragging beneath her feet.

Ugly, she'd thought when she'd first seen the outfit she now wore. It was the top layer of a bag of clothes a lady from the church had dropped off at the apartment back in September. I'll never wear that, she'd thought at the time. Taylor will get a job and stop drinking and then we'll be happy again. Like we were when we got married. We won't be needing this kind of charity. But she'd been well brought up, so she'd smiled and thanked the woman for her help, invited her in for a soft drink, and made sure she was gone long before Taylor came home. Taylor hadn't liked her having folks over to the apartment, and she'd done everything she could to keep Taylor happy.

Now, she smiled again, genuinely grateful for the woman's help—the woman's stubborn persistence—and the warmth of the ugly outfit. For a while, she concentrated on the stream of holiday travelers moving in and out through the rest stop's double doors. Most of them stood for a moment, brushing snowflakes off their coats or stomping their feet on the heavy rubber mat as their eyes moved around the big, open room. She watched, hoping that the kindest looking of them would notice her and smile. But each pair of eyes swept past the pregnant young black woman, usually seeking instead the appropriate restroom. Some travelers spent a few minutes in front of the long row of vending machines before making their selections and going back into the weather to continue their journeys.

An hour later, almost 10:00 p.m., and the crowd of travelers had thinned to a trickle. The young woman stood slowly, pressed her hands into the small of her back and stretched. Then she visited each of the vending machines in turn, entertaining herself by imagining what she would buy if she found money in one of the change dispensers. She decided on the hot chocolate and, when the machines yielded no coins, dug through her pockets, hoping that somehow she had overlooked a few quarters. When she discovered she hadn't, she shrugged and turned her back on the food.

It wasn't the first time she'd been hungry, but she regretted the loss of the money she'd so carefully saved and kept hidden from Taylor—almost twenty dollars in ones and loose change. But Taylor had shown up unexpectedly. She'd heard his key, heard the door catch on the chain, heard him shouting in an alcohol-slurred voice for her to open the g-d motherfucking door right now or he'd fucking kill her.

She'd snatched up her flannel shirt and run out the back door, leaving everything else behind, deciding in a heartbeat what she'd been agonizing about for days. A car would be waiting, they'd told her. It would wait for her on Monday and Wednesday and then again on Friday. At 6:00 p.m. All she had to do was make the commitment to begin the journey. On Monday, she'd been sure things between her and Taylor would be better, if only she tried harder. By Wednesday, she hadn't been sure, so she'd retrieved the money from a hole in the mattress and hidden it underneath the torn lining of her purse. Just in case. On Friday, with Taylor at the door, she'd known she had no other choice.

She'd run to the subway station, keeping to the back alleys just in case Taylor followed her. In her panic, she'd left her purse behind, but she knew how to get onto the subway for free, especially at rush hour. She picked up a discarded transfer from the sidewalk near the station, waited until a

CTA bus disgorged a load of passengers, and joined the crowd transferring onto the subway, impatiently pushing past the ticket agent who took the transfers without giving them a second glance. In the commuter lot at the end of the line on the Blue Route, she looked for the green mini-van parked next to the *Chicago Tribune* newspaper box. They'd promised her it would be there. And it was.

Mary's stomach rumbled as she walked away from the vending machines, and she wished that she hadn't already eaten the Christmas cookie that the woman had given her when she'd dropped her off at the rest stop. Beneath the wrapping of white tissue and red ribbon, the cookie was shaped like a Christmas tree. It was the size of both of her hands held side-by-side and was covered thickly in green icing. Tiny multicolored candies brightened the icing and, at the top of the tree, there was a star. She had eaten the star last, eaten it as she'd looked up at the night sky through the rest-stop window and said a prayer for herself and her baby. And a little prayer for Taylor, even though that made her feel guilty.

She wandered over to the big state map anchored to the brick wall behind a layer of Plexiglas. A red dot marked a spot on I-57 south of Kankakee, Illinois. *You are here.*

Here.

What would happen if no one came for her? What if the woman who had visited her hospital room and offered her this chance to escape had lied? What if she had to go back to Taylor, who would know she had tried to run away? Would she live through the next beating? Would her baby? Mary wished her mama was still alive. She wished she knew where her older sister had disappeared to. She wished she knew someone she could call for help. She folded her arms tightly around herself and prayed again. Hard. And she hoped that God wasn't too busy to give a poor pregnant black girl an answer to her prayer.

A gust of cold air blew through the rest stop as someone new came in. She shivered and turned toward the doorway, hoping for salvation. And was disappointed. A tall white man walked in, the wind whistling through the open door with him. For sure, he's not the one, she thought. All the people who'd helped her were women.

The door swung shut behind him as he paused, running a hand through his crew-cut red hair, brushing away a layer of clinging snow. Mary noticed that a nasty scar—the kind she'd seen inflicted in a knife fight—snaked along the side of his jaw.

He wore an nice leather jacket, a thick flannel shirt and worn jeans, and Mary immediately figured him for an undercover cop. Or maybe just an off-duty cop. But a cop for sure. Something about the way he stood there, quiet like, and looked around the room. For a moment, his eyes rested on her, and she noticed they were green. Cop eyes, she thought. Hard and mean.

As his gaze moved on to examine the rest of the room, she began worrying that he might decide she was breaking some law, might arrest her for loitering or maybe even accuse her of doing something like selling drugs. She bent her head so he wouldn't think she was staring at him, and kept her eyes on his booted feet as they crossed the room.

He stopped just a few feet from her, stood in front of the map.

I should get up and go into the women's room, she thought. Wait there until he leaves. But she was afraid that would make him even more suspicious.

He began whistling "Silent Night." Then, midsong, he abruptly switched to the chorus of "Jesus Loves Me."

The woman who'd brought her as far as the rest stop had

told her that was the signal. The person whistling those songs would be there to help her.

She caught her breath, looked down at the tattered sneakers that covered her feet, and was suddenly afraid, suddenly indecisive. Easy enough to trust a woman. But a man? A white cop? She'd be a fool to trust him, she told herself. He might hurt her worse than she'd already been hurt.

Maybe going back wouldn't be so bad. Maybe Taylor'd been drinking enough that he hadn't even noticed she'd been gone. Or maybe he would hit her, but probably not as hard as the last time. Besides, she deserved a beating for running away and getting him mad. She should have known better.

Then her baby moved, its tiny heel or knee or elbow tapping an odd, fluttery rhythm within her. A reminder of why escape was so important. Two weeks earlier, Taylor'd beaten her so bad she'd almost lost the baby. She took a deep breath, lifted her head and spoke softly.

"I'm Mary."

"Well, hi there, Mary," he said. "My name's Chad."

His words were accented by a soft, down-home drawl and the smile that brightened his face made his scar seem not so ugly.

"I'm here to take you down south. To a place called the Cherokee Rose," he continued. "My wife and her aunt run the place. They'll take real good care of you. Find you a nice place to raise your baby. A place to call home."

Then he stripped off his jacket and wrapped it around her.

"By the way," he said, "my wife's pregnant, too. Doc says it's going to be a little girl."

* * * * *

Set in darkness beyond the ordinary world.
Passionate tales of life and death.
With characters' lives ruled by laws the everyday world
can't begin to imagine.

Introducing NOCTURNE, a spine-tingling new line
from Silhouette Books.

The thrills and chills begin with UNFORGIVEN
by Lindsay McKenna

Plucked from the depths of hell, former military sharpshooter
Reno Manchahi was hired by the government to kill a thief,
but he had a mission of his own. Descended from a family of
shape-shifters, Reno vowed to get the revenge he'd thirsted
for all these years. But his mission went awry when his target
turned out to be a powerful seductress, Magdalena Calen Her-
nandez, who risked everything to battle a potent evil.
Suddenly, Reno had to transform himself into a true hero and
fight the enemy that threatened them all. He had to become a
Warrior for the Light....

* * * * *

Turn the page for a sneak preview of UNFORGIVEN
by Lindsay McKenna.
On sale September 26 wherever books are sold.

Chapter 1

One shot...one kill.

The sixteen-pound sledgehammer came down with such fierce power that the granite boulder shattered instantly. A spray of glittering mica exploded into the air and sparkled momentarily around the man who wielded the tool as if it were a weapon. Sweat ran in rivulets down Reno Manchahi's drawn, intense face. Naked from the waist up, the hot July sun beating down on his back, he hefted the sledgehammer skyward once more. Muscles in his thick forearms leaped and biceps bulged. Even his breath was focused on the boulder. In his mind's eye, he pictured Army General Robert Hampton's fleshy, arrogant fifty-year-old features on the rock's surface. Air exploded from between his lips as he brought the avenging hammer down. The boulder pulverized beneath his funneled hatred.

One shot...one kill...

Nostrils flaring, he inhaled the dank, humid heat and drew it deep into his massive lungs. Revenge allowed Reno to endure his imprisonment at a U.S. Navy brig near San Diego, California. Drops of sweat were flung in all directions as the crack of his sledgehammer claimed a third stone victim. Mouth taut, Reno moved to the next boulder.

The other prisoners in the stone yard gave him a wide berth. They always did. They instinctively felt his simmering hatred, the palpable revenge in his cinnamon-colored eyes, was more than skin-deep.

And they whispered he was different.

Reno enjoyed being a loner for good reason. He came from a medicine family of shape-shifters. But even this secret power had not protected him—or his family. His wife, Ilona, and his three-year-old daughter, Sarah, were dead. Murdered by Army General Hampton in their former home on USMC base in Camp Pendleton, California. Bitterness thrummed through Reno as he savagely pushed the toe of his scarred leather boot against several smaller pieces of gray granite that were in his way.

The sun beat down upon Manchahi's naked shoulders, grown dark red over time, shouting his half-Apache heritage. With his straight black hair grazing his thick shoulders, copper skin and broad face with high cheekbones, everyone knew he was Indian. When he'd first arrived at the brig, some of the prisoners taunted him and called him Geronimo. Something strange happened to Reno during his fight with the name-calling prisoners. Leaning down after he'd won the scuffle, he'd snarled into each of their bloodied faces that if they were going to call him anything, they would call him *gan,* which was the Apache word for *devil.*

His attackers had been shocked by the wounds on their faces, the deep claw marks. Reno recalled doubling his fist as they'd attacked him en masse. In that split second, he'd gone into an altered state of consciousness. In times of danger, he transformed into a jaguar. A deep, growling sound had emitted from his throat as he defended himself in the three-against-one fracas. It all happened so fast that he thought he had imagined it. He'd seen his hands morph into a forearm and paw, claws extended. The slashes left on the three men's faces after the fight told him he'd begun to shape-shift. A fist made bruises and swelling; not four perfect, deep claw marks. Stunned and anxious, he hid the knowledge of what else he was from these prisoners. Reno's only defense was to make all the prisoners so damned scared of him and remain a loner.

Alone. Yeah, he was alone, all right. The steel hammer swept downward with hellish ferocity. As the granite groaned in protest, Reno shut his eyes for just a moment. Sweat dripped off his nose and square chin.

Straightening, he wiped his furrowed, wet brow and looked into the pale blue sky. What got his attention was the startling cry of a red-tailed hawk as it flew over the brig yard. Squinting, he watched the bird. Reno could make out the rust-colored tail on the hawk. As a kid growing up on the Apache reservation in Arizona, Reno knew that all animals that appeared before him were messengers.

Brother, what message do you bring me? Reno knew one had to ask in order to receive. Allowing the sledgehammer to drop to his side, he concentrated on the hawk who wheeled in tightening circles above him.

Freedom! the hawk cried in return.

Reno shook his head, his black hair moving against his

broad, thickset shoulders. *Freedom? No way, Brother. No way.* Figuring that he was making up the hawk's shrill message, Reno turned away. Back to his rocks. Back to picturing Hampton's smug face.

Freedom!

* * * * *

Look for UNFORGIVEN by Lindsay McKenna, the spine-tingling launch title from Silhouette Nocturne™. Available September 26 wherever books are sold.

Silhouette

nocturne™

Save $1.00 off

your purchase of any
Silhouette® Nocturne™ novel.

Receive $1.00 off
any Silhouette® Nocturne™ novel.

**Available wherever books are sold, including most
bookstores, supermarkets, drugstores and discount stores.**

Coupon expires December 1, 2006. Redeemable at participating
retail outlets in the U.S. only. Limit one coupon per customer.

5 65373 00076 2   (8100) 0 11265

SNCOUPUS

Silhouette

nocturne™

Save $1.⁰⁰ off

your purchase of any
Silhouette® Nocturne™ novel.

Receive $1.00 off
any Silhouette® Nocturne™ novel.

**Available wherever books are sold, including most
bookstores, supermarkets, drugstores and discount stores.**

Coupon expires December 1, 2006. Redeemable at participating
retail outlets in Canada only. Limit one coupon per customer.

RETAILER: Harlequin Enterprises Limited will pay the face value of this coupon
plus 10.25 cents if submitted by the customer for this specified product only. Any
other use constitutes fraud. Coupon is nonassignable. Void if taxed, prohibited or
restricted by law. Consumer must pay any government taxes. Mail to Harlequin
Enterprises Ltd., P.O. Box 3000, Saint John, New Brunswick E2L 4L3, Canada. Limit
one coupon per customer. Valid in Canada only.

52607136

SNCOUPCDN

THE PART-TIME WIFE

by *USA TODAY* bestselling author

Maureen Child

Abby Talbot was the belle of Eastwick society;
the perfect hostess and wife. If only her
husband were more attentiive. But when
she sets out to teach him a lesson and files
for divorce, Abby quickly learns her husband's
true identity...and exposes them to scandals
and drama galore!

On sale October 2006 from Silhouette Desire!

*Available wherever books are sold,
including most bookstores, supermarkets,
discount stores and drug stores.*

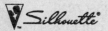

COMING NEXT MONTH

#109 DRESSED TO SLAY by Harper Allen
Darkheart & Crosse

On the eve of her wedding, trendy society-girl and triplet
Megan Crosse found out about her mother's legacy as a vampire
slayer the hard way—when her fiancé turned on her and her
sisters, fangs bared! Now it was up to Megan to trade in her
bridal bouquet for a sharp stake and hunt down her mother's
undead killer....

#110 SHADOW LINES by Carol Stephenson
The Madonna Key

Epidemiologist Eve St. Giles had never seen anything like it—an
influenza outbreak that *targeted* women. But this was no natural
disaster—someone was manipulating the earth's ley lines to wreak
havoc. Could the renowned Flu Hunter harness the ancient healing
rites of her Marian foremothers in time to avert a modern medical
apocalypse?

#111 CAPTIVE DOVE by Judith Leon

When ten U.S. tourists were kidnapped in Brazil, the hostages'
family connections to high political office suggested a sinister
plot to bring American democracy to its knees. Only CIA
operative Nova Blair—code name, Dove—could pull off a rescue.
But would having her former flame for a partner clip this free
agent's wings?

#112 BAITED by Crystal Green

Pearl diver Katsu Espinoza was never one to turn down an
invitation to cruise on multimillionaire Duke Harrington's yacht.
But when her dying mentor announced he was disinheriting his
assembled family and making Katsu his heir, the voyage turned
deadly. Stranded on an island in a raging storm, with members
of the party being murdered one by one, Katsu had to wonder
if she was next—or if she was the bait in a demented killer's
trap....

SBCNM0906